$6 -
+ cd

013840

T H E
Passersby

List of Characters

I do not have genius and I
   do not know it   *student at I Study*

I do not marry   *student at I Study*

I brown myself in the sun   *student at I Study*

My mouth is twisted   *student at I Study*

I'm sick of living To respond *student at I Study*
   to Auschwitz

Rabbi I love to walk   *rabbi at No's wedding*

List of Characters

If I could, I would grant myself the luxury of being sick	*patient at the sanitarium*
I need poison	*patient at the sanitarium*
I love beauty so much She refused me	*sponsor of the arts*
I believe in fairy tales I fight so that they become true	*family friend who runs I Study*
I have a tender heart and I hide it	*his wife*
I Study	*young man killed in the war; Jewish school is named after him*
Nylon	*student at I Study*
Dreamer Skinned Alive I, II, III	*students at I Study*
I know everything and I am unhappy	*teacher at I Study*
I am in mourning for my mother and my brother	*his former fiancée*
No of Montpellier	*student at I Study*
No of Rabat	*student at I Study*
I talk a lot and I have much charm	*student at I Study*

List of Characters

Pinched and Superior I will discover the secret of life	*No's husband*
The Passersby:	
Holiday	*one of No's lovers*
Little lamp held in secret	*another lover*
Better than nothing	*another lover*
Spare tire	*another lover*
I have three first names and two thousand women	*paramour of No's before marriage*
I wonder what I did to remain loyal to our ideal	*No's friend*
I drink my two pints a day	*family chauffeur*
Me I live	*family maid*
Above all no man	*family cook*
I speak alone but I still am sound of mind	*family nurse*
I will make myself tubercular	*No's friend*
Dr. Leave it to me	*doctor treating No's anorexia*
Dr. Deranged My money above all	*head doctor at the sanitarium*
Dr. Out of control Danger	*doctor on duty at the sanitarium*
Dr. I make men run	*Little No's doctor at the sanitarium*
Dr. I say nothing and I take	*analyst No visits*

List of Characters

No (Moon) But I'll get out of
  it
I'm dying   *No's mother*
God does a bad job, I'll take *No's father*
  over
Yes   *No's sister*
Do not talk about me   *Yes's husband*
YesNo   *No's sister*
NoNo   *No's sister*
YesYes   *No's sister*
Give me a discount   *No's grandmother*
Marked with genius of unity *family name of some of*
                                  No's ancestors

I will create myself And I   *No's adopted brother*
  will get out of it
She knows how to love   *his wife*
Frivolous and frivolous   *their son and daughter*
She has given all   *She knows how to love's*
                                  mother

Little No   *No's daughter*
Little Yes   *No's son*
God of Joy, Joy of God,   *Little No's children*
  Endowed for friend-
  ship

need only feel what is written, to feel every word, to live it, each of you in your way, as your own story. You can read the book aloud: it is a tale to be listened to. If you wish, you can also try to discover for yourselves what Kabbala is: the esoteric source of wisdom and life."

As the translator of *The Passersby*, I have tried to transmit the insights and eloquence of Atlan's testament to the durability of humanity in the shadow of disaster. Her work is a personalized story as well as a myth of return and re-creation, of meaning and consolation, that speaks to the condition of our time.

In consultation with the author, I have created a brief glossary to define French and Hebrew terms and identify unfamiliar names. The glossary appears on page 85.

I wish to acknowledge with gratitude the following people for their encouragement: Liliane Atlan, George Economou, Marc Aronson at Henry Holt, Ann Farber, and Mary Victoria Wilson.

—Rochelle Owens

Preface

Liliane Atlan was born in Montpellier, France, in 1932. She was kept hidden during World War II, first in her home country, then in Monaco, because she is a Jew. She began writing at a very early age, poetry first, then drama and fiction. Her work has always been centered on her experience as a European Jew growing up during the Holocaust. In *The Passersby*, Atlan narrates the story of a young girl suffering from anorexia in the aftermath of the war; however, this simple tale of a girl named *No* is also a timely and timeless allegory. Its themes are the pain of alienation, the despair of loss, the complexities of family, friendship, and love—all of them examined in light of a spiritual quest. This quest reflects the wisdom of a body of mystical writings known in Jewish tradition as the Kabbala. Profoundly influential in the past and still relevant for modern life, Kabbala seeks understanding of the links between the human and the divine, and of the ways the divine reaches into human life. As Atlan wrote me in one of her letters, "Kabbala has made a strong, visceral impression on me." In *The Passersby*, she shares that tradition with us, exploring the mysteries of the human spirit and revealing the vital and healing force of the divine presence. "I would tell my young readers," Atlan suggested to me, "if you want to understand *The Passersby*, you

I am and I will no longer be.
Apart from that, I believe in miracles.
—Liliane Atlan

Henry Holt and Company, Inc., *Publishers since 1866*
115 West 18th Street, New York, New York 10011

Henry Holt is a registered trademark of Henry Holt and Company, Inc.

First published in the United States in 1993 by
Henry Holt and Company, Inc.
Published in Canada by Fitzhenry & Whiteside Ltd.,
195 Allstate Parkway, Markham, Ontario L3R 4T8.
Originally published in France in 1988 by
Éditions Payot under the title *Les passants*.

Library of Congress Cataloging-in-Publication Data
Atlan, Liliane.
[Passants. English]
The passersby / by Liliane Atlan; translated from the
French by Rochelle Owens; illustrations by Lisa Desimini.
p.   cm. — (Edge Books)
Summary: As a teenage Jewish girl struggles with anorexia,
her decisions about whether or not to live affect those close
to her and are influenced by survivors of the Holocaust.
[1. Anorexia nervosa — Fiction.   2. Holocaust survivors — Fiction.
3. Jews — Fiction.]
I. Owens, Rochelle.   II. Desimini, Lisa, ill.   III. Title.
PZ7.A8655Pas 1993   [Fic] — dc20   93-17678

ISBN 0-8050-3054-9 / First American Edition — 1993

Printed in the United States of America on acid-free paper. ∞

1   3   5   7   9   10   8   6   4   2

T H E
Passersby
Liliane Atlan

Translated from the French by
Rochelle Owens

—

Illustrations by
Lisa Desimini

Henry Holt and Company • New York

POETRY
IN THE
ELEMENTARY
CLASSROOM

Poetry in the Elementary Classroom

BY

Flora J. Arnstein

A PUBLICATION OF
THE NATIONAL COUNCIL OF TEACHERS OF ENGLISH

APPLETON-CENTURY-CROFTS
Division of Meredith Publishing Company
New York

ACKNOWLEDGMENTS

The author and publishers wish to thank the following publishers, authors, and agents for permission to reprint poems published in this book:

CURTIS BROWN, LTD. for "Jonathan Bing," by B. Curtis Brown. From *One Hundred Best Poems for Boys and Girls,* compiled by Marjorie Barrows. Whitman Publishing Co.

BURNS, OATES, AND WASHBOURNE, LTD. for "The Shepherdess," by Alice Meynell. From *The Poems of Alice Meynell.* Copyright ©, 1923, by Wilfred Meynell.

CONSTABLE AND COMPANY, LTD. for "Storm," by H. D. From *Sea Garden* by H. D. London: Constable and Co., Ltd., 1916.

NORMA MILLAY ELLIS for "Afternoon on a Hill" and "Travel," by Edna St. Vincent Millay. From *Collected Poems.* Harper & Row, Publishers. Copyright ©, 1917, 1921, 1945, 1948, by Edna St. Vincent Millay. By permission of Norma Millay Ellis.

HOLT, RINEHART AND WINSTON, INC. for "The Pasture" and "The Road Not Taken," by Robert Frost. *From Complete Poems of Robert Frost.* Copyright ©, 1916, 1921, 1930, 1939, by Holt, Rinehart and Winston, Inc. Copyright © renewed, 1944, by Robert Frost. Reprinted by permission of Holt, Rinehart and Winston, Inc. For the same poems, LAURENCE POLLINGER, LTD. From *Complete Poems of Robert Frost.* Published in the British Commonwealth by M/s Jonathan Cape, Ltd.

THE MACMILLAN COMPANY for "The Snare," by James Stephens. Reprinted with permission of the publisher from *Collected Poems,* by James Stephens. Copyright ©, 1915, by The Macmillan Company. Copyright ©, 1943, by James Stephens. And for "Full Moon," by Sara Teasdale. Reprinted with permission of the publisher from *Collected Poems,* by Sara Teasdale. Copyright ©, 1926 by The Macmillan Company; copyright ©, 1954, by Mamie T. Wheless.

A. D. PETERS for "Tarantella," by Hilaire Belloc, as Literary Agents for the Estate of Hilaire Belloc and his publisher, Gerald Duckworth and Company, Ltd.

THE SOCIETY OF AUTHORS for "The Listeners," by Walter de la Mare. Reprinted by permission of The Literary Trustees of Walter de la Mare and The Society of Authors as their representative.

STANFORD UNIVERSITY PRESS for poems quoted from *Adventure into Poetry,* by Flora Arnstein. Stanford University Press, 1951. Copyright ©, 1951, by the Board of Trustees of the Leland Stanford Junior University. All children's poetry in this book not reprinted from the volume above are manuscripts in the author's possession.

THE VIKING PRESS, INC. for "The Noise of Waters," by James Joyce. From *Chamber Music,* copyright ©, by J. W. Heubsch; copyright ©, 1946, by Nora Joyce. In *Collected Poems,* Viking Press, Inc., 1937. Reprinted with permission of Viking Press, Inc.

FOREWORD

THE ONLY TRUE POETS are children, someone has said. Their fascination with language, their "built-in" ability to use it in unique and original ways, their skill in making language work for them in conveying their experiences and their thoughts are most pronounced among the very young. This is true because only the young child has not lived long enough to be influenced in his use of language by adults. Very early in life well-meaning adults often shape and bind the child's naturally poetic use of language into stilted, conforming, "correct" speech. Teachers are the most vulnerable on this score.

The three-year-old, resting for a moment in the play area on a New York nursery school roof, explained to her teacher that she was being "quiet as smoke." Here is truly poetic language. Any parent or teacher of the threes to sixes can match this illustration with equally potent expressions of the creative use of language by children.

The young child's zest for and skill in using language creatively must be fostered as he grows toward maturity. Mrs. Arnstein's *Poetry in the Elementary Classroom* becomes for the sensitive teacher, and hopefully for the sensitive parent, a tool which can make poetry a living force in the development of children.

If poetry is to make a difference in the lives of children, we must look at the teacher and the goals he has for his children. Next to parents, the teacher frequently exerts the greatest influence in the life of a child.

A good teacher is primarily concerned with the full flowering of personality. He knows the "ingredients" necessary for personality development:

—a climate which fosters freedom to explore, discover, and dream

—opportunities to share emotions, thoughts, and ideas

—skills which conserve rather than squander the creative powers of children.

A good teacher believes that poetry encompasses the "ingredients" necessary for the fruition of personality. He not only believes this; he communicates it to children in many ways:

—Through awareness of the beauty and power of words. His appreciation of words is as deep as that of the child in Mary Ellen Chase's delightful bit of autobiography, *The White Gate,* who upon being given a tiny safe for her choice possessions, kept within the depository pink slips of paper upon which were written favorite words. These were taken out from time to time and savored. The good teacher will help children discover their own unique ways of collecting words which have meaning for the collectors. Rich and frequent experience with poetry will stimulate word collectors to greater effort.

—Through recognizing that feelings are as potent as facts; that feelings *are* facts. And in no aspect of the curriculum is there as rich a source of "feelings" as in poetry. The teacher of tens to eighteens, concerned with developing concepts of the American heritage, may cram all of the knowledge he possesses into the minds of his social studies students, but unless these youngsters get the "feel" of those who helped establish a great nation, information soon departs. The good teacher will make sure that the great poetry of the American heritage is as much in the consciousness of his youngsters' experience as is the history of our nation. He will read appropriate passages from Benét's *Western Star,* for example, where children living in the present period of social revolution will find reflected the past tradition of "man's inhumanity to man." They will find within the beauty of Benét's great narrative poem the hostility of old New Castle and feel with the stranger as the inhabitants "whip the first Quaker bloodily through the streets."

—Through stimulating children to find in the commonplace a spur to the imagination. Only a teacher who is alert to the magic in the first snowfall of the season or the eeriness of thick fog will find the opportunities to make the world of reality and the world of the imagination one world for the child. Herein are opportunities for helping children become sensitive to the fact that poets express their own experiences in ways that are distinctly unique. "Fog" is the title of equally delightful poems by Sandburg, Farjeon, and Rossetti; each is different; yet each tells us as much about the subject.

In this book the author shows how teachers may work creatively with the individual child or with children in small groups and in large classes. For teachers eager to enrich their own content resources as well as their skills in conveying to children the "use value" of poetry in their lives, Mrs. Arnstein has provided an instrument of great value. Of greater value, *Poetry in the Elementary Classroom* has the potential for bringing to fruition the poet that is in every child.

MURIEL CROSBY

Wilmington Public Schools
Wilmington, Delaware

PREFACE

THE IDEA FOR THIS BOOK suggested itself to me after a talk I gave to a gathering of teachers. I became aware that during the "question-and-answer" period the identical questions were posed whenever I spoke to teacher groups: How do you get children interested in poetry? How do you get them to write? What can a teacher do on being required to teach poetry when he feels his background in the subject inadequate? It occurred to me that perhaps a book dealing with their common problems might be of service to teachers and help to provide them with confidence in their ability to handle the teaching of poetry.

But more than this, I felt that such a book might give the needed assurance that poetry by its nature is not antipathetic to children, as is generally supposed; also that it is not forbidding to teach. Through examples of poetry written by children, by quotations from their own comments I hoped it would be demonstrated that children bring to the study of poetry an eager and lively interest; likewise, as the result of this interest and through their engagement with writing, that children achieve a notably enhanced awareness and appreciation of poetry which may serve as a firm foundation for future poetry study.

So in the hope that not only the children might prosper through my sharing the fruits of my experience, but that teachers themselves might derive new-found pleasure in poetry and fresh encouragement and incentive to teach it, this book was undertaken.

F.J.A.

CONTENTS

1

Why Poetry?

THE PASTURE

I'm going out to clean the pasture spring;
I'll only stop to rake the leaves away
(And wait to watch the water clear, I may):
I shan't be gone long.—You come too.

I'm going out to fetch the little calf
That's standing by the mother. It's so young,
It totters when she licks it with her tongue.
I shan't be gone long.—You come too.[1]

HERE IS A POEM by Robert Frost, one of the great poets of today. It is a poem accessible to everyone. There is no word in it that is not comprehensible to any eight-year-old. It is simple in syntax and in meaning —even the below-the-surface meaning that older children are quick to discern. And it is poetry—that bugbear which many readers and teachers claim they cannot understand, much less enjoy.

What has produced this widespread distaste for poetry? Poetry is an art, as are music and painting, and as such it is intended for our enjoyment. There are, of course, a few tone-deaf people, or some unresponsive to the graphic arts. But by and large people enjoy listening to music and viewing paintings, as is attested to by the numbers who attend concerts and visit galleries. Why, then, is poetry alone of the arts so neglected?

For many teachers it presents a bewildering subject. They recognize that something about the teaching of poetry differs from the teaching of social science, arithmetic, or even English in general. They feel ill at

---

[1] From Robert Frost, *Complete Poems of Robert Frost* (New York: Holt, Rinehart and Winston, 1949). Originally in *North of Boston* (Holt).

ease when called upon to teach even the token amount of poetry included in most English courses. They are not to be blamed for their bewilderment. They themselves are the product of teachers who have shared their own lack of preparation. The poetry to which each group was exposed in its youth seemed as meaningless, as devoid of value as today's teachers suspect will be the poems they are called upon to present to their own pupils. How this vicious circle can be broken, how poetry can become meaningful to children will be the burden of this book.

We shall have to begin by revising our own concepts of poetry. Many of us are responsive to music and art; yet the aesthetic response to poetry is as available to us as that of the other arts if we are able to approach it in an amenable spirit. That we feel ourselves unable to do so is mainly the result of two deterrents: 1, the manner in which poetry was presented to us in our youth, and 2, the idea that poetry is something remote, esoteric. Let us deal with the last mentioned first.

We have already noted that in "The Pasture" there is nothing, even at a first reading, that is not readily understandable. It deals with an *experience* on a farm—the farmer going out in an early month of the year to clean a spring that has become clogged with the winter's debris. He is also planning to bring into shelter a newborn calf. Regarded at this level, the poem presents simply an experience which must be a common one for farmers, but which is not beyond the imaginative grasp of city people. Boiled down to its essence it is merely a reconstruction of an experience. And, here is the point, all poetry is just that: the presentation in words of experience either actual or imagined. Of course it goes without saying that poetry is something more than that as well; we shall explore the "more" as we proceed. But for the moment let us be concerned with poetry as recorded experience.

Even the youngest child is constantly involved in experiencing. Before he can speak he is feeling and either consciously or unconsciously recording and remembering experience. So here is something that we may build on—the child's own experience, the most necessary adjunct to his growth, indeed to his living. What we have to do is to relate his experience to that of other people and, in the matter of poetry, to that of the poet. Let us take, for example, the experience of climbing a hill. We might talk with the children about the various aspects of climbing a hill, of looking down, of noting what things look like from this vantage point, and we might invite the children to relate their own experiences of hill-climbing. After each has had the opportunity to make his contribution to the subject, the teacher might say, "Here is what one poet felt and thought about going up a hill." Then she might read them "Afternoon on a Hill" by Edna St. Vincent Millay.

> I will be the gladdest thing
> Under the sun!
> I will touch a hundred flowers
> And not pick one.
>
> I will look at cliffs and clouds
> With quiet eyes,
> Watch the wind bow down the grass,
> And the grass rise.
>
> And when lights begin to show
> Up from the town,
> I will mark which must be mine,
> And then start down![2]

Through the children's recalling and relating their own experiences, they have built a bridge between themselves and the poet; it has been brought home to them, not in so many words, of course, that poetry deals with experience and that experience is a two-way road that may be shared with poets.

The concept of poetry as experience and the invitation to children to relive their own experiences serve to rob poetry of that remoteness that bedevils our usual attitude toward it. Unless children are conditioned unfavorably to poetry, they are not inclined to feel this remoteness. And if the teacher evaluates his own experience, examining it in the light of what it has brought to him in his own life, he too may begin to feel at home in the world of poetry. No one is so insensitive that he has not at some time been awed by the power of waves crashing on rocky shores, or has not been moved by the silence and majesty of a moonlit night. Bringing back to mind our own reactions at such times, we can reactivate our sensitivity to the less spectacular but no less meaningful day-

[2] From Edna St. Vincent Millay, *Collected Poems* (New York: Harper & Row, 1956).

to-day experiences. This recalling may in turn make us more aware of the child's constant experiencing. We may then become more sympathetic to and more understanding of his thoughts and feelings regarding those matters which touch upon his daily life.

By giving respectful attention to his genuine reactions we can hope to lead him toward values of more significance than some of those offered him in our present culture. Many movies that children are exposed to are designed mainly for adult consumption, and the subject matter dealt with as well as the frequent depiction of violence is hardly conducive to the children's developing a response to the more meaningful values our culture is heir to. The same may be said of advertising with its stress on material possessions. If we permit rock and roll to replace all other music, the "quick draw" to supplant sounder dramatic presentations, the possession of "the latest" in clothes and gadgets to take precedence over everything else, we rob the child of the ability to relate to the significant features in our culture; we close down to him the opportunity to enjoy the great music, the art, the poetry that the past makes available.

What can be offered our children to counteract the merely sensational which tends to deaden response to all less titillating offerings? It may seem fantastic to suggest as antidote the quiet, seemingly unexciting adventure into poetry. To anticipate the skepticism that such a suggestion will arouse is not difficult. How can poetry compete with the suspense of a movie, a jazz session, a ride in a speeding car? Well, let us admit from the start that we are not speaking of competition. We speak of something on quite another plane. The case for poetry rests on what this plane has to offer that no other aspect of our culture does to today's children.

What is it, let us first ask, that children today are deprived of? Is it not the opportunity to experience life in a deeper sense than the superficiality, the speed of today's living makes possible? Are not children too often deprived of experience at first hand—or if not that, then are they not exposed to experiences following so closely, one upon the heels of the other, that there is no time to absorb, to assess, to do more than skim the surface of any single one? Against this superficiality, poetry allows a child a certain perspective, allows him to stand off from his own experience, to recall it, to relate it to the experience of others, and by so doing to accord the experience a value that it would not otherwise have for him. And this value takes on greater dimensions as the child realizes the significance that adults and, in this special case, poets place upon it. The wealth and scope of poetry offer children a wide range for thoughtful consideration. What other subject matter can draw upon so extensive a field, and what other can touch so closely each person's private store?

It is this personal relation to poetry and the satisfaction such a relation entails that is responsible, I believe, for the continued interest of the children I have taught. In a lifetime of teaching I have found group after group responding happily to the poetry sessions. Much of the children's satisfaction derives from their own writing, from the tapping of their creative resources; this aspect will be dealt with later. But that the reading and discussion of the matter of poetry, the opportunity offered children to explore, to formulate their own thoughts and feelings —that all this is meaningful to them has been proved to me beyond a doubt. What is in question here is not alone satisfaction and enjoyment; it is a deeper realization of life, a fuller appreciation of the world around us, a more sensitive ability to identify with others, in effect, a capacity to bring to living something more than a cursory glimpse in passing.

In addition the discussing and airing of ordinarily repressed thoughts and feelings affords the child a therapeutic outlet. Visitors to our classes have commented upon the relaxation attendant upon the poetry sessions. Also the poems of some of the children have attested to a release of tension and pressure. One girl says, "Sometimes when I am troubled, I feel the most like writing," and in illustration she writes:

It's funny that sometimes when I'm most quiet and peaceful
It is hardest to write poems.
Sometimes when it's noisy,
And I am disturbed in my mind,
Poems come quite easily.[3]

Many restless children have become calmer during the hour devoted to poetry and, surprisingly, many children say "thank you" on departing from class.

In contrast to the approach to poetry that I have outlined is that to which we were subjected in our youth. I might guess that my own

[3] From Flora J. Arnstein, *Adventure into Poetry* (Stanford, Calif.: Stanford University Press, 1951).

experience was fairly typical. In my preteens I was required to memorize "Thanatopsis" by William Cullen Bryant, a poem whose subject is death, and, it must be admitted, death treated in rather a grisly fashion:

> When thoughts
> Of the last bitter hour come like a blight
> Over thy spirit, and sad images
> Of the stern agony, and shroud, and pall,
> And breathless darkness, and the narrow house,
> Make thee to shudder, and grow sick at heart . . .

Also I was required to memorize lines from Milton's "L'Allegro." Now neither of these poems is in any way appropriate for children. The first, both in vocabulary and concept, is not within the range of a child's experience. The philosophic exhortation to resort to nature "when thoughts of the last hour" beset us has little to offer to a child; actually all I brought away from it was a sense of horror that it required years to efface. The second, beginning

> Hence, loathèd Melancholy,
> Of Cerberus and blackest Midnight born . . .

deals in its opening lines with a state of mind that is, hopefully, not related to a child. The entire poem is so stylized and so alien in vocabulary as to make the memorizing of it a dread chore. Such memorization imposes upon many children a real hardship that is responsible, I believe, along with remote subject matter and forbidding vocabulary, for the frequent distaste of children for poetry. I might interpolate here that I have never required memorizing of my children—I have avoided it as I have any other task that might seem onerous, since my object has always been to make the poetry experience a pleasurable one.

Some of the more accessible poems offered children I believe to be equally inappropriate for them. "The Village Blacksmith" and many others of the sort have a sentimental aura unacceptable to today's children,[4] and the didactic poems particularly are not calculated to

---

[4] One twelve-year-old girl, a member of one of my out-of-school classes, reported: "We had the most horrible poem in school today," and then she grimaced and in a mincing voice recited: "Blessings on thee, little man,/Barefoot boy with cheek of tan."

contribute to a love of poetry. Is it any wonder, considering what we were offered in the name of poetry, that when the school demands were over we should never turn to poetry in the hope of any pleasure to be derived from it? If we, as teachers, try to efface these early memories, we can then approach poetry with an open mind and enjoy what poets have to tell us that is relevant to our lives today. Only then can we bring to children our newly discovered pleasure in poetry and invite them to share with us what it offers.

2

The Teacher's Dilemma

ONE OF THE MOST FREQUENT questions teachers ask me is, "How can one teach poetry when one has insufficient background in it oneself?" Understandably this situation seems almost impossible to resolve. Teachers know only too well that they will be unable to instill in their pupils an interest in poetry if they possess none themselves. The answer is there is no immutable law requiring that they continue without interest in poetry. Here is a field that will be enriching for personal reasons as well as for teaching. And what if, in the exploring, teachers are only one jump ahead of their pupils? Jumping is fun and the imminence of having one's heels trod on is a prime incentive to effort on one's own part.

The first step might be to secure an anthology of modern poetry—perhaps not the latest anthology, since it must be admitted that some modern poetry (just as some modern art and music) is difficult to understand. But many paperbacks are readily available—notably anthologies by Oscar Williams[1]—that contain a wealth of poetry that is readily grasped.

Guides to one's first faltering footsteps are the very readable books of Babette Deutsch and Elizabeth Drew. The latter has recently issued, under the imprint of the Dell Laurel Poetry Series, a book entitled *Poetry: A Modern Guide to Its Understanding and Enjoyment,* which is to be recommended most highly.[2] If the teacher is primarily interested in the creative approach to poetry, there are the invaluable volumes of Hughes Mearns, a pioneer in creative work with children: *Creative*

[1] E.g., Oscar Williams (editor), *The New Pocket Anthology of American Verse* (New York: Washington Square Press, 1961) and *Pocket Book of Modern Verse* (New York: Washington Square Press, 1960).
[2] The National Council of Teachers of English has compiled a bibliography of Critical Anthologies for the Teacher and a list of Collections of Standard Verse.

Youth[3] and *The Creative Adult.*[4] The first gives a picture of a school environment which sets free the creative spirit. It contains stories about the children, their conversations, and along with these the author's illuminating commentary on the means for kindling and encouraging the writing of poetry. *The Creative Adult* is not specifically addressed to teachers but contains much valuable material and a heartening encouragement to experiment. An excellent book, unfortunately out of print, but possibly available in some libraries, is *Enjoying Poetry in School* by Howard Francis Seely.[5]

But the main suggestion is that the teacher read poetry, that he forget any obligation to "appreciate" or indulge in any critical appraisal. Appreciation grows with exposure to poetry as one's own preference and taste develop. To plunge in, to get the "feel" of poetry as something to be savored—that is all that is necessary for a start; this, and for the teacher to rid himself of two holdovers from his early conception of poetry: the idea that poetry must "teach a lesson" and that it has to do with sentiment. Poetry does deal with emotion, but the sentiment which is popularly associated with it from the past is more likely to be sentimentality. The gap between sentiment and sentimentality is a great one, though the distinction for the beginning poetry reader may be difficult to make. We all tend to accept conventional "sentiment," so that we fall into the trap of the easy and familiar. But by enlarging our vision, putting it to the test of the genuine in emotion—emotion that is truly felt and rooted in reality—we need no longer be beguiled by the facile, the trite. However, the new poetry reader need not worry. Taste and discrimination grow as one reads, and the teacher may be guided by the poems in anthologies collected by acclaimed and established poets. Let him select poems that appeal to him and reread these to find how much a poem has to give beyond its first impact.

Turning again to "The Pasture," which, as printed in Robert Frost's volume *North of Boston* appears in italics before the table of contents, the teacher might ask himself, and later his children, why the poet chose to place the poem where he did instead of in the body of the

---

[3] (New York: Dover Publications, 1959).
[4] (New York: Doubleday, 1940).
[5] (Richmond, Va.: Johnson Publishing, 1931). My own *Adventure into Poetry,* while containing some material included in this present book, goes into greater detail regarding the children's poetry and deals with other matter that will not be herein included.

book. The children answer the question with one of their own: "Was Frost intending the invitation to the pasture as an invitation to the poetry?" Also he might ask why (aside from the rhyme) does the poet say that the little calf "totters when she licks it with her tongue," instead of something to the effect that it was unsteady on its feet? The children are quick to discover that the last is merely a flat statement, whereas the phrase "tottering when she licks it with her tongue" gives a vivid picture of the precarious stance of the little calf far better than an explanatory phrase could do. This picture-making quality of poetry is illustrated in the following poem by Sara Tearsdale:

FULL MOON
(Santa Barbara)

I listened. There was not a sound to hear
  In the great rain of moonlight pouring down,
The eucalpytus trees were carved in silver,
  And a light mist of silver lulled the town.
I saw far off the gray Pacific bearing
  A broad white disk of flame,
And on the garden-walk a snail beside me
  Tracing in crystal the slow way he came.[6]

Here the moonlight "pours down" in a "great rain"; the eucalyptus is "carved in silver"; and notably we have the snail "tracing in crystal the slow way he came." I venture to say no child after reading this will ever look at a snail's trail as he has before—the crystal tracing will have become part of his mental baggage.

Joseph Conrad in his preface to *The Nigger of the Narcissus* expresses the credo of a great artist. He says: "My task which I am trying to achieve is, by the power of the written word, to make you hear, to make you feel—that is, before all to make you *see*. That—and no more, and it is everything." Robert Browning in his poem "Fra Lippo Lippi" has his painter say:

> For, don't you mark, we're made so that we love
> First when we see them painted, things we have passed
> Perhaps a hundred times nor cared to see;
> . . . .
> Art was given us for that.

[6] From Sara Teasdale, *Dark of the Moon* (New York: Macmillan, 1926).

Matthew Arnold assigns to poetry the "power of so dealing with things as to awaken in us a wonderful, new and intimate sense of them and our relation to them."

All these artists, the prose writer, the painter, the poet, are asking their readers and viewers to see with the inner eye, with the imagination, and by doing so to re-create for themselves the emotion that gave rise to the work of art. This re-creation of the emotion is one of the essential objects of poetry. For poetry is not a purely intellectual fabrication. It has its roots in the feeling world—all the way from the tactile sensations, the auditory, the visual, to the most complex feelings arising from our most subtle, deeply felt emotions. The poet John Ciardi says, "A poet thinks with his senses, his nerve endings, his whole body . . . He *feels* what he thinks."[7] And this is primarily the way children think.

The sensory aspect of poetry is particularly related to children, for their senses are not yet jaded and respond eagerly to experience which is still to them delightfully fresh and new. Fay, eight years old, writes:

> I love to work in clay
> And get my hands all sticky
> And then I squeeze it,
> And then it gets all dry,
> And then I can't work with it
> Because it crumbles up.[8]

Sylvia, seven, dictates:

> I love to hear the sea roaring,
> And then go wading,
> And then come out
> And watch the little bugs
> Crawl along the sand,
> And then pick up shells.
> Oh, how I love to hear the sea roaring.

Alan, ten, writes:

SWIMMING

> I love to feel water's icy fingers
> (That wrap me like a blanket)
> Grasping me.

[7] *Saturday Review* (November 22, 1958).

[8] From Flora J. Arnstein, *Adventure into Poetry* (Stanford, Calif.: Stanford University Press, 1951).

Ruth, eleven, writes:

> The sand is yellow golden,
> But when you dig down deeper,
> It becomes a darker brown.
> The water is blue with white foam,
> With shells down in the bottom.
> Sometimes the shells are washed up on the shore,
> But when I see them
> They are all smashed and crushed.
> You can see jelly-fish down by the shore, too,
> The sky is a lovely deep blue
> With a great big enormous round sun.

These and countless more of the children's poems describe in exact terms their sense impressions—feeling, hearing, seeing.

When the teacher comes to read poetry with the children, he need not be surprised that there already exists in them a bond with poetry. No barrier blocks their direct response, and, in some inexplicable way, this response induces an interplay between him and the children that provides for him an unanticipated pleasure in the poetry he is sharing with them. Sharing is the key word. Let the teacher forget he is teaching poetry; let him rather share it and together with the children discover and enjoy what it has to offer. The more he is able to derive enjoyment himself, the more will the children do likewise, for nothing is so contagious as enthusiasm, provided that it is genuine and not forced.

As to the teaching of a lesson, previously referred to, while our literature contains many didactic poems, most people, and especially children, do not savor being preached at. It might be better to allow poetry of this nature to go by the board. In addition, in some didactic poetry the lesson takes precedence over the poetry, which is an added reason to eschew it, since it is the poetry with which we are primarily concerned. Poetry should not be made the vehicle for moral instruction —that is, if it is to minister to enjoyment, nor should the poetry session be the occasion for moral pronouncements upon what the children say. Discussion, if it is to have any value, can result only if the children feel free to talk spontaneously.

Another aspect of poetry that the novice reader may enjoy is the connotative as against the denotative function of words. To simplify—

denotative words are those essential to science and to informative writing. They are the words that are most exact, that strictly delimit meaning in order to pinpoint fact. Connotative words are valuable to poetry. They are the words that have accrued to themselves a wealth of meanings, overtones of feeling, latitudes that stimulate the imagination. John Ciardi says in the article previously quoted: "A word [in poetry] has far more meaning . . . than in factual prose. A word is not a meaning but a complex of meanings consisting of all its possibilities: its ability to identify something, the images it releases in making that identification, its sound, its history, its association in context with other words of the passage. Good poets use *more* of a word than most readers are used to."

Robert Frost has been quoted as saying that poetry is that which escapes in translation, which in effect means that the words of poetry have for those who speak the same language an aura of meaning, of feeling, of allusion that cannot be exactly duplicated in a foreign language. For words are an integral part of the culture of a people and evoke in the reader memories and associations that are not necessarily shared by readers of an alien culture. The poet avails himself of just this evocative power inherent in words so that his readers may approximate his own feelings in relation to the matter that concerns him at the moment.

Let us look at the following poem by Alice Maynell for pertinent illustration.

THE SHEPHERDESS

> She walks—the lady of my delight—
>   A shepherdess of sheep.
> Her flocks are thoughts. She keeps them white;
>   She guards them from the steep;
> She feeds them on the fragrant height,
>   And folds them in for sleep.
>
> She roams maternal hills and bright,
>   Dark valleys safe and deep.
> Into that tender breast at night
>   The chastest stars may peep.
> She walks—the lady of my delight—
>   A shepherdess of sheep.

She holds her little thoughts in sight.
　Though gay they run and leap.
She is so circumspect and right;
　She has her soul to keep.
She walks—the lady of my delight—
　A shepherdess of sheep.[9]

This poem, selected almost at random, contains words that most happily illustrate what is meant by connotation. Take the word "fragrant," which might stir our remembrance of perhaps gardens at night, of the warm scent of newly ripened fruit; a host of other associations might come to mind, so that the "fragrant height" becomes something that is not a description of height, but of height trailing lovely odors rarefied in the upper air. So too the "maternal" hills, in which maternal has no precise meaning as applied to hills, but carries the connotation of something warm and protective, which concept is reinforced by the "valleys safe and deep." Neither adjective, "fragrant" or "maternal," is used literally, yet how much more dynamic and effective each is than literal, descriptive words would be.

If this stressing of the value of connotative words seems to contradict the earlier example of the "tottering" calf, it is just to make the point that poetry includes both the most happily chosen exact words to paint specific pictures and the most suggestive evocative words to arouse appropriate emotions. Also, in some instances, a word may be at the same time denotative and connotative, as in a sense "tottering" is. This encompassing scope of language in poetry may be the source of continuous aesthetic enjoyment. The reader arrives at a sense of discovery when he finds shopworn words revitalized by use in a fresh context, and he finds himself rejecting the clichés that are so prevalent in sentimental poetry.

One way in which poets use what John Ciardi calls "more of a word" is notable in the following poem by James Joyce.

NOISE OF WATERS

All day I hear the noise of waters
　Making moan,

[9] From Alice Meynell, *The Poems of Alice Meynell* (New York: Scribner's, 1923).

Sad as the sea-bird is, when going
Forth alone,
He hears the winds cry to the waters'
Monotone.

The grey winds, the cold winds are blowing
Where I go.
I hear the noise of many waters
Far below.
All day, all night, I hear them flowing
To and fro.[10]

Observe how the poet's choice of words with long "O" sounds—*moan, alone, monotone, go, below, fro*—contributes to the mood of melancholy. The new readers of poetry will discover many instances of this relation of the sound of words to mood. They will note, too, the use of onomatopoeia—that jawbreaking word which means simply the use of words that imitate or illustrate natural sounds, such as *crack, break, tinkle*. At the appropriate time the teacher may initiate the children into this magic power of words; he will find them eagerly responsive and avid to make their own discoveries.

Imagery, which plays such a large role in poetry, is another aspect that may engage the new reader. Describing one object in terms of another is such a common practice that we do not realize we are making use of imagery when we say, "He was quiet as a church mouse," or something is "as cold as ice." In poetry the juxtaposition of two disparate objects by reference to a characteristic that is shared by both is a deliberate device. In some strange way the very difference of the two objects compared seems to add to the impact of the image, to add another dimension to the description.

In "The Shepherdess," quoted earlier, the entire poem is an image. The lover likens his lady to a shepherdess—her thoughts are flocks—and he sustains this image throughout the poem. But there need not be such continuity. In "Full Moon" we have the images of moonlight compared to rain and the snail's trail to a tracing of silver. We may, then, expect to find in poetry much expression that is not literal; rather, the play of imagination makes use of words for their power of sugges-

[10] From James Joyce, "Chamber Music," Stanza XXV, in *Collected Poems* (New York: Viking, 1937).

tion, for their power to arouse emotion, and for their ability to make us contribute our own imaginative identification with the poet and what he is saying.

Children are very receptive to images, although, needless to say, this would not be true of very young children. Also they are frequently surprised to find that they have made spontaneous use of images in poems of their own writing. Image-making is natural to all people, children as well as adults: one little girl in an elevator asked me, "What shelf do we get off at?" and my little grandson once remarked that he couldn't look at the sun long because it made his "eyes all out of breath."

Imagery, then, the picture-making quality of words, and the use of words for their sound-inducing mood are some of the aspects of poetry that the beginner-reader may explore. A wider vista will open up later, but these suffice for a beginning as well as provide discoveries that may be shared with children.

3

A Favorable Climate

To WHAT EXTENT a child's learning is influenced not only by his teacher's competence but also by the latter's attitude toward him is only a matter of speculation. Teachers have often had the experience of the arrival of a new class whose suspicion and antagonism suggest that an unfavorable relation had existed between them and their former teacher—one not conducive to learning. I once visited an extremely successful teacher whose work along creative lines drew such acclaim that her classroom became a mecca for visitors. I noted that the walls of her room were lined with paintings of hideous caricatures of people, indicating such violence of feeling that I wondered what had given rise to such an outburst. She explained that they had been painted in response to her request that the children paint the "horridest person they had ever known." "These children," she said, "came to me from a lower grade teacher who had employed excessively repressive measures to control her class, in consequence of which the children had built up a seething inner storm of resentment. I thought perhaps that if they could rid themselves of some of this feeling by channeling it off in external action, they would find relief and also present a more amenable attitude to me and to learning. You'll note," she went on, "that none of the pictures represent their old teacher." They did not—instead there was one of a threatening Hitler-like person, another of a grimacing devil, and other horrendous figures, either male or female. Apparently the children were still too frightened to risk any overt statement, but all the pictures without exception gave evidence of extreme emotions of fear and hatred.

How much relief the children derived from this channeling off I had no way of knowing, for by the time of my visit to the class, the relation between the children and their new teacher was serene, relaxed, and respectful. And I have never seen a happier or·more creative group, though the principal of the school responded with a tinge of indignation on my asking to visit this particular teacher's room, "Why does everyone ask to see Mrs. X's creative work? The work her children do in their regular studies is just as exceptional and outstanding."

Of course this teacher was one of those rare creative souls, the artist-teacher, but aside from her particular gifts she had established a "climate" in her room that any teacher may aspire to. After my visit, in trying to analyze what such an elusive matter as climate consists of, I came to a few conclusions. I noted the presence of a tone of mutual respect between her and her children. In giving instructions she was quiet and relaxed, though obviously in command of the group. Without availing herself of the "permissiveness" too often associated with a creative program, she accorded each child the courtesy and respect usually reserved for adults but not so often for children. And she listened to what they said.

This last may strike the reader as an absurd statement. Doesn't everyone listen when spoken to? Well, there are kinds of listening. One kind is the equivalent of lip service, a superficial attention given in passing. The other is an aroused awareness that what the child is saying is meaningful, that it can often be for the teacher a clue that may guide him in meeting the child's needs. It may make all the difference between the teacher's failing him and being able to extend the helping hand that will make his next step in growth and development not only possible but also happily inevitable.

But what such listening does for the teacher is only half the story. His courteous respect builds in the child a sense of his intrinsic worth and the desire to be worthy of a respect generously offered. Nothing can build security in a child more effectively than the feeling that his teacher has an abiding regard for him. This security is of the utmost importance in order to assure that a child may be free to apply himself to the effort involved in learning.

For some two years I conducted an office for remedial study for children who were having difficulties in their school work. I was surprised to find that all the children, no matter what their specific problems in any subject, had one attribute in common—they were all more or less discouraged. What this discouragement stemmed from I was not in a position to determine, though in some instances the parents' attitude toward the child suggested the cause. I found that what these children needed as much as, perhaps more than, help in subject matter was a buildup of confidence in themselves and in their own ability. Surprisingly, this buildup did not require too much time to establish. Given a graduated program involving a series of small successes, the children were able to achieve the confidence that is often manifested in their slightly scornful comment, "Oh! That's easy!" Arrival at this point is the beginning of clear sailing and ultimate accomplishment.

Everything that tends to build up a child's feeling of being adequate is necessary to successful learning. For creative achievement it is essential. How can a child have access to his creative sources when he does not believe in himself? How can he dare exhibit in the open his thoughts and feelings if he denies their validity? A child's paintings and modelings may afford him a measure of anonymity, but in his poetry everything is out in the open. He has revealed himself and must take the consequences. Unless he feels assured of sympathetic understanding, he dare not give free rein to his creative impulses. But by "sympathetic understanding" I am not advocating the teacher's emotional involvement with his pupils; in fact, I would emphasize that such involvement is detrimental to children. An "impersonal-personal" relationship, so to speak, relieves the child of a sense of obligation to gratify his teacher. He is then free to address himself wholly to the task in hand without being disturbed by any inner division of feelings, while at the same time he is secure in the assurance of his teacher's support and faith.

Faith in the child is the cornerstone upon which is built a relationship that will accord him the maximum in encouragement. This faith need not be manifested in any overt expression, but where it is present it will be recognized by the child—faith in him as a person, regardless of what he may be able to accomplish. For not all children have equal intellectual ability, and a fine achievement may be the result of small effort on the part of a child gifted with words, while a mediocre achievement by a child not so gifted may represent true striving. In some subjects where the standard of *correct* and *incorrect* must be applied, as in arithmetic or spelling, a child may be rated competitively. In creative activity, such as poetry or art, high intellectual ability is not always a requisite for achievement. I have had in my classes at times children of somewhat meager ability who have been able to produce delightful poems. I had one child whose output was enormous in quantity but of poor quality. But the point I want to make is that this last child was functioning to the best of her ability, and in unrestricted fashion, in contrast to her strivings in other fields in which she could not have helped but feel her inadequacy. Do we not owe every child the opportunity to function in some area in which he does not anticipate defeat before he starts? We are overprone to value end results, whereas it is the process of functioning and the growth consequent upon functioning that are important to a child. I am not, however, unaware that teachers are required to meet certain standards in their work, but happily in the field of poetry such standards are neither required nor should they be imposed.

To return to the climate in the classroom described at the beginning of this chapter—from which I have digressed—another factor was brought home to me. I remembered that I had nowhere seen any evidence of competition. At no time had the teacher compared one child's work to another's or singled out any child for special commendation or criticism. Acceptance, unconditional, was offered each child, and such acceptance is available to every teacher. Whatever a child presents is worthy of respectful consideration—even inept offerings, since these may be all a given child is capable of tendering. But aside from the fact that acceptance is a prime stimulus to further effort on the child's part, it provides an additional value—an immensely salutary effect on interchild relationships. As many teachers know, their class will pattern its behavior on their own: where the teacher adopts a critical attitude, the children will do likewise for two reasons—one, because criticism is the sanctioned behavior, and two, because they believe it will curry favor with him. What may be the damning effect of criticism will be dealt with later when we speak of the children's writing.

In an atmosphere of acceptance, then, the child is able to relax and does not need to bolster up whatever inadequacy he feels in himself by detraction of others. Instead, noting the teacher's appreciative response to ideas and suggestions from the children and his favorable commenting on a happy use of words in some child's poem, or a thoughtful observation, the child is inclined to accord the other children the same respect that the teacher does. A teacher will be most gratified to observe the generous acclaim with which children receive a poem which they like. One child, in an editorial meeting when the children were engaged in selecting poems to be submitted to a yearbook, said:

"We shouldn't just read a poem and vote on it. Someone ought to tell the nice parts. If you don't think about it, you discard it at once, and you miss the good things." Another girl added, "It's funny—if you like it for this and don't like it for that, it spoils it to analyze." To which the first girl replied, "I think it's a good point to bring out the good parts but not the bad." As the poetry work progresses, so does the children's ability to recognize and value poetic felicities—sometimes only a word or a phrase that gives distinction to a poem.

These, then, seem to be the pillars of a room in which a climate favorable to creative work may flourish: respect, the building up of a child's faith in himself—which can only grow out of his teacher's faith in him—and acceptance which gives him the courage to be himself. The relaxation inherent in such a climate affords the child the alternative to assuming a "face" that he ordinarily feels he must present to a more or less hostile world. In the climate of such a room, a child can dare to be himself and dare to probe that self, secure in the belief that he is not only an accepted member of his world but also one who is valued for what he is regardless of what he may be able to accomplish.

4

What Poems?

CONFRONTED with the enormous body of poetry readily available, teachers are understandably at a loss concerning which poems to select for their classes. Anthologies are the most fruitful source. They are organized in a variety of ways: some merely give the names of authors and their poems in chronological order; others are organized around subject matter, as in the excellent anthology for young people, *This Singing World* by Louis Untermeyer.[1] The categories in this volume read, to name a few: Songs of Awakening, Breath of the Earth, Common Things, Places, Children, Birds and Beasts. However, neither of the two types of organization will be particularly helpful to the teacher. In his search for poems appropriate to his age group he will of necessity have to select those best suited to his own children.

While there is a difference between the poems suitable for seven- and eight-year-olds and for children of ten and older, certain common principles may guide the teacher in his choice. The first, mentioned in an earlier chapter, is that poems should deal with experience familiar to children. In the main, the poems should have been written in comparatively recent times, since these treat of a world with which our children are acquainted. An exception to this restriction is poetry of the nature of Robert Louis Stevenson's, whose *A Child's Garden of Verses* taps the more or less ageless preoccupations of childhood. Poems of today likewise employ a vocabulary more readily understandable than that of earlier times. The teacher will find that children respond to poems about natural phenomena—the sun, the moon, rain, rivers, animals—as well as to poems of personal experience such as "Afternoon on a Hill," previously quoted. To sustain interest, poems should be chosen that may be grasped at a first hearing. Any poem containing too many unfamiliar words tends to disrupt interest, though at times a poem

[1] (New York: Harcourt, Brace & World, 1926.)

22

may contain one or two words that are foreign to a child's vocabulary. This fact need not be a deterrent to the choice of that particular poem. It is desirable, of course, to enlarge a child's vocabulary. The difficulty may be forestalled by an explanation of the words in question before the reading of the poem.

The length of a poem is another matter that should be taken into consideration. For the younger children poems should be short, since any too protracted demand on attention is fatal to interest.

I would suggest that poetry of the jingle variety be only infrequently presented—not that all jingle is to be decried. The delightful verses of A. A. Milne, like the nursery rhymes, are appropriate in their place, but in the classroom they are too facile and serve to identify poetry in the child's mind with verse that adheres to a certain bouncy rhythm. Many children have arrived in my classes convinced that nothing is poetry that is not of the "Dee-dum, dee-dum, dee-dum, dee-dee / Dee-dum, dee-dum, dee-dum, you see" variety, so that it takes some time to displace this concept with a more valid one. What actually constitutes poetry need not be overtly defined. Through the years no definition of poetry that is all inclusive and universally acceptable has been, or perhaps ever will be, arrived at.

But infallibly the children learn to sense the nature of poetry when they have been exposed to it over a period of time. An identical phrase has cropped up surprisingly often in different classes. Commenting on a poem of their own or on that of another child, they say, "That sounds more like a story than a poem." What they are sensing by this observation is that something more than blunt statement is necessary in a poem—that there exists such a thing as "prosiness," though they are unable to formulate the concept. They sense also that the absence of cadence is detrimental to poetic expression. Cadence is an elusive thing to define, but here again there is no need to attempt a definition with the children. They eventually recognize consciously that absence of cadence may make the difference between what is and what is not a poem, as more specific commentary than the one noted above appears during the progress of the poetry study.

A ten-year-old girl writes:

> The moon is like a silver plate.
> It breaks as some one breaks a real one.

>Other times it is put together again
>By strong fingers of sky and clouds.

On rereading this at the session following its writing, she says, "It is not good," and amends it to read:

>The moon is like a silver plate.
>It is broken by strong fingers of sky and clouds,
>And then put together by them again.[2]

While not notably poetic, the latter version is an obvious improvement over the first. The child has recognized the prosy ineptitude of line two. We shall have more to say of the children's development of criteria later. At this point what we want to bring home is the fact that children have, perhaps instinctively, a keen sense of what constitutes poetry not only in rhythmic but in free verse as well.

In order to further such recognition it is advisable to read to the children a considerable amount of free verse. So much of modern poetry falls into this category that there is a wide field upon which to draw. In the absence of regular rhythm and rhyme the children learn to focus attention on the essentials of poetry; and this concentration is of especial value to them when they come to write their own poems.[3] Regular rhyme and rhythm are difficult to handle. The attempt to manipulate their thoughts and feelings into a more or less rigid framework forces the children to distort their spontaneous expression and resort to other undesirable practices, all of which will be discussed when we speak of the writing program.

By advocating the choice of much free verse I do not wish to imply the exclusion of rhythmic verse. The response to rhythm is basic in all people, and a great deal of aesthetic enjoyment of poetry rests upon an either unconscious or conscious realization of its presence. I advocate the choice of much free verse not only that the children may feel the sanction to write in this form but also because heretofore emphasis in

---

[2] These two versions are from Flora J. Arnstein, *Adventure into Poetry* (Stanford, Calif.: Stanford University Press, 1951).

[3] Sean, a twelve-year-old, says: "A poem with regular rhythm and rhyme sometimes distracts you from the idea by the rhythm. With free verse you notice the meaning." And Rachel adds, "Sometimes words are put in just to rhyme, and that ruins it."

the teaching of poetry has been placed almost exclusively upon rhythm and rhyme, so that other aspects of poetry often have been overlooked.

Another caution with regard to choice is perhaps not necessary, but attention might be drawn to the fact that a great deal of poetry for children tends at times to a certain archness and is "written down" to them. In accordance with what I have previously said of maintaining a respectful attitude towards children, I feel that poetry of this order violates such respect. The first acts on the assumption that "cuteness" is acceptable to children and that it is a desirable quality to foster; the second, that children are not capable of a serious approach to poetry. Of course not all poetry written for children presents these undesirable aspects, and the teacher of young children especially will need to draw upon some of these, since the amount of poetry understandable to young children is necessarily limited.

For the older children narrative verse and ballads prove most acceptable and, as the poetry program continues, poems demanding thought and presenting increasing use of poetic devices may be offered. The teacher will indeed be surprised to find that children are able to come to grips with poems he would have initially believed to be far beyond their understanding.

5

How Young?

THE SIX-YEAR-OLDS enter my classroom wide-eyed and somewhat dubious. Shepherded by their class teacher, who aware of the poetry work taking place throughout the school has asked me to read poetry with her group, they take their places around our ample table. I myself have certain misgivings. I have never taught such young children, but I reassure myself with the thought that they cannot be too different from my seven-year-olds. In any case, that which has guided my choice of poems for the sevens will apply no doubt as well to the younger children.

However, another factor enters here. Because I shall not have continuous contact with these children, I cannot plan any long-range program for them. Since our meetings will be few and occasional, my aim must be restricted to making poetry immediately pleasurable, so that the idea of poetry may have only happy connotations for them. Of course pleasure should be one of the concomitants of the poetry experience for all ages; with these particular children it may have to be the end-all.

I decide to read one poem which has proved "sure-fire" for the sevens and even for some of the older children, "Jonathan Bing" by B. Curtis Brown.[1] Though it is a type of poem I have cautioned against in my last chapter, it is one that fills the need on certain occasions. Before reading it I ask the children whether they forget things sometimes. Up go the hands as each child is impatient to tell some instance of his forgetfulness. When all have had the opportunity to speak, I say, "Here is what one poet had to say about forgetting."

[1] From *One Hundred Best Poems for Boys and Girls*, compiled by Marjorie Barrows, Whitman Publishing Company, Racine, Wisconsin. This book is out of print, but perhaps it can be found in some libraries.

JONATHAN BING

Poor old Jonathan Bing
Went out in his carriage to visit the King,
But everyone pointed and said, "Look at that!
Jonathan Bing has forgotten his hat!"
    (He'd forgotten his hat!)

Poor old Jonathan Bing
Went home and put on a new hat for the King,
But up by the palace a soldier said, "Hi!
You can't see the King; you've forgotten your tie!"
    (He'd forgotten his tie!)

Poor old Jonathan Bing
He put on a beautiful tie for the King,
But when he arrived an Archbishop said, "Ho!
You can't come to court in pyjamas, you know!"

Poor old Jonathan Bing
Went home and addressed a short note to the King:
"If you please will excuse me I won't come to tea,
For home's the best place for all people like me!"

The procedure of introducing a poem by discussion of the experience
with which it deals is one I consistently employ. It sets the stage for the
poem and relates the child to the experience and hence to the poem's
content.

Here let me interpolate that, as I go along, I shall necessarily refer
to certain of my own procedures which seemed to foster favorable
results. However, I want to disclaim any pretense of presenting these as
"a method." Reducing procedures to a hard-and-fast mold robs them
of life; it is far better for a teacher to experiment, to employ his own
approach than to accept literally the formula of another. What works
with one person may not work with the next. Unlike the teaching of
arithmetic, for which a method may be outlined, the teaching of art is
most successful when the teacher ventures into paths of his own choosing. If he is sensitive to the children's responses and flexible enough to
discard procedures that prove headed in the wrong direction, he is more
likely to be successful—for the more creative the teacher, the more

creative the child will be. I suggest, then, that the practices I shall describe may be most happily regarded as a jumping-off place for the teacher's individual venture.

There are innumerable approaches to teaching, and some that are congenial to one teacher may not be so to another. The artist-teacher to whom I referred in an earlier chapter made use of a diametrically different approach from my own. Whereas she was a very dynamic person who was able to carry the children along on the wave of her own enthusiasm, I am inclined to be retiring and resort to drawing the children out. But the difference in our ways of working diminishes in no respect my regard for her achievement. Certain practices of Hughes Mearns, as described in his *Creative Youth*, I admire unreservedly, but they would be impossible for me to apply.

In the *English Journal* for April, 1951, Marjorie Braymer wrote of her experience in the teaching of poetry to reluctant high school students. Her approach was novel. She started by exploring the role that poetry has played in the lives of primitive and civilized peoples: "how poetry evolved to meet man's need for songs that would make bearable the monotony of hard labor." She dealt with the "historical and psychological reasons for poetry in everyday life." And when she had established for her students the validity of poetry, she embarked upon the discussion of the nature of poetry, of different forms of poetry, of layers of meaning, until she had not only won over her class to poetry but had also developed a group of enthusiastic explorers who were bringing to class new discoveries of their own. The titles of some of their papers speak for themselves: "The Truth of Poetry"; "A Precious Discovery"; "Poetry Is Fun"; "'Growing Up' about Poetry"; "A Change of Attitude." So, I repeat, what in this book I have to offer is merely my personal approach along with whatever my experience has taught me.

To return to "Jonathan Bing." Some of the qualities in this poem may suggest to the teacher poems of a similar nature suitable for young children. At this age children delight in rhythm—it is, perhaps, as much the rhythmic quality of *Mother Goose* as its content that has endeared it to children over the years. "Jonathan Bing" has just such a seductive rhythm and attractive rhymes as well. At times, on a second reading, I have read the first line of the rhymed couplets and then omitted the rhyming word of the second, which the children have shown great gusto in supplying. The poem contains repetition, so dear to young children's hearts, and a humor which appeals especially to them. Finally, it deals with the experience of forgetting, shared alike by young and old.

Having won over the children to poetry, the teacher may turn from the type of poem quoted to poems of a more serious content. "Who Has Seen the Wind?" by Christina Rossetti provides discussion for the experience of a windy day. "Tired Tim" and "The Little Green Orchard" by Walter de la Mare draw upon child experience, and "Fog" by Carl Sandburg might be an introduction to free verse.

After reading a poem I have found it a valuable practice to ask the children what they have noticed in the poem. I do not favor paraphrasing, the saying of a poem "in your own words." The words of a poem and what the poem says are really one—to say a poem in different words is to destroy it as a poem. But to ask the children what they have noticed serves to whet their attention. They are eager to enumerate all the "things" they have noticed, and I have found that after a little practice eight-year-olds are able to recall the entire content of a poem. In order to refresh memory they frequently ask for a second reading, which is of course to be desired. What one can "do" with a poem in the teaching of young children is necessarily limited, but a pleasurable introduction to poetry is in any case a worthy aim.

My work with this particular group of six-year-olds was of short duration because of the conflict in their teacher's schedule and mine. But some years later I had the pleasure of reading poetry with another group of the same age. We began the program with the making of books. How this procedure suggested itself to me I do not remember, but it proved so far-reaching in results that I adopted it with all subsequent classes. Stiff-covered blank books, a selection of attractive cotton materials with which to cover them, spatulas, vegetable glue, and colored paper for lining the inside covers were the only equipment necessary. After the children had made their choice from among the materials, they settled down to the business of covering the books.

The making of these books has a particular value for the teacher. Observing the children working provides him with the opportunity of getting acquainted with a new group of children, noting their characteristics, the differences between those who go about the work confidently and those who are tentative and require help and encouragement. Also the book-making provides an informal atmosphere, one in which the children can be themselves without self-consciousness. For the children it affords an activity that all ages enjoy and has the added advantage of engaging each child immediately and sending off the poetry hour to a pleasurable start. Two sessions are generally necessary for the younger children to finish their books, the first for pasting the outer covers, the second to add the linings. Of course after both sessions the books must be pressed under heavy volumes or any other weights available.

Many teachers have classes of such a size that the making of books is not feasible. I used these procedures in poetry classes of about sixteen children. However, another procedure is open to the teacher of large classes—he may procure an attractive book in which children may paste poems he brings to class. The object of the books in both cases is to provide a more personal anthology than is represented by published anthologies. These last cannot offer the child the personal, intimate feeling that arises from a collection of poems of his own choice; often anthologies contain many poems unsuitable to a child's age, hence neither invite nor foster reading.

I have referred above to poems brought to class. What are these poems that are destined for the books? At each session I would read a number of poems from which the children would make a choice. I would type these and bring them to the succeeding session for the children to paste in their books. The opportunity for the exercise of choice I believe to be of prime importance. Choice is the first step in the development of "appreciation." I place *appreciation* in quotes, as I am somewhat wary of so-called appreciation classes in the arts. Appreciation, I believe, cannot be taught. Along with the development of taste, it results from growth, from maturing, and from the exposure to poetry and the opportunity to write. Any designation of a work of art as "good" or "bad" is only confusing to a child. Criteria supplied from without have no meaning because to a child they seem arbitrary, and an acceptance of them without understanding leads more often than not to misapplication. But more of this will be said when we deal later with the children's writing.

What a child likes, then, is a valid base upon which to build appreciation. Because of the expectation of having to make a choice from among the poems read, the children's initial attention is aroused and focused, and often this same expectation leads to the request for the rereading of certain poems, as has been already mentioned. The advantage of such rereading need not be labored. Altogether the exercise of choosing implies an act of discrimination, and discrimination has its value even if this is only the expression of personal preference.

The teacher of a large class is obviously not able to type poems for individual books, but for the class book it may not be too burdensome for him to write or type single poems. After a reading at a particular session he might ask the group to vote on the poem they liked best, and the majority's choice would then be included in the class book. A careful distinction should, however, be made. The children should not be asked to vote for the "best" poem—since the evaluation of a poem as good or bad is not within their ability—but they should be invited to say which one they *liked* best. And I suggest that the children be not required to copy the chosen poem, since, as I mentioned earlier, anything that savors of a chore should be avoided in the poetry program. Of course if a child volunteers to copy a poem, that is another matter. Each child may be allowed his turn to paste the poem in the class book, which would make him a participant, to a certain extent, in the compiling of the anthology.

After the entering of the poem in the book, the teacher might read the poem aloud with this particular child. There is a good reason for not permitting children to read the poems alone. A stumbling rendition is fatal to a poem, but even when a child reads fluently, he is not equipped to give due value to certain words or to pauses, or to other aspects of the poem: needless to say a poem should always be presented in its best light. By reading with the teacher, the child learns the appropriate pace, for poetry usually should be read more slowly than prose. I explain to the children that, whereas in a story the author is eager to carry the reader along with the story's progress, in a poem what the poet desires is to have the reader linger, so that he may enjoy the words, the pictures, and get the feeling of the poem. Thus the children acquire the habit of reading a poem slowly and quietly. One little girl in her eagerness to conform to these requirements read a poem in such a subdued, almost unintelligible manner as to bring forth the comment from another child: "It's all right to read quietly, but she doesn't need to read as if she is a ghost!"

Many readers of poetry adopt a somewhat self-conscious or declamatory rendition. Either they pause overlong at line endings, or too scrupulously do not pause at all in such run-on lines as Tennyson's:

Till the great sea snake under the sea
From his coiled sleeps in the central deeps
Would slowly trail himself sevenfold
Round the hall where I sate . . .

Now the fact that a line ends at a certain place, in free verse as well as in metrical, suggests that there is a reason for its so doing. The new line may imply a certain emphasis, since a word in this position acquires a slight stress, or it may mean that a breath is taken, or the line ending may accentuate the rhyme (sleeps and deeps) in the quotation above, or a number of other reasons may be responsible for certain lines ending at specific places. I feel that a fraction of a pause should occur at line endings—perhaps the equivalent to the ears of what the moving to the following line entails to the eyes. What I am trying to say is that a poem should not be pedantically read in accordance with preconceived ideas. A simple forthright reading invites the readiest interest and response, since children react negatively to anything that savors of affectation.

My own poetry sessions after a time fell into something of the regularity of a routine: a familiar framework which, when flexible enough to allow some variation, provided the children with the security of the known and expected. Each session started with their pasting in the books the poems chosen at the previous session and their reading them aloud—in unison with those who had chosen the same poem and with me. Then followed the reading of new poems, generally not more than four, as this number allowed time for discussion, reading, and choosing. In all, the procedure involved approximately twenty minutes, at which point I brought the lesson to a close—unless the children had embarked upon writing. How the writing came about will now be taken up in our consideration of the seven- and eight-year-olds.

6

We Like to Write

FOR THE PAST YEAR a group of four twelve-year-olds, two boys and two girls, have been coming to my home once a week to read poetry. We started as a summer project last year, but the children asked to continue during the winter and now have expressed the desire to go on into next year. This would seem to argue that they like poetry. Said one of the boys, "When my mother wanted me to start, I thought I would hate it. I thought poetry was 'sissy' stuff. Now I like it—and writing is the best part." This remark is the first overt expression of liking to write that has come from any child I have taught, but the fact that I have accumulated some sixteen typed volumes of poems the children have written over the years corroborates what this boy has said.

Getting young children to write is not so difficult as some teachers might imagine. Given the room climate earlier referred to and a period of time devoted to the reading of poetry, during which no mention of writing has been made, the children take the next step naturally in their stride. The request to write has often followed upon my bringing to class a book of Hilda Conkling's poems. The picture of the little girl on the frontispiece and the fact that her poems had been accorded the dignity of a printed book impressed the children greatly and brought forth the spontaneous question, "Can't *we* write some poems?" Previously it had been explained to them that Hilda's "writing" did not mean that she actually had transcribed the poems herself but that she had dictated them to her mother. The children then naturally assumed that they would dictate their poems to me.

It became amply evident by the unself-consciousness with which the children unburdened themselves in their poems that they enjoyed expressing and sharing their thoughts and feelings. They would write of anything that came to mind, and quite simply, for they were not as yet hampered, as were some of the older children, by any preconceived ideas of what is and what is not poetry. Reading these poems, teachers, however, may be inclined to question "Is any of this poetry? And if not, of what use is it?" They may be reassured. If this is not poetry, it is the stuff of which poetry is made, and the writing of it affords the child the opportunity and the sanction for tapping his own creative sources. I have had two children in my poetry class for as long as five years, others for not such extended periods, but all long enough to indicate that these early poems are the preliminary exercises, the gropings toward a more authentic poetic expression. And many of these young children's poems might be considered poetry in their own right.

The business of dictating involves a practical problem: how to occupy the other children when one child is dictating. My solution was to ask each child to raise his hand when ready to dictate and to call each to my desk in turn. While waiting, the other children are preoccupied with the poem they have in mind, thinking it through and trying to remember it. But after dictation, then what? I have generally made available several books of poems for the children to look through, or I have permitted them to continue with any book they may have been currently reading.

The teacher of large classes has an additional problem. He may have to do some organizing in advance, perhaps by dividing his group into two, allowing one group to read or pursue some other school activity while addressing himself to the other group. It is of course necessary that quiet be preserved, an atmosphere of relaxation, for the "poetry-feeling" to be achieved. Or a teacher might explain to all the children that each will have the opportunity to dictate, even if all will not be able to do so at one session. Or one period may be given to poetry reading, another to writing. A resourceful teacher may feel his way for the best procedures.

Of prime importance is the manner in which the teacher receives the child's poems, because upon his attitude will hinge the continuance of the child's writing. If the teacher is unresponsive to what the child produces in his first halting attempts, the child is forced to reject his ideas and feelings and to substitute for his spontaneity something he feels will be acceptable to his teacher, if indeed he will make any further attempt to write. Too great expectancy of him beyond his immediate ability discourages further effort, and, since our aim is to enable him to continue to develop his powers, as teachers we should accept whatever a child writes at a given time as valid for him at that stage in his development. I have heard many teachers say to a child, "You could do better," but who knows what any child can do? In their creative work I have been surprised too often by both superior and inferior performance to presume to guess a child's potential.

In what manner, then, should a teacher receive a child's poem? It would seem that all that is necessary is a favorable response, worded somewhat vaguely, such as "That is nice" or "I like that." The children, I have found, neither expect nor desire more. Actually many walk away from the desk while still dictating, and many do not recognize the poems of their own writing when these are read at a later session. Praise or comment is not required. Unless children have become accustomed to expect praise for everything they do, they treat their poems as casually as they do a finished arithmetic assignment. And this is as it should be. However, at times it is advisable for the teacher to draw attention to Johnny's accurate observation as illustrated in his poem or to Jane's well-chosen words in a description. Such observations may be made provided they are done lightly and that the child is not made to feel singled out for praise. The justification for comment in these cases is that indirectly the children are led to sense that a certain accuracy of observation and a happy use of words are desirable elements in writing. At the same time the light, impersonal character of the observation does not lead to any competitive feelings. It might not be amiss to state here that such indirect teaching tends to bring about results unobtainable by head-on instruction. There is little that can be dogmatically taught children in the creative pursuit of poetry. There are no "rights" and "wrongs" in the sense that a word is spelled correctly or incorrectly. Rather there are desirable modes of expression, but these cannot be formulated step by step or reduced to formal "rules." Instead, what is desirable can only be suggested indirectly by attention being drawn to certain acceptable practices. The child then makes his own inferences and incorporates in his writing as much of the suggestion that at the time he is able to assimilate. An example of indirect approach may be found in our earlier discussion of the word "tottering" in the poem, "The Pasture." It would be ill-advised to enjoin the child to search for words of comparable effectiveness in his own writing. Such a conscious search would block the spontaneity one wishes to preserve and foster, since it is just this spontaneous expression that provides the groundwork upon which the child can build.

An adult poet, mature in the practice of his craft, often substitutes a dynamic word for one that is dead or shopworn, but even for him the *trouvé* word comes by the grace of God. All of us make use of the phrase, "It just came to me," without questioning the authenticity of ideas arrived at without deliberate planning. The best we teachers can offer the child is the opportunity to draw upon his native gifts in an atmosphere in which they may continue to flourish. We need not be concerned if some of what "comes" in the beginning is awkward or naïve. For it is only by the exercise of his own powers that a child becomes proficient; Hughes Mearns speaks of the "muddy water" that must be allowed to flow before the stream becomes clear.

The poems of some six-year-olds are appended here to give the teacher an idea of what may be expected of children of this age. He may expect to find certain modes of expression appearing again and again, not only at this age but later in the poems of the sevens and eights. One of these is exemplified in the tendency of a child to fall into stereotypes. For example, John begins every poem with the phrase, "It's fun to . . ."

> It's fun to sail.
> As I watch all the sights,
> Miles and miles away.
> It's fun to walk on the deck
> And watch the sailors scrub and rub the boat.
> It's fun to sail,
> Especially when you're going to strange docks.

Karen begins her series of poems with, "When I . . ."

> When I am sick in bed,
> I always put out all the toys I have,
> And play and play till I have to put them away,
> And I don't want to.

After a short time she relinquishes the "When I's" for another repeated expression: "I have . . ."

> I have a little book.
> I wonder what's in it.

> I'll read it out loud
> So I'll know what's in it . . .
> Then I'll know what's in it.

Mary Anne starts all of her poems "Once when . . ."

> Once when I went to the beach,
> I played in the sand,
> And then went in the water,
> And when the waves came up and splashed,
> They felt so good.
> And when it was time to go home,
> I didn't want to.

The teacher need not be concerned about this repetition and feel he ought to direct the children into other modes of expression. Repetition at this point may answer some need of the children who employ it. In any case, without comment from the teacher, the children of their own accord relinquish stereotypes when these apparently have served their purpose.

Beginning writers are inclined to dictate little stories that bear small relation to poetry. Jane dictates:

A ROSE AND A BUTTERFLY

> The butterfly was sitting on the rose,
> And the little girl came and scared it away.
> The butterfly flew away to a palm tree,
> And then a boy climbed up the palm tree,
> And scared the butterfly away.
> Then it found another plant.
> It flew into the bramble bushes,
> And a boy climbed again in the bramble bushes.
> He scared the butterfly away.
> The butterfly this time got the boy away from him—
> He went up on top of an incinerator.

The incinerator delightfully proclaims its independence of anything poetic. That stories occur in the poems of the seven-year-olds is not surprising, for until the children have been exposed to poetry they naturally write in the prose forms to which they have been accustomed.

It is also possible that most of the poems they have heard have been narrative ones.

Many children, however, draw upon the subject matter of lyric poetry: they write of nature, of the objects around them, and of their own reactions to these. Martha writes:

> Magic chair, can you walk?
> Can anybody sit in you?
> Could I sit in you?
> Do you have any friends around the living room?
> Could you walk down the streets
> With your little bare feets?
> Do you talk to the lamp,
> The big old lamp in front of you?
> When do you eat, old magic chair,
> What do you eat today?

Martha has a vivid imagination. She invests inanimate objects with human qualities as in the following poem:

> Old house, are you lonely,
> With no windows in your window-pane,
> In the tree-tops down in the forest alone?
> Does anybody come to stay in you?
> The breezes ask you.

This has a genuine lyric quality rare in such a young child; one has only to compare the cadence with that of the previous poem.

Rachel also has a lyric feeling:

> When it's morning I wake up,
> And say I had a long, long dream.
> And I go in the sun
> And it's blooming like sky,
> And it's sunny and the flowers are starting to grow.
> Then my poor nice day started to rain,
> 'Cause I was going to a little tea-party.
> After the tea-party the sun came out,
> And the flowers started to bloom again,
> Then they started to go down,
> 'Cause night was coming.

Rachel seems a bit hazy about the relation of sun, rain, and night to flowers, but the sun "blooming like sky" is a charming lyric touch.

Many children inject subjective matter into their poems as does Kenny in the following:

> The black clouds are flying in the dark sky.
> At first they are white, when they are in the sky,
> When the wind is blowing them.
> Then I go to sleep at night.
> Suddenly the windows start banging and banging,
> And the dark clouds
> Throw great little pieces of ice down,
> And they hit the street,
> And make the street all white.
> Then it starts to pour,
> And the rain taps on the window
> Forever and forever until the rain is stopped.

He continues this with a prosy schedule of getting up, breakfast, and play, but in the portion of the poem quoted here is indication of observation of color and sound along with the childlike phrase, "great little pieces of ice."

In the following poem, which incidentally is the longest a child of any age has written in my classes, he again gives evidence of acute observation and a dramatic quality of a somewhat breathless variety.

> The firemen slide down the pole.
> They jump onto the engine.
> The siren blows.
> The firemen hang on tight.
>
> One sits in the driver's seat and drives the engine
> As fast as it can go.
> Sometimes they turn around the corner so fast,
> They turn on two wheels.
>
> When they get to the fire
> They ask the chief what they're 'sposed to do.
> The chief is already there.
> He has a bright red coat and so do they,
> And a bright shiny bell,
> And bright red lights,
> And so do they have bright red lights.

Clang, clang goes the hook-and-ladder truck,
Going down the street as fast as it can go.
There's a man in back of the engine
With a steering wheel,
And he's strapped on top of the ladders.

When they get to the fire they set up a ladder,
Right up to the building.
The flames shoot out every place in the building.
The firemen take a hose and put it right up the building.

They take an axe and run up the ladder,
And chop the burning pieces of the wood.
Sometimes they have to get up late at night,
And the roaring engine comes out,
And the siren blows as loud as it can.
Sometimes they have to do it on foggy nights.
Sometimes when they're doing it on foggy nights,
Boats catch on fire,
And they hear the fog horns tooting to make them hurry.
Sometimes they have to have a lot of fireboats come,
'Cause lots of boats have a wreck,
And they all catch on fire,
So a tug boat has to come and pull them,
So a fireman can get in between the boats,
And get water from the bay and the ocean.
Sometimes they're in the bay or the ocean,
    The Pacific Ocean.

Sometimes they have to get a search light
On the foggy nights to see where they are,
So they won't let the fire burn worse.
Sometimes the bridge gets on fire,
And they have to come very fast.
Sometimes the bridge breaks on them,
And then they have to get water from the ocean,
And when the bridge breaks the fire is out.[1]

Only the fact that at this point the class period came to an end put
a stop to Kenny's "inspiration." But he was not discouraged. We met

[1] From Flora J. Arnstein, *Adventure into Poetry* (Stanford, Calif.: Stanford
University Press, 1951).

almost a month later and he continued (without having heard a repeat of his poem) with another thirty lines on the same subject. By this time he has come around to forest fires and his poem ends:

> Sometimes about three months, the place where the fire was
> Is still scorching, sometimes more.
> And sometimes when it's still scorching,
> Cigars and cigarettes are thrown from a road,
> And that starts another big fire,
> And burns up the things that are scorching.

Aside from being unusually articulate for a child of six, Kenny demonstrates a characteristic common to the poems of young children—that of exploring a subject from many angles; though it must be said no child has been so thorough in exploration as he.

Susan is another able child. She dictates:

> The rose is pink in the spring,
> It turns yellow in the summer,
> And the butterfly that stands on it
> Looks velvet.

> The roses that are pretty in the garden
> Sometimes yellow, red and pink,
> And the violets look so pretty—
> The purple ones like velvet,
> And the white ones like silk.

> And sometimes the pansies' green stems and yellow.
> The country is full of all those pretty flowers,
> But still I can't decide which of the flowers I like the best.
> But I think all day long,
> But I can't think in the night,
> Because I'm sleeping.

> And all the flowers have green stems,
> But some have purple stems—
> I don't know which ones have purple stems.
> And the daphne smells so good,
> And so do gardenias, and so do roses,
> But gardenias and roses and daphnes look pretty—
> I wonder why the little daphne
> Sparkles so in the sunshine.

In this poem Susan forecasts many modes of expression which will appear with great frequency in the poems of the seven- and eight-year-old children. One is that of enumeration. Susan enumerates the different flowers, their different colors, and the different colors of the stems. However, she enumerates somewhat incidentally, whereas the older children often start their poems with enumerative lists. It is as though at this age children are impelled to assemble all the data that they know on a given subject in order to be able to envisage it.

The expression "I like" is another one common to the older children—which Susan touches upon here in her inability to decide on her preference between the different flowers. The "I like's" may serve in some way to relate the child to phenomena outside him; in any case the use of the phrase is too common to be dismissed as of no significance. Susan also evaluates her subjects in terms of aesthetic appeal: the flowers are pretty; the daphne smells good. Like Kenny she has a staying power unusual in children even of a later age; she is not deflected from her subject.

All in all, the poem has the charm of childhood in its minuteness and freshness of observation, but in addition Susan avails herself of one of the essential devices of poetry, imagery. The butterfly "looks like velvet"; the "purple violets like velvet, the white ones like silk." And the poem ends on the delightful query of why the daphne "sparkles" in the sun.

These, then, are some of the poems of six-year-olds. What the sevens write now follows.

7

The Sevens and Eights

THE SEVENS AND EIGHTS are eager and articulate. They write about what they see, hear, touch, or feel inwardly. Inanimate objects, nature, animals engage their attention; in fact there is nothing that is not grist to their mill. They assess the world about them and their own relation to it. Fay at eight writes:

MOON

When I go to bed at night,
I turn off my light
And I look at the beautiful moon
And the thousand pretty little stars,
When the sky is clear.

Eric at seven also writes about nature:

The clouds are so fluffy and white.
I wonder if they're strong enough to lie down on,
And maybe if they're strong enough,
I might sit on one and sing myself a song.
If I sat on a cloud I might see a twittering bird,
Or maybe a robin flying toward the south.
And maybe I might see a plane
With its glistening wings
As it goes sailing by.

Roger at eight:

RAIN

The rain pours down upon the leaves
While I lie in bed.
I hear the leaves rustling in the night,
And when I get up in the morning,
I see everything wet with bubbles all around.

Eric now turns his attention to

A TRAIN ON A JOURNEY

A train is in the railroad yard.
It is going on a great long journey
It is off on its way now.
Where does it go?
The winds are passing—
They whistle, they sing a song,
And this is what they sing:
"Go fast, go fast, you're on your way."
"Oo, Oo," this is what I sing—
"Oo, Oo."

These poems deriving from direct experience are a far cry from the poems of children printed in so-called "Kiddie Columns." Recently I heard a radio program of children reading and discussing their poems under the leadership of a woman who could not have been their teacher for, among other questions, she asked under what circumstances the poems had been written. The program, with its implied achievement and the importance given to the poems by the questions asked, seemed to me to be the most ill-advised procedure for the children, who were made to feel that they were in some way especially gifted. Their poems did not bear out this assumption. They were facile jingles that bore no relation to genuine experience—the sort any bright child can turn out a dime a dozen. In contrast, the poems I have quoted above represent children's natural preoccupations and have none of the pretentiousness that invariably arises when children are made to feel self-conscious about their writing.

Ellen at eight writes:

A BEAUTIFUL COLOR

Blue is a beautiful color.
Blue is in the waters of lakes,
Rivers, streams and oceans.
And the sky is blue.
A flame is blue.
Just as the flowers are.
Blue is in the most beautiful things
In the world.

While I make no great claims for this as poetry, I should like to contrast it with an adult poem on the same subject. Placing them side by side may serve to illuminate that elusive matter of sentimentality I referred to in an earlier chapter.

BLUE

So many radiant things are blue—
Heavens of fragile turquoise tint;
This curling smoke, a sea-ward view;
The eyes of laughing girls, that hint
Of sudden stars or sun-touched dew;
So many dear, delightful things—
Forget-me-nots, and gentians, too;
A blue-bird's crisp and curving wings—
I think the soul's own hidden hue
Must be some lovely shade of blue!

Let us note first the trite adjectives the adult poet employs: *radiant* (as applied to "things"—with the noun's lack of specificity); *fragile, curling* (of smoke), *sun-touched* (dew), *curving* (wings)—not a fresh observation is among them; nothing is seen with the individual eye. Then let us note the blue objects the author has chosen to enumerate and contrast these with those the child has noted: *heavens,* as against the child's more direct *sky; stars, dew,* the sentiment-laden *forget-me-nots* and the eyes of *laughing girls,* as against the child's fresh observation of the blue of a *flame* and the straightforward *flowers.* The banal ending caps a poem that is further removed from true poetry than is the unpretentious one of the child. For poetry is that which is seen and experienced at first hand. The child is writing out of experience; the adult, in language that suggests less a personal reaction than one derived from the parlor gift book.

The poems quoted above are less common than the usual poems written by children of the same age. As mentioned in the previous chapter, the children employ certain recurrent types of expression, such as enumeration which recurs with surprising frequency in the poems of the sevens and eights. No teacher need be told that measurement by chronological age is far from accurate, that some children at seven have a mental age of nine or more, and conversely, a child without really being less able, may perform at an age level younger than his own. In the creative field these variations are especially pronounced. What may seem to be reluctance or unreadiness in any given child may occur when he has been cut off from his creative self, either by some emotional disturbance or by any of a number of other causes. Cultural factors enter the picture as well. A child from an environment where reading is a matter of course, and one who has read widely by himself, will have at his command a vocabulary and a handling of language that are not available to children with a more limited cultural background. Hence the age designations employed in this book should be regarded more as a convenience of classification than as an indication of what children at any given age may write.

Enumeration, though, seems especially characteristic of the sevens and eights. That the children are not imitating one another, as might be surmised, is evidenced by the fact that this mode of expression arises spontaneously in different groups at different times and places. The process of assembling all the data they know on one subject seems to be a phase of development through which children pass. Here follow some typical examples.

John at seven writes:

> There are all kinds of animals:
> There are brown animals,
> Red animals, and yellow animals.
> There are some funny animals,
> And there are some baby animals.
> There are animals that have big, big noses,
> And big feet, like the pelicans.

Emily at seven writes:

> Books, books,
> Red books, yellow books,
> Orange books,
> All sorts of kinds of color books.
> Sometimes there are magazines,
> In the shelves of the library.
> Usually there are.
> There are yellow, blue, red magazines,
> And orange magazines,
> Not only books and magazines,
> But fairy tales.

Adolph at eight enumerates:

> Flowers are growing,
> And some are yellow,
> And some are red,
> And some are blue,
> And some are big,
> And some are little.
> The sun makes them grow.
> At night-time they go to sleep,
> And let their little heads hang down.

In the last three lines the child makes some general observations accompanying enumeration, and this variation occurs in many of the poems.
Kay at seven dictates:

> There are big horses
> And little horses,
> There are horses that are wild,
> And horses that buck,
> And you cannot ride them
> Unless you ride very, very well.
> There are tame horses
> That ride very smoothly.
> Mostly little children ride ponies.
> Ponies mostly don't buck.
> I would like to ride a pony, but I cannot,
> For I don't know how to ride.

Along with poems containing general statements appear other forms of expression: "I like" or "I love." Among the seven-year-olds there occur in the course of three terms 67 instances of the use of the former, and in the eight-year-olds in five terms 104. In the nine-year-olds in six terms the expression occurs 61 times, and from then on it tapers off with only occasional appearances in the poems of older children. It is as though in the employment of these expressions the children were relating themselves in terms of feeling to their subject matter and at the same time, by expressing preference, envisaging it in a subjective rather than objective fashion.

The following by a seven-year-old is a poem in point. It starts with the familiar list, then expresses a preference.

TREES

There are big trees and little trees,
There are eucalyptus trees and pine trees.
I like the eucalyptus trees better
Because they are more healthy
And smell better.

Whether this little boy likes the eucalyptus trees because they are healthy themselves or presumably because he believes them to be wholesome for people is engagingly ambiguous.

The same boy in a few months progresses from strict enumeration and the blunt statement "I like" to a more extended assembling of data, and from the expression of personal preference to a commentary on the behavior of other people.

FLOWERS

There are all kinds of flowers
In the big garden—
Marigolds, pansies, roses
And other flowers.
They grow in the spring,
And go down in the autumn.
I should think they'd stay up
All the year,
But they do not.
When you forget to water them,
And you forget to pull out the weeds,
They die—they die of thirst
And of the weeds.
I think it is very cruel,
But some other people do not.

Long, long ago
I had a very big garden
With all these flowers,
And they all died,
And we never, never wanted to see them again.[1]

[1] Hughes Mearns in his *The Creative Adult* comments upon this poem, as well as on my teaching.

Ellen, aged eight, also makes the transition from mere listing to personal evaluation and commentary:

> Trees are plants,
> Just like flowers.
> I see them in the flower-pots,
> I see them in the bowers,
> I see them in forests,
> I see them in yards.
> But best of all I like
> The daffodils on the hill.

> Roses red,
> Pansies all colors,
> Daisies white,
> And all those flowers,
> But best of all
> Are the daffodils
> Sitting on the glowing hill.

Here too we have the child making use of a refrain.

While in the stage of writing the "I like" poems, these children also fall into employing stereotyped phrases. They begin every poem with an identical sequence of words. Some children riot through a series beginning "I like"—as does eight-year-old Fay:

> I like to draw pictures
> And color them too,
> And sometimes I go over the line;
> And then I scribble it.
> And sometimes it is easy,
> And I can do it.

> I like the little jelly-fish.
> He's awfully sticky.
> I like to pick them up,
> And then I throw them into the water,
> And then the fishes get them.

She varies the "I like" to a series of "I love":

> I love to write in ink,
> And smear it all over my hands,
> And when it gets too smeary,
> Then I have to use pumice stone—
> What I hate. It's so rough, you know.

Gradually, as has been previously noted, the children relinquish stereotypes in favor of more varied expression. Here is the same child some time after writing the above:

REDWOOD TREE

> Tall, green redwood tree,
> Spreading its great bough over me,
> Patches of blue sky,
> I see as I lie
> On my back at the foot of the tree.

Incidentally this poem shows unusually successful use of rhyme; we will speak of children's use of rhyme in a later chapter.

Other stereotypes begin with "When I . . ." Kathy, eight, dictates:

> When I go on the river,
> When I go through the waves,
> I always think it's a sort of blue cloth
> That spreads over the water.

And

> When I play with chalk,
> It always gets in my nose,
> Mamie always says, "Go wash your face,"
> Or else, "How did that chalk
> Get in your nose?"
> I always have to wash my face anyway.

Stereotypes are so common with young children that any teacher may expect to find his children employing them. He may be inclined to wonder why I have not suggested directing the children's expression into different channels. It seems that anything that serves to induce self-consciousness in the children tends to block their spontaneity, and inasmuch as the children of themselves presently progress to different types of expression there is no reason to make an issue of the matter.

The sevens and eights, like their younger brothers and sisters, dictate what might better be designated stories than poems. Doris writes:

THE LITTLE OLD LADY

Once there was a little old lady.
She was only about twelve years old.
Oh, yes, I mean she was only 1200 years old.
This little old lady thought
She was the youngest person in the world.
She went running about and said,
"I am the youngest person in the world."
And everybody laughed at her. They said,
"You're just the opposite from the youngest,
You're the oldest."
Then she laughed a funny kind of laugh,
And said, "Ho, ho, you think so,
But you're very, very wrong."
And then she went walking down the street proudly,
Laughing and laughing and laughing.
Then she went home and said,
"They don't know anything.
I'm the youngest and not the oldest."
And then she laughed herself to sleep,
And not cried.

Many children begin their poems "Once upon a time," thus indicating their concept of poems as stories. Seven-year-old Mark does not start off with the familiar phrase, but his "Two Pennies" is nonetheless a little story:

I had two pennies.
I went down to a book store.
I asked the man for a book that cost two pennies.
He said, "No! Most certainly not!
It takes paper and ink and typewriters
To make a book.
Wouldn't you think a book would cost more
Than two pennies?"

I said, "Bah!" and went out,
And I went to another book store.
I asked for a book that cost two pennies.
The man said, "Take one."
And I looked around and found a nice little book.
All it had in it was little poems,
But I liked it very much
Because there were pretty little poems,
Like about buttercups and that sort of thing,
And spring times.[2]

It is significant that the book Mark finds is one containing "little poems" which he likes very much.

On the whole the children write fewer "stories" than might be expected. For one thing, they tend to write in short units. Even older children are more at ease in nonexpository writing. One has only to remember the groans with which an assignment of a "composition" is greeted, and the perfunctory and dull performance resulting, to realize that exposition is difficult for children to handle and is distasteful to them. Poetry, dealing as it does with a unit of experience, comes more easily and is more congenial.

Incidentally, short poems receive justification from no less a poet than Edgar Allan Poe, who contended that there is no such thing as a long poem—it is made up only of a sequence of short ones.

In order to suggest to the children that short poems are acceptable, I have frequently read them translations from Japanese poems all of which employ only condensed forms. For the same reason, when the children come to write their own poems, I distribute small paper, six by four inches, so that they are not confronted with a large formidable space that they feel they must fill. The small sheets do not seem to limit them, since when they wish to write more extended poems, they ask for additional paper.

Teachers may be troubled at times by the children's tendency to imitate what they have heard or read. They need not be. Children are natural mimics. Is not learning to speak in itself largely an act of mimicry? Children are likely to adopt either content or actual expres-

[2] From Flora J. Arnstein, *Adventure into Poetry* (Stanford, Calif.: Stanford University Press, 1951).

sions from poems they have heard—whole lines in some instances. They do this without compunction, announcing freely, "I got that from"; or another child will comment on someone's poem, "He copied that from. . . ." Cribbing was not always regarded as it is today. Did not Shakespeare appropriate the plots of his plays from whatever sources he chose, and is it not difficult for the listener sometimes to distinguish the early Beethoven from his predecessor, Mozart? So the children may be forgiven behavior sanctioned by their illustrious forbears. It is generally those children who have been early readers or who have read considerably who are inclined to crib. They take over familiar forms, such as the following adopted by Carol, age eight:

> Five pink toes,
> One pink nose—
> That makes a baby.
> Two eyes,
> One mouth,
> That makes a baby.
>
> One neck
> And one baby,
> Makes a baby,
> And an extra neck.[3]

On dictating this, when Carol arrived at the line, "One neck," she stopped, at a loss how to proceed. She shifted from one foot to the other, hesitated a few minutes, then came up triumphantly with the "extra neck." Her solution of her problem, which has convulsed adults to whom the poem has been read, seemed in no way humorous to Carol or to her classmates.

The influence of A. A. Milne is clearly discernable in seven-year-old Kay's

DICTATING

> I'm dictating to my mother,
> I'm dictating to my brother,
> I'm dictating to my sister
> A poem that I read.

[3] From Arnstein, *Ibid.*

I'm dictating to my aunt,
I'm dictating to my uncle,
I'm dictating to my cousin
    A poem that I read.

I'm dictating a poem—
A poem isn't funny,
A poem isn't silly,
 A poem is a poem,
    And that is all it is.

It's only just a poem,
It's only just a poem,
It's only just a poem
    A poem that I read.[4]

It is not irrelevant that Kay says she is dictating a poem that she *read*. However, despite the cribbing, the poem indicates that Kay has an innate sense of form—the four-line stanza (with one exception) and the refrain persisting throughout.

At times a child is disturbed by another's "copying" of his poem. In such cases the teacher may observe that nobody can write a completely original poem. Since writing has been going on over the ages, necessarily everything must have already been written about. And one might add that whenever the child who is accused of copying feels he wants to draw on his own ideas he will do so. This reply has seemed to mollify the child who considers himself injured, while it places no stigma on the cribber. It is seldom, though, that children borrow from one another. In cases where they do, it is generally those insecure children who have little confidence in themselves who feel the need to take over another child's ideas. Once faith in themselves has been established, they are only too eager to draw upon their own experience and to explore their own ideas and feelings. Again for the teacher, the indirect approach seems advisable. His continued approval of material that derives from the children's personal experience tends to discourage borrowing and directs the children back to their own sources.

Expressions which the children believe to be "poetic" are apt to appear in poems of beginners. The use of "a" preceding the verb, as "a-sailing,"

---

[4] From *Ibid.*

and such expressions as "I pray" or "at play" turn up now and again. The observation that people today generally write in the way we speak nowadays seems all that is necessary to direct the children to their natural mode of expression. In any case the use of archaic terms is short-lived. On the whole the teacher will find it desirable to ignore such practices and to allow the children to write whatever comes to them without comment or direction. She may be reassured that many children who start with a very indifferent performance often are able, in the course of the poetry study, to achieve original and delightful writing. Such a one is Carol, who at eight dictates:

> Trees are very useful things:
> Tables, chairs, stools
> And even paper.
> When you see an oak tree
> Standing peacefully in the woods
> You sort of say to yourself,
> "Maybe you'll be turned into a book tomorrow,
> Maybe a fairy-tale will be written on you,
> And maybe you will be turned into
> That particular geography book
> That I hate."

This has little to commend it as a poem, and as an early attempt it gives no indication that this child is to develop into an exceptionally gifted writer.

After a few months' exposure to poetry, however, she writes the following:

> The sea is deep and blue.
> The sea is sometimes green.
> The waves crash on the shore
> Loud as thunder,
> And the clouds above are grey.
>
> The sea gulls must be very cold
> As they sit upon the posts,
> For they quiver and shiver and vibrate.
> Sometimes they are grey,
> And sometimes they are white,
> And they look like the clouds.

The waves with all their white caps
Come clashing into land—
It deafens you.

But when the day is nice,
And the sun shining merrily,
And there are thousands and thousands of sail boats,
The waves are not big at all.
They are not grown up.
It is all so beautiful at sunset,
For the sun makes everything red,
And the sea gulls have a lovely time.
Oh, the sea is beautiful at all times,
Even though the times are very, very different.

Here are shown firsthand observations, a response to different facets of the sea, a smoother cadence, and the use of imagery in the gulls resembling clouds. Of course not all the poems of a child, as is true as well of adults, are of the same quality at any given time, but those of children who have attended poetry classes over a period of years give ample evidence of growth in poetic expression. It can never be assumed what a child may ultimately be able to accomplish; the process of maturing, the exposure to poetry, his ability to gain access to his native resources, and finally the quality of those resources—all will determine what the outcome will be. Nothing grows from nothing, and with the constant exposure to poetry the children unconsciously absorb those characteristics that distinguish it from prose and draw upon these in their own writing.

8

We Come into Poetry

A COMMON PRACTICE in the teaching of music appreciation tends, I believe, to destroy rather than to foster the children's enjoyment of it. Along with the playing of the music, stories of the lives of the composers are presented, with little inconsequential anecdotes concerning them. Notably absent is any commentary on or elucidation of the music itself. The same practice is current in the teaching of poetry. Dates of the poets may be mentioned, their nationality and other factual material concerning them are dwelt upon, but little consideration is given to the poetry as poetry. Content is stressed, but that this content is presented in the context of poetry is ignored. Yet it cannot be dismissed as a matter of no moment that since the writer has employed poetry rather than prose as his medium, there is good reason for discussion of the poetry as poetry.

The same lack of emphasis on poetry as poetry is evidenced by many poetry programs on radio and TV. The discussants concern themselves with the poet's subject matter, his philosophy, his place in history, everything in effect but what constitutes the particular character of his poetry, or what distinguishes it from the poetry of another poet. Reference is seldom made to his individual handling of language, of form, his personal style, or of any other specific attributes of his poetry. While the historical or philosophic approach may have relevance for adults, for the child anything extraneous to the poem itself is irrelevant and misleading. What *is* relevant for the child is the question, "What is this poem saying to me now?" For the younger child it is enough that the poem be related to his understanding, his feeling. But as the children grow older, they are well able to grasp and enjoy those features of poetry that distinguish it as poetry. The shared experience with the poet having already been established, it remains to be recognized that a poem is an experience in itself.

In "Why Poetry?" I mentioned some of the aspects of poetry that the teacher might explore for his own enjoyment. Having done so, he may now share these with his children. At the age of nine or ten some of the children may be ready for an introduction to the elements of poetry, though the age at which these may be presented will be for the teacher to decide. Considerations such as the maturity of his group and whether his children will have been exposed to previous instruction in poetry will enter into his decision.

For example, while a young child will spontaneously employ imagery in a poem of his own writing, he is often unable to entertain the concept of an image. Even in his own poems he sometimes demonstrates confusion with regard to images, as is illustrated by the following poem which John at seven dictates:

THE LITTLE SEA ANIMAL

In the sea the animal roams.
He looks like a horse,
But he does not have eyes,
He does not eat.
He is just foam
That comes up on the sea-shore.
I like to play with the sea horse.
It roars when I get up in the morning,
And also splashes all over me,
So that I should live.
I could not live without the sea horse.
I like to bathe in the sea horse.

Here in likening the foam to a horse, he pushes the analogy beyond reason or sense.

Again in another poem he says, "The wind is blowing just like skirts in the sky," a somewhat more rational use of image though as yet he does not realize its nature. It is as though he senses a need for comparison but has not arrived at the precise concept of an image. When he writes, "The rain looks like water coming down from heaven," he is employing what might be called an abortive image, and this is a form common with beginners. The juxtaposition of two objects not completely dissimilar (since rain *is* water) removes the analogy from the realm of true imagery. The true image compares two disparate objects, heightening the first by underlining the common element in the two. Thus, when a child writes, "A sailboat is like a bird," he is noting the common element in both objects—a certain wing-like structure; it is this common element that performs the function of the image—heightening the picture, giving extension to the meaning.

By the age of ten or thereabouts children are not only able to grasp the concept of image but are avid in identifying these in poems they read. They are ready to discuss the value the particular simile lends to the poems, and they make increasing use of imagery in their own writing. At times certain of my groups have suggested a sort of game—choosing a word and finding images appropriate and applicable to it. On one such occasion Grace, ten, writes:

MOUSE

Tail like a whip,
Size like a door knob,
He sneaks in and out of his hole.[1]

DEER

His antlers like bare trees,
His eyes like hard buttons,
He nibbles the green, green grass.

Louise, eleven, contributes:

GOLD FISH

Darting in and out,
Gold as the sun,
Fast as an arrow,
With fins like the dew in the morning.

Sometimes the children surprise one with outstanding images, as does nine-year-old Joyce:

---

[1] All five poems from Flora J. Arnstein, *Adventure into Poetry* (Stanford, Calif.: Stanford University Press, 1951).

BAT

He flies through the night
Like a black surprise . . .

and

TIGER

He leaps through the forest
Like a striped hurricane.

Many an adult poet would have been happy to have created such
striking and vivid images as the "black surprise" and the "striped
hurricane."

The sound of words in relation to their meaning interests the children
greatly. One might read them, as two contrasting uses of "sound" words,
the "Noise of Waters," quoted earlier, and "Storm" by "H. D."[2]

STORM

You crash over the trees,
you crack the live branch—
the branch is white,
the green crushed,
each leaf is rent like split wood.

You burden the trees
with black drops,
you swirl and crash—
you have broken off a weighted leaf
in the wind,
it is hurled out,
whirls up and sinks,
a green stone.

In this poem the children enjoy identifying the words that express action
by their sound, such as *clash, crash,* and also those words or phrases that
are "picture-making."[3]

[2] From H. D., *Sea Garden* (London: Constable, 1916).
[3] See "The Teacher's Dilemma," p. 8.

Older children are responsive to the symbolic content of a poem. Matthew indicates this readiness at twelve when he says, "I like poems that mean more than they mean." "The Road Not Taken" by Robert Frost provides an example of the symbolic in poetry.

It might be helpful at this point to illustrate one of the many possible presentations of this poem. Just as it has been suggested earlier with reference to the younger children that the children's own experience be explored before reading a poem, so with the upper elementary children, before reading the poem, the setting or the general idea of the poem should be touched upon. There need be no extended exposition of the poem's content, just enough so that the children are enabled to orient themselves to it. "The Road Not Taken" might be summarized in this fashion: "This poem deals with the experience of walking in a wood and arriving at a spot where two roads diverge or separate. The poet chooses one of the roads." If possible the poem might be written on the blackboard since it might be difficult to deal with it analytically only by hearing it—we are all today to some extent "eye-minded."

THE ROAD NOT TAKEN

Two roads diverged in a yellow wood,
And sorry I could not travel both
And be one traveler, long I stood
And looked down one as far as I could
To where it bent in the undergrowth;

Then took the other, as just as fair,
And having perhaps the better claim,
Because it was grassy and wanted wear;
Though as for that the passing there
Had worn them really about the same,

And both that morning equally lay
In leaves no step had trodden black.
Oh, I kept the first for another day!
Yet knowing how way leads on to way,
I doubted if I should ever come back.

> I shall be telling this with a sigh
> Somewhere ages and ages hence:
> Two roads diverged in a wood, and I—
> I took the road less traveled by,
> And that has made all the difference.[4]

One might begin by taking up the content of the poem. Questions might be asked: What road did the poet take and why? What does his choice tell you about the man? What is the implication of the title? Such questions lead directly to the matter of symbolic interpretation. Is the poet speaking exclusively about a road? Or it might be asked, if the children have not already brought the matter up, is the poet saying anything about the making of choices? And this in turn might lead to a discussion of the universal predicament of choice and where this leads.

But, as I mentioned earlier, one must not be restricted to dealing with the content of a poem alone, or as a matter of fact with any one aspect of a poem to the exclusion of others. A young teacher told me of the tendency of her group while in teacher training to embark on what she called "a safari of image hunting," to the point where they became so obsessed with this exercise that their interest was limited solely to this one phase of poetry.

With relation to the poem noted above the question might be posed, why should this subject be presented in poetic form? Someone might come up with the remark, perhaps not entirely innocent of the intent to disconcert the teacher, that it is written in poetry because the writer was a poet. If the idea was to slightly discomfort the teacher, it miscarries with his reply, "Precisely. But what does the presentation as poetry do for the subject that prose might not have done equally well?" In order to bring out one point he might ask each member of the class to write in prose the content of the first three lines, through the word "traveler." Such a prose rendering might read: "I was walking along a road in a wood to where the road separated into two forks. I was sorry I could not take both forks, but being only one person I could not do so." Now the class might be asked to count the words in the poetic version—they add up to eighteen—then to count those in their prose version. In mine they add up to thirty-six.

---

[4] From Robert Frost, *Complete Poems of Robert Frost* (New York: Holt, Rinehart and Winston, 1949).

The difference between the number of words necessary to express the same thought in poetry and prose brings up another aspect of poetry: that of condensation, compression. Poetry expresses by a sort of short-hand, by suggestion, or by other means what it is not possible to express in the same space in prose. And, as any condensation leads to tension, so too a subject gains a certain dynamic quality by the tension inherent in poetic rendering. (Of course one need not express the matter in these terms to children.) They may be shown, for example, how much is implied by the final line: "And that has made all the difference." In these seven simple words are suggested the idea of how a person's whole life may be changed in the moment of a single choice. And one may note the understatement, as again expressed in, "I shall be telling this with a sigh." How much emotion is conveyed and how much of recollection and regret are carried by the phrase, "Somewhere ages and ages hence"! Content and condensation, however, do not exhaust the matter for discussion offered by this poem. They have been presented here merely as examples of the varied approaches which may bring to the children aspects of poetry that will be new to them.

Condensation is also illustrated through the poetry of the Japanese. The forms employed, the *hokku* and the *tanka*, the first consisting of only seventeen syllables, the last, thirty-one, are telling examples of how much may be suggested by restricted means. One may speculate that for the Japanese the short poem serves to stimulate the imagination to carry the thought onward. One might compare the effect with that of a pebble thrown in a lake, the concentric circles expanding wider and wider; just so the thought is carried on beyond what is said to the limits of the readers' imaginative powers.

I append a couple of examples since I employ these and similar poems in my work with the children.

> O Pine-Tree
> At the side of the stone house,
> When I look at you,
> It is like seeing face to face
> With men of old time.[5]

[5] All these Japanese poems are from Elias Lieberman (editor), *Poems for Enjoyment* (New York: McGraw-Hill, 1931).

This poem by "The Priest Hakatsu," translated by Arthur Waley, by its delicate suggestion stimulates one's thoughts to the recollection of the old days and then men living then. The past is brought to the present by the confrontation "face to face" with the living pine trees (associated with the old men), whose ridges are of today and yet have been made by the passing years.

Similar imaginative evocation occurs in the following two poems:

My heart thinking
"How beautiful he is"
Is like a swift river
Which though one dams it and dams it,
Will still break through.

This, by "The Lady of Sakanoye," is rendered in English by the same translator. Another poet, Okura, is translated by Mabel Lorenz:

THE MOUNTAIN TOP

Because the plum trees on the peak
Are up so high,
The buzz of bees about their bloom
Comes from the sky!

Poems such as these allow the child a congenial play of imagination and lead him to search behind the literal facades for further meanings. And such reading-with-the-imagination is especially to be cultivated in connection with poetry.

Here a word may be interpolated concerning the teacher's response to the children's comments. These are bound to be in many cases immature and irrelevant, or may even contain false inferences, but whatever their nature, they should be accorded respectful reception. Nor need the teacher acclaim any "correct' or particularly significant remark; by doing so he will be diverting the children's concern from the matter under discussion to that of offering observations that presumably will gain his approval. To single out any one child for special commendation is as undesirable as to single him out for condemnation. Response is to be encouraged, and the quality of the response will improve through continued exposure to poetry.

Suggestion, in addition to explicit exposition, whether with condensation or not, occurs in English poetry as well as in Japanese. "The Listeners" by Walter de la Mare lends itself admirably as an example. The children's interest is immediately aroused by the poet's having placed the reader squarely in the middle of his story without any hint of the incidents leading up to the climax, or elucidating to what commitment the traveler is referring. Searching for interpretations and trying to envisage possible situations that might have given rise to the incident described offer an imaginative challenge to the children's inventiveness.

THE LISTENERS

"Is there anybody there?" said the Traveller,
    Knocking at the moonlit door;
And his horse in the silence champed the grasses
    Of the forest's ferny floor:
And a bird flew up out of the turret,
    Above the Traveller's head:
And he smote upon the door again a second time;
    "Is there anybody there?" he said.
But no one descended to the Traveller;
    No head from the leaf-fringed sill
Leaned over and looked into his grey eyes,
    Where he stood perplexed and still.
But only a host of phantom listeners
    That dwelt in the lone house then
Stood listening in the quiet of the moonlight
    To the voice from the world of men:
Stood thronging the faint moonbeams on the dark stair,
    That goes down to the empty hall,
Harkening in the air stirred and shaken
    By the lonely Traveller's call.
And he felt in his heart their strangeness,
    Their stillness answering his cry,
While his horse moved, cropping the dark turf,
    'Neath the starred and leafy sky;
For he suddenly smote on the door, even
    Louder, and lifted his head:—
"Tell them I came, and no one answered,
    That I kept my word," he said.

> Never the least stir made the listeners,
>   Though every word he spake
> Fell echoing through the shadowiness of the still house
>   From the one man left awake:
> Ay, they heard his foot upon the stirrup,
>   And the sound of iron on stone,
> And how the silence surged softly backward,
>   When the plunging hoofs were gone.[6]

The poem lends itself to a wealth of poetic discovery. One feature that has not been previously mentioned is that of the music inherent in poetry. Reading this poem aloud, one becomes more aware of the music of the lines, the smoothness of their flow, and harking back to the "Noise of Waters" quoted in "Why Poetry?" one can note here a similar cadential quality.

The mood evoked by the poem can also be explored, notably the passage from "the host of phantom listeners" through to the "Traveller's call." The "faint moonbeams," the "dark stair," the "empty hall," the "air stirred and shaken"—all these phrases are calculated to arouse the feeling of eeriness, of strangeness. And attention might be drawn to the exactness of description of hoofbeats as "the sound of iron on stone," and how this is another telling example of condensation—the sound of the horse galloping away suggested merely by the "iron on stone." The contrast in the following line might be noted, as the poet resumes the mood of strangeness by the words "the silence surged softly backward" with their "S" sounds (like the admonition "Sh") reinforcing the idea of silence. I have made a point of calling to the children's notice the feeling a poem gives one, since children are sensitive to feeling, and attention drawn to it brings the realization that poetry is directed to the emotions as well as to the mind. It is obvious that not every poem lends itself to evaluation in terms of feeling.

Repetition of lines and the use of refrain open up another area of interest. The children might be asked, for example, what does the poet intend to convey by the repetition of the final line in each stanza of "The Pasture"? What function does the repetition of the last two lines of each stanza in "The Shepherdess" perform? Again, in the poem "Recuerdo" by Edna St. Vincent Millay, what does the repeated "We

---

[6] From Walter de la Mare, *The Listeners* (New York: Holt, Rinehart and Winston, undated).

were very happy, we were very merry" do for the poem? Or Robert
Frost's repetition of "And miles to go before I sleep" in his "Stopping
by the Woods on a Snowy Evening"?

In the next poem quoted there is a novel use of repetition which the
children will be interested in discovering. One might explore the use
of refrain in the old ballads—and speaking of ballads, a wealth of material here in both the old and new will delight the children. Such
comparatively modern ballads as "The Highwayman" by Alfred Noyes
and "The Inchcape Rock" never fail in appeal. It will interest the
children likewise to be made aware of the condensation employed in
the ballads—how much of the story is told by implication or by snatches
of conversation.

We may now turn to the consideration of rhythm in poetry which I
have delayed discussing because it, and rhyme, are too often treated as
the only components of poetry. Let us begin by having the children
clap the number of beats (the stressed syllables) in the following poem
by James Stephens:

THE SNARE

I hear a sudden cry of pain!
    There is a rabbit in a snare;
Now I hear the cry again,
    But I cannot tell from where.

But I cannot tell from where
    He is calling out for aid;
Crying on the frightened air,
    Making everything afraid.

Making everything afraid,
    Wrinkling up his little face,
And he cries again for aid;
    And I cannot find the place!

And I cannot find the place
    Where his paw is in the snare;
Little one! Oh, little one!
    I am searching everywhere.[7]

[7] From James Stephens, *Collected Poems of James Stephens* (New York:
Macmillan, rev. ed., 1954).

We find here consistent lines of four beats each. Looking back at "The Shepherdess," we find lines of four beats alternating with lines of three. In "The Pasture" we have two stanzas with the first three lines containing five beats and the fourth containing, roughly speaking, four, though practically every word is stressed. Countless variations of rhythm occur in poetry, and the children, once they are introduced to the possible variations, eagerly pursue their own discoveries in this field.

I would not suggest any more extensive analysis of meter with children, but the teacher might be interested in examining further subtleties of rhythm. Clapping the rhythm of the first stanza of "The Snare," we get the following general pattern of stressed (−) syllables and unstressed (◡):

$$\underset{\text{I hear a sud/den cry/ of pain!}}{◡ \; - \; ◡ \; - \; ◡ \; - \; ◡ \; -}$$

$$\underset{\text{There is/a rab/bit in/a snare;}}{◡ \; - ◡ \; - \; ◡ \; - ◡ \; -}$$

$$\underset{\text{Now/ I hear/ the cry/ again,}}{- \; ◡ \; - \; ◡ \; - \; ◡ \; -}$$

$$\underset{\text{But/ I can/not tell/ from where.}}{- \; ◡ \; - \; ◡ \; - \; ◡ \; -}$$

The basic pattern then, is unstress-stress (the iambic which is employed in the bulk of English poetry). The pattern of four beats to a line, however, is not affected by the omitted unstress at the beginning of the last two lines. Examining the lines more carefully and reading the words as they would be accented in speech, we find that we give a sort of intermediate accent, for example, on the word "I" and "Now." Using the symbol of ″ for this intermediate accent, we find the verse gives us the following pattern:

$$\underset{\text{I hear/ a sud/den cry/ of pain!}}{″ \; - \; ◡ \; - \; ◡ \; - \; ◡ \; -}$$

$$\underset{\text{There is a/ rabbit/ in a snare;}}{◡ \; ◡ ◡ \; - \; ◡ \; ◡ ◡ \; -}$$

$$\underset{\text{Now I hear/ the cry/ again}}{″ \; ″ \; - \; ◡ \; - \; ◡ -}$$

$$\underset{\text{But I can/not tell/ from where.}}{◡ \; ″ \; - \; ◡ \; - \; ◡ \; -}$$

The pattern, now, instead of being the consistent ∪ — of our clapped verse, becomes a very different and more complicated rhythm.

$$\begin{array}{l}'' \_ / \cup \_ / \cup \_ / \cup \_ \\ \cup \cup \cup / \_ \cup / \cup \cup \_ \\ '' \;'' \_ / \cup \_ / \cup \_ \\ \cup \;'' \_ / \cup \_ / \cup \_ \end{array}$$

However one may divide the beats into units (and there might be different ways of doing this), the pattern is notably different from the clapped one. Thus within any all-over fixed pattern there may be innumerable variations. This interplay of the natural stress of words against the basic rhythm—a sort of counterpoint—adds immeasurably to the interest of the rhythm, and the reader senses this interplay even if he is not consciously aware of it. The presence of this counterpoint is an added reason for a poem not to be read with the jingly rhythm common with some readers.

Another type of rhythmic variation may be of interest. In a stanza from a poem by Edna St. Vincent Millay, "Travel," we find the lines:

> The railroad track is miles away,
> And the day is loud with voices speaking,
> Yet there isn't a train goes by all day
> But I hear its whistle shrieking.[8]

This, too, has the basic iambic rhythm, but note lines two and four. Here, instead of starting with one unstressed syllable, the poet starts with two: And the day, Yet there isn't, and such additions of extra syllables may occur at any point in a line—as, for example, it does in the third line: isn't a train. Another variation is the "feminine" ending of a line, with an unstressed final syllable as in speaking, and shrieking.

Departures from basic patterns add life and interest to rhythm. Should the rhythmic stress coincide consistently with the word stress, or if there were no occasional additions of syllables to vary the basic beat, the lines would be of an intolerable monotony.

[8] From Edna St. Vincent Millay, *Collected Poems* (New York: Harper & Row, 1956).

The many possible variations of rhythm are of continuing interest to children. Here is an amusing free use of rhythm in the following poem by Hilaire Belloc.

TARANTELLA

Do you remember an Inn,
    Miranda?
Do you remember an Inn?
And the tedding and the spreading
Of the straw for a bedding,
And the fleas that tease in the High Pyrenees,
And the wine that tasted of the tar?
And the cheers and the jeers of the young muleteers
(Under the vine of the dark verandah)—
Do you remember an Inn, Miranda?
Do you remember an Inn?
And the cheers and the jeers of the young muleteers
Who hadn't got a penny,
And who weren't paying any,
And the hammer at the doors and the din?
And the Hip, Hop, Hap!
Of the clap
Of the hands to the twirl and the swirl
Of the girl gone chancing,
Glancing,
Dancing,
Backing and advancing,
Snapping of the clapper to the spin
Out and in—
And the ting, tong, tang of the Guitar!
Do you remember an Inn, Miranda?
Do you remember an Inn?

Never more, Miranda;
Never more.
Only the high peaks hoar;
And Aragon torrent at the door.
No sound
In the walls of the Halls where falls
The tread

Of the feet of the dead to the ground.
No sound:
But the boom
Of the far Waterfall like Doom.[9]

In this poem there is no commitment to regularity of rhythm. The beginning gives the effect of a wild dance, with its short single-syllabled words, together with the skillful juxtaposition of two-syllabled and the short vowel sounds contrasted with the long (short "i's" in *Inn*, short "e's" in *tedding*, as against the long "e's" in *fleas*, and the long "i's" in *wine*). The internal rhyme, *cheers, jeers,* rhyming with mule*teers,* also adds to the speed, the dancelike quality of the verse. Notice also how the poet alters the mood in the last stanza, passing from the jingling words, *tedding, spreading,* the short crisp ones such as *clap, snap,* to a sequence of words containing long vowel sounds, as in *more, hoar, door, ground, sound*—all reinforcing the idea that the old happy times are now gone. With the opening words "never more" we are immediately introduced to the somber present whose mood culminates in the final lines "Only the boom/ Of the far Waterfall like Doom."

The use of rhyme may be studied with the children. With the letters of the alphabet as symbols, the rhyme scheme of "The Snare" is charted:

> pain—a
> snare—b
> again—a
> where—b

and so on. In "The Shepherdess" the rhyme scheme is

> delight—a
> sheep—b
> white—a
> steep—b
> height—a
> sleep—b

In "The Pasture" we have a, b, b, c, for the first stanza and d, e, e, c for the second. All the possible variations of rhyme will be of interest to

---

[9] From Blanche Jennings Thompson (editor), *More Silver Pennies* (New York: Macmillan, 1939).

the children—the regular and the irregular, as illustrated in "Tarantella." A stimulating discussion would result from the question why
rhyme is employed and what function it serves in a poem.

Here, then, summarized, are some of the elements of poetry that may
be brought to the children's notice: imagery, symbolism, mood, repetition, condensation, suggestion, alliteration, rhyme, and rhythm. By the
time the children have been introduced to all of these they will be able
to respond to poetry with an enthusiastic awareness that will challenge
and delight the teacher. And with this freshness of vision and enhanced
perception of poetry will come evaluation and appreciation that will not
be restricted to poetry alone but that will extend the children's general
outlook and bring a new enrichment to their lives.

9

We Write to Learn

Tom comes to my desk when the poetry writing is in progress. He is obviously troubled. "I can't think of anything to write about," he says. In any teacher's group whenever writing is in progress there will occasionally be found several such Tom's, and this is not to be wondered at. Having been assigned specific topics to write on during his school life, Tom is naturally overwhelmed when the whole world of subject matter is open to him to choose from. What can be done to help him? We might embark on a private conference in which we talk about things that interest him, his hobbies, how he spends his free time. Before long, Tom's face kindles and he says, "Oh, I know! I can write about . . ." such and such. Tom is now on his own. He knows where to turn for his material. Where else should this be than to himself and what interests him? For the teacher to suggest subject matter would be to direct him away from his creative self which alone is the source of his authentic impulse. I have tried both suggesting subject matter and allowing the children to choose their own, but I have found that it is wiser to direct the child to his inherent creative sources. It may be more difficult in the beginning to lead some children to tap their own resources, but in the long run it is the most rewarding— since they do better work when "sparked" from within than from without.

Jane is less articulate. She doesn't come to my desk. She sits, pencil in hand, observing her classmates absorbed in composition, and slinks past me when the period is over. Jane really wants to write. We find that out when she and I talk. With her it is not a question of not knowing what to write but of not knowing how to get started. And this, too, is not surprising. How does one have the courage to express one's thoughts and feelings? How does one dare to expose oneself to criticism or perhaps even ridicule? Many young people grow wary as they grow

73

older, and with wariness unfortunately comes the possibility of loss of access to their deeper selves. Jane needs, above all, reassurance. "You don't *have* to write," I tell her. "Write only when, and if, you feel like doing so." And I add the further reassurance, "Anything you write that you don't want read aloud, just tell me and I won't read it." With the pressure off, Jane also finds reassurance in the fact that none of the poems handed in are either corrected or criticized. All, she notes, are met with acceptance, none singled out for acclaim, none rejected as inadequate. Jane comes to feel that the teacher's attitude toward writing is in no way different from that which he assumes toward work in any other field, arithmetic or spelling; no more is made of it. This realization is often all that is necessary to enable the timid child to take her first step and, once launched, to go forward without fear.

Often creative work seems to some people to call for a sort of special consideration—as though the mere fact of writing a poem casts some sort of aura around the activity. If the teacher's attitude does not overweight the writing, the children are relieved of certain fears surrounding it.

Though the teacher may place no pressure on the children's writing, and though they may interpret his attitude as one of not being over-concerned with it, they are far from undervaluing the experience themselves. The feeling already quoted of the boy who said, "Writing is the best part of it [the poetry session]," is corroborated by the behavior of the many children who have cherished poems of their own writing over the years. The children have made small looseleaf binders in which to collect their poems; these have proved an additional incentive to writing, in that both in anticipation and in the accumulation of a volume of one's own poems resides an additional satisfaction. There is value in having such a compilation available—the children not only enjoy rereading their earlier efforts, but they are often able to chart progress and achieve a sense of accomplishment. In a large class the teacher cannot, of course, type the children's poems as I did, but small notebooks may be provided in which the children may copy their own poems, after these have been corrected for spelling, punctuation, line spacing, or for any flagrant errors in grammar. This type of correction is unlike the correction of the poems themselves, which I do not sanction. Though the poetry sessions should not be made the occasion for the teaching of spelling, punctuation, etc., there is no reason why the mistakes should be perpetuated.

Any corrections other than these seem inadvisable, since, as I have said earlier, no specific "rights" and "wrongs" may be applied to creative writing. What a child writes at any given time is valid as an expression of his development at that particular stage. Teachers are constantly asking, "How are children to improve if they aren't given specific instruction?" They *do* improve, and any doubts on that score I believe will be allayed when we turn our attention later to the children's development in poetic criteria. In my opinion the most fruitful method of teaching in the field of creative writing is one of indirection. The constant reading of poetry, with attention drawn to felicities of expression, to the poetic practices described in the last chapter, brings to the child the sense of what constitutes poetry. And though this sense is in the main unconscious, it is nonetheless valuable; in fact, perhaps because it is unconscious it is the more operative in the writing. Does not what we call "inspiration" derive largely from the so-called unconscious? We pay verbal tribute even if we do not actually acknowledge this fact when we say of something we have written, "It just came to me."

From the behavior of the Tom's and the Jane's, the teacher will discover that it is not so easy to initiate writing with the older as with the younger children. Many things have happened to a child in the process of growing older that may tend to inhibit freedom of expression. Not the least of these is self-consciousness. Assurance of acceptance is even more essential to the older than to the younger child, since the former is more inclined to be critical of his own performance. Often this criticism is not valid on poetic grounds. It may grow primarily out of the child's lack of confidence in himself. He forestalls the criticism of others by asserting, in advance, "It's no good." Here is an example of faulty evaluation in a poem written by twelve-year-old Prue:

WINDOWS

> There is a house on the hill that has many windows:
> Windows in the cellar, windows in the garret,
> Windows everywhere.
> Some look cross and frowning
> As if they dared anyone to look inside them.
> Some look inviting, some happy, some sad.
> One bay window looks out haughty and proud,
> And a tiny attic window, like a smiling child.

The windows on the first floor are very slim,
Tall and beautiful, but they look as though they had
    no feeling.
The windows in one of the bedrooms
Look from behind some lacy curtains,
As if smiling knowingly
To remember the good times they have seen.
The windows of the big bedroom look imposing,
Not deigning to notice the others.
Every time I go by the house, I nod to the windows.
I feel that I know them,
That they are old friends.[1]

This is a poem no twelve-year-old need be ashamed of, and yet after writing it, Prue crumpled it and threw it in the waste basket. When I asked to see it, she gave the usual reply, "It's no good." But after I had told her that sometimes even an adult poet is not able to decide immediately after the writing whether a poem is good, and when I assured her that I would show it to no one, she overcame her reluctance and handed it to me. Later, as evidence of her growth in self-confidence, she submitted it to the school magazine, where it was accepted. Should she have discarded it, she would in all probability have felt discouraged and have discontinued writing, with a consequent loss to herself of a significant experience.

An added difficulty for the older child results from his having built up preconceptions of poetry that the younger child has not as yet acquired. Thinking, as he generally does, of poetry in terms of rhythm and rhyme, he is often fearful of attempting what seems to him a difficult undertaking. And in these terms it *is* difficult. To acquire a technique in the handling of rhythm and rhyme is an arduous task and obligatory only on those who are dedicated to becoming poets. Since our objective in the poetry study is not to make poets of our young people, but rather to open up the field of poetry to them, it would seem wiser to suggest that in their writing they avail themselves of the latitude of free verse. Having been introduced to free verse through our reading, the children feel this to be a legitimate form of poetry. They realize in addition that they are better able to express their thoughts

[1] From Flora J. Arnstein, *Adventure into Poetry* (Stanford, Calif.: Stanford University Press, 1951).

and feelings in this medium than when constricted by the exigencies of meter and rhyme. The attempt to force their thoughts into strict forms obliges them to abandon their initial ideas or so manipulate them that they lose authenticity. A poem such as the following illustrates into what banalities the commitment to rhythm and rhyme drives the child:

DULL DAY

On a dreary, dreary morning,
A dull, dull day,
As I sat at my window,
Sleeping the day away,
My cat was lying and mewing,
Just as if to say,
"If you have nothing to do,
Please pet me, I pray."[2]

What does this poem say that derives from a child's observation and feeling? Note the obsolete expression, "I pray." Strangely enough, the children often fall into such archaic usages (the *a-sailing, a-riding* noted earlier) when writing in metrical form.

In distinction to the above poem, here are poems by the same child, when after a prolonged addiction to trite rhythmic verse, she finally abandons it in favor of free verse. At nine she writes:

THE OCEAN FROM DIFFERENT POINTS OF VIEW

1

O mighty ocean,
O roaring waves, and banks of foam,
How can we, small and feeble as we are,
Plunge into your depths unafraid?

2

O scaly, shiny dragon,
How can the waves break through your hard coat
To make the little ripples in the water?

[2] From Arnstein, *Ibid.*

3

What are you chasing,
Ocean, great ocean,
That you rush upon the shore
Only to fall back again discouraged, fatigued?

At ten she writes:

WEATHER

A warm murkiness is hanging on the air.
Every once in a while it rains in little torrents,
And then it stops.
The sky cannot make up its mind what to do,
So it just lets the clouds play tag with the sun.

Here, in these poems, we find accurate observation, individual reactions, imagery, and a general play of imagination totally lacking in her rhythmic poems.

One eight-year-old writes in meter and rhyme:

Down by the brook in the middle of spring,
I look around and things seem to sing.
Around the brook are little flowers,
And up above there are no towers.

Aside from the absurdity of the towers, introduced solely for the rhyme, we have here the absence of specificity in the "things" that seem to sing. Ineptitudes such as these occur constantly in the children's rhymed and rhythmic poems.

In contrast the same little girl writes the following at a later poetry session:

THE CLOUDS

In the daytime
Sometimes the clouds blot out the sun.
Sometimes they are all different colors,
Like reddish pink, light pink,
And like blue, lavender,
Purple and green.

Sometimes they are big grey clouds
Floating in the sky.
Sometimes they look like popcorn,
Or little lost sheep in a valley.

In the night time
Sometimes they are white.
Then they look very pretty.
Sometimes they blot out the stars,
So you can't see the stars at all.
But I like the clouds in the day time
Best of all.

Here we have the real child, expressing herself in accordance with her
age (note the enumeration and the phrase "I like") and giving evidence
of personal observation in such comparisons as the clouds to popcorn
and the charming resemblance to "little lost sheep in a valley."

She turns to consideration of herself in the following:

ME

Me is always me
When I look at myself in the mirror
It is me.
I am always me.
The "Me" in me never goes away.
I am always here—
Me and myself.

The question of identity which preoccupies many writers of today is
here invoked by a child of eight! One is continually surprised by the
children's concern with matters that we tend to think the exclusive
province of adults.

Carol provides a prime example of the crippling effect of the attempt
to adopt metric forms.[3] She is a particularly gifted child and at the age
of ten is able to handle rhythm and rhyme with a certain dexterity. The
following poem is an illustration:

[3] See *Ibid.*, page 30, for a more extended examination of this child's writing.

And through the willow leaves,
Behind the birches' white bark,
Far beyond the ferns and grasses,
The river flows on dark.

And in the happy sunlight,
Beyond the grey rocks' way,
Among the reeds and rushes,
The sparkling brooklet lay.

And in the gurgling fountain,
In lovely gardens of kings,
Making the grass wet and dewy,
The brook flies on without wings.

Slipping down from ridges,
Rushing into the lane,
It joins the mighty river
Swollen large with rain.

In essence this poem says nothing, though it indicates that this child has
read some poetry and has achieved a glib command of language. It is
full of irrelevance—such as the garden of kings, and the brook rushing
down a *lane*; it contains a change of tense from the present used
throughout in order to supply a rhyme for "way."

Contrast it with the following poems written later:

Golden trumpets of the spring,
Announcing the day—
The daffodils are breathing.
Are breathing away the winter.
Quivering to the wind—
The spring daffodils.

. . . .

On a low hill
Lit by the moon.
A row of young pine trees
Stood silhouetted against the night.

. . . .

The tide-line is on the shore now.
It is where the ocean puts its ripples to dry,
And stores its freshness.

It's where the ocean puts the sprouting onions,
And heaps the brown sea-weeds.
They look like dead lions
Scattered on the sand.

While likening the daffodils to trumpets is not an original observation,[4] the statement that they are "breathing away the winter" is a delightful concept. Also the picture of young pine trees silhouetted against the night arises from authentic observation. And the ocean putting its ripples to dry on the tide-line is an amusing imaginative touch. At twelve Carol has travelled from the literal into the realm of suggestion, as she well knows by entitling this poem "Impressionistic":

I went one night to where the marshes meet the moon,
To where the last oak of the world stands alone.

All the free verse here quoted, whatever its limitation as written by children, is still imbued with the genuine stuff of which poetry is made —with personal commentary and imaginative evocation. And the same is never true when the children employ metrical forms, for in such practice they invariably lose touch with their subjective world. Since the world of their thoughts and feelings is alone meaningful and of value to them, inasmuch as it is the source of whatever creative impulses they may have, it would seem wise to direct them to it, and, without being insistent, suggest they avail themselves of free verse rather than metrical as being better adapted to their expression.

But we have anticipated ourselves. A question teachers most frequently ask is, "How do you get the writing started?" Often merely the remark, "How would you like to try your hand at writing?" is all that is necessary to get the children under way. Another incentive grew out of the fact that previously the children had made the looseleaf booklets in which to keep their original poems. As I mentioned earlier, I would type the poems written at each session and return these at the

---

[4] This simile is of course not original to adults, but it may be to a child. This, however, involves no problem, since no comment is made to the child on the quality of the simile. While it is true that much that might be trite to an adult is new to a child, it is equally true that children's observations are rarely trite. They do see things freshly, and many an adult poet envies the fresh vision of the child.

following, when the children would enter them in their books. During the term the poems were held in place by brass clips which were replaced at the end of the year by permanent cords.

Reading the poems written by other children, such as those of Hilda Conkling, also stimulates the desire to write, as do those contained in my own *Adventure into Poetry* or in *Creative Youth* by Hughes Mearns.[5] Actually the launching of the writing is easier than teachers anticipate. But assuring the continuance of writing is more difficult. Many teachers, not only of children but also of college students, have observed that the impulse to write is inclined to flag after a time. This need not happen. Given the room climate already outlined, and the teacher's acceptance, the children continue, I have found, to write indefinitely.

There are, however, certain pitfalls which the teacher may fall into that lead to discontinuance of writing. Perhaps my experience in having fallen into these has brought me a certain awareness which may be of help to other teachers in avoiding them. One that contributed to unfortunate results for a child was my not having apprised the parents in advance of the nature of the creative writing program. Parents are naturally, and in some cases justifiably, proud of the achievements of their offspring, but in certain instances the expression of such pride is likely to place barriers in the way of the child. Matthew, aged twelve, instead of handing in his poem at the end of the writing session asked, "Would it be all right if I take my poem home first to show to my mother?" Not foreseeing any unfavorable consequences, I made no objection. Here is the poem:

NEWS

A click-click-click,
Half a hundred typewriters pounding,
Like the music of a machine gun.
They crash, they pound,
And then one breaks.
All the typewriters pounding,
Pounding out news for the press—
Bad news, good news, tabloid news
All for the daily press.

[5] (New York: Dover Publications, 1959.)

In the next building is a telegraph office,
With the steady dot-dash, dot-dash of the telegraph equipment,
Echoing, re-echoing through the building,
Sending news all over the world—
Bad news, good news, important news,
Sent over the whole world.

Down the street a telephone office,
With its honeycomb of little holes,
With little plugs to match—
A myriad of little buttons,
Plugs, switches, and electrical connections,
A network of wires running in and out,
And a steady, running buzz of conversation,
Conversation everywhere,
Sent everywhere,
Received everywhere—
A telephone office is a busy thing.

News, news being sent everywhere,
To all parts of the world—
News of business failures, business successes,
News of death, news of sickness,
News of joy, news of happiness . . .
What would you, what could you do
Without news?[6]

This is a very acceptable piece of work, especially as an early attempt. But Matthew's mother was so impressed by it that she read it to a friend who was in some way connected with publishing and who suggested the poem's publication. Matthew's mother arrived at school the next day to discuss the matter. I advised her against taking such a step, but unfortunately the damage had already been done to Matthew. He had been made to feel he had accomplished something especially noteworthy, and as a result he became self-conscious about his writing. Whether he was wondering before embarking on a new poem if it would "be as good as 'News'," or whether in the writing the same idea obtruded, there was no knowing. In any event a long time elapsed before

[6] From Arnstein, op. cit.

he could write spontaneously again. His subsequent poems were stilted and wooden. Overpraise, strangely enough, seems to block a child's creativity, and this is an additional reason for the teacher to accept the child's poem in a casual manner.

A conference with the parents of individual children ahead of time or some general talk with the parents of the class, in which the teacher outlines the aim of creative writing, would have obviated such an incident as the above and insured the children's continuance of writing. In my later classes, until such a conference had been held, I did not permit the children to take their poems home.

Another unfortunate situation might have been avoided if I had followed this last procedure. Irene, a member of an after-school high school group that met with me informally for two years, wrote the following poem:

FLY

O Fly,
Climbing glass panes,
Why not go out
When I open the window?
Are *we* all like that?

O Fly,
The air outside's free.
Beautiful air—
(Just a bit lower, Fly,)
What's wrong, Fly,
Can't you see?
Are *we* like that?

O Fly,
Struggling desperately,
Mastering the slippery false glass,
You only fall back bruised.
Are *we* like that?

O Fly,
What is glass?
A delusion and a snare
With no meaning for you,

Or a big thing
With a meaning
Great as the world?

O Fly,
Are we comrades,
You and I?
Of what good are you,
Or I?
Are we all like that?

O Fly,
Climbing glass panes,
It's time you *knew* that glass is glass!
Learn then, O Fly.
But you won't.
I won't.
The world won't.
O Fly,
We are all like that—
We are comrades, O Fly,
You and I.[7]

I think we can agree that this poem gives indication of a native gift for expression and a marked feeling for form, for structure, [illegible] for climax. Had this girl, along with being exposed to poetry [illegible] to write, she would, in my opinion, have undoubtedly dev[illegible] of cadence and a generally more poetic mode of expre[illegible]. But wh[illegible] happened was that Irene was eager to take her poem home to show her father. A close relationship existed between the two, and his approval was meaningful to her. But he did not approve. "It's no poem," he told her. "It has no rhythm and no rhyme." Irene had nothing at her command with which to counter this verdict and came to class next week crestfallen. The fact that her father, as she admitted, never read poetry did not seem to affect her acceptance of his dictum. I reminded her of the Psalms we had read, of Carl Sandburg and of Walt Whitman, and she regained enough confidence to submit the poem a short time l[illegible] to her school paper. But here again she met rebuff. The tea[illegible]

[7] From *Ibid.*

passed upon contributions rejected the poem on the same grounds as her father. The combined repudiation was apparently too much for Irene. She never attempted to write again. Perhaps I should have been skillful enough to have helped her overcome her discouragement, but sometimes discouragement strikes so deeply that all attempts to surmount it are unavailing.

Criticism seems to strike at the very root of the creative impulse. Even in the case of adults, I have observed that ill-advised criticism has often resulted in such bewilderment as to inhibit writing. Only the rarest and most skillful teacher and one with long experience in the creative field can offer fruitful criticism, and, what is of as great importance, know the correct time to tender it. But for the child, criticism is invariably fatal to writing. Aside from making for self-consciousness, that prime deterrent to creation, it leads to confusion which has a like result. For criticism means the application of adult standards to the work of a child, and a child is not ready for such standards. Preoccupation with them induces in him the concern, "Is this correct or all right?" And this concern should not be forced upon him. He should be permitted to write and write, untrammeled by any outside considerations. Only by continuous writing will he learn, as the title of this chapter states: "We Write to Learn," which some readers may have taken for a misprint, thinking it should read "We Learn to Write." But the wording was advised, for nowhere is the old precept of learning by doing more applicable than to the writing of poetry.

We err in lack of faith in the child. In a skill such as skating, a child learns propulsion and balance by himself, by means of trial and error. Just so will he learn in writing. Only when he has had continuous access to his creative sources and has had a long experience of writing should he be concerned with the application of standards. And these standards will then be his own. They will have been arrived at by exposure to poetry and by his own experience in writing. He will have earned them in the process of growth and discovery.

10

As Poets Write

IT IS AN OPEN QUESTION how much is native to a child in his use of poetic devices and how much he has learned through exposure to poetry. We have already given some examples of the early use of imagery and we append here further ones by children of eight. Rachel writes:

> The sky is blue,
> The sun is yellow,
> And the grass blooms when the sun is yellow,
> And the flowers, too.
> Trees are *lighted up like Christmas trees,*
> They are so green.

Ellen writes:

THE SHADOW ON THE HILL

> When I look at the big red mountains,
> With the city below,
> I see the shadow of the city
> Lying on the mountains *like a sheet of grey paper*
> The shadows of the trees
> Are sometimes lying on it, too.

FAR-AWAY CLOUDS

> The far-away clouds
> Look just like the snow—
> A *mountain of snow,*
> A *mountain of marshmallows*
> Floating in the sky.

Sometimes when they are way up in the sky
They look *like cotton*—
All in little puffs.

A COLD WINTER EVENING

When a cold winter night comes,
The little snowflakes outside
Look *like spring blossoms*
Falling from their tree.

The sky *is their tree*,
And the *clouds are clusters*
Of more blossoms.

Again she writes, "The creek looks at me with its golden eyes," and
Karen, also eight, sees "the river in a golden dew."

When the children are older and have been reading poetry for some
time, they continue the use of imagery in their own writing, but how
deliberate this is it is impossible to determine. The same might be said,
however, of an adult poet. One can hardly imagine the latter saying
to himself, "I will put an image in here." The practice of poetry brings
with it a vocabulary of poetic usage, and the children draw upon this
as do their elders. Here follow examples of the use of imagery by older
children.

Rhoda, eleven, writes:

DREAMS

Dreams are queer—
Some are like walking in a labyrinth
Full of dusty cracks and holes,
With strange and weird creatures
Staring at you
From hidden places,
And an adventure
Ready to jump out and catch you,
When you are forced into a dark room
With cobwebs brushing and swinging past your face.
Then as you turn a corner,

A beautiful dream
Dressed in a starry gown,
With moons glittering in her hair,
And downy, golden wings
Flies away from you
To a place in the sky.

Rhoda was about to destroy this when I retrieved it and persuaded her
to keep it. The poem contains telling images: the labyrinth "full of dusty
cracks and holes," and the "dream dressed in a starry gown, with moons
glittering in her hair." In another poem she likens a leopard to "A
shadow that has no fear."
   Bill, twelve, writes:

> Off in the distance there is a small lake,
> Set among the mountains like a glittering sapphire
> In a dull setting.
> It nestles there—mercury held in a cloth.

The last, "mercury held in a cloth," is an original concept and an apt
picture of a lake in the high altitudes.
   Ross, eleven, likens the stars to "confetti some giant threw in the
sky," and Frank, eleven, likens darkness to "the last act in a play: The
scene changes, houses are changed into ghosts." (Curiously enough,
Frank now has taken up acting as his profession—one of two boys whose
early poems foreshadowed their later activities.)
   Rose and Rena, twelve and thirteen respectively, avail themselves
of images. Rose:

GOLDFISH

> Goldfish, I wonder how you feel in your house like a bubble.
> Don't you ever get tired of going round and round,
> Making the cat's eyes pop out,
> Longing for just a bite of you?
> The visitors admire your coat of golden sunset.
> When I am lonely, I watch you open and close your mouth.
> It makes me feel as if you were talking to me,
> Then I no longer feel lonely.

Rena:

> The sky is like a huge ocean
> Which stretches forever,
> But unlike the sea,
> It is calm and serene,
> The clouds like small boats
> Floating on its waters.

Sean, twelve, writes:

NIGHT

> Night is still and dark and calm.
> The moon pours its silver generously
> Over the town.
> 'Most everyone sleeps at night
> In a calm and sleepful rest,
> Like an old flower
> Wilting its petals so quietly.

Sleep "like an old flower wilting its petals" is a beautiful and original image. In another image he likens the sea to a poem, "an endless poem which never stops."

Rae Jean, ten, in the first five lines of the following poem writes in true lyric cadence:

> It is late afternoon now.
> The shadows are long on the grass.
> The flowers gently wave to and fro
> And the birds rustle the leaves
> Under the oak trees as they walk.
> Now the sun is setting
> Behind the hills.
> Soon a swift breeze springs up.
> As the twilight deepens,
> The flowers turn into fairies,
> And dance in the light of the moon
> On into the night.
> Sometimes they sway and bend briskly

But now they are almost motionless,
Listening to the soft music
Played by the waving grasses.
Now the dawn breaks, and the gold of the morning
Washes over the fairies,
But look more closely,
They are not fairies at all,
But just flowers
Gleaming in the sunlight.

Except for the conventional intrusion of fairies, the poem contains
fresh vision in the fairies bending "briskly," then being "almost motionless,/ Listening to the soft music/ Played by the waving grasses." And
the "gold of the morning" is a charming designation of day.

The fact that the children know themselves to be engaged in writing poetry seems to impel them to avail themselves of the tools of
poetry. The older they get the more they incorporate in their writing
those devices that through their reading they have come to associate
in their minds with poetry. As with their use of imagery, they employ
certain devices unconsciously while they are still unaware of these as
elements of poetry. John writes:

THE STEAM ENGINE

The steam engine starts with a snort,
The wheels creaking, the steam hissing,
The bell ringing, the fire-box glowing.
Faster, faster it goes,
Until it seems as if it is flying.
Through villages, through towns
It passes crossings with its whistle blowing.
Slower now, slower now.
Hiss goes the brake as it stops—
Its work is finished for the day.

Here we find the onomatopoetic words *snort, creaking, hiss* employed
before the child had been introduced to them in a poetic context.

The children likewise employ inversion, the use of words out of their
natural order. Katy, at eight, writes:

OUT BEYOND THE MOUNTAINS

Out beyond the mountains
There is a rushing river,
Trees at either end.
Tiny fish are living in the river,
Birds build their nests in the trees.
Bordering it are flowers.
Butterflies spread their golden wings
As they fly to the flowers for a rest.
There is grass all around the trees
Next to the flowers.
In the grass are little bugs,
They hop and chirp all day long.
They have a merry little song.
They sing, "This is a nice place to be."

In lines one, six, and eleven Katy makes use of inversion, thus giving a variety to the syntax.

Ross, at ten, writes: "A foggy day it is today," and, at eleven:

Softly, softly through the grass it moves,
Silently, peacefully and calm.
Paying no attention to people and their ways,
But snorts in disgust and moves on
Softly, silently and calm,
Paying no heed to wars, but goes on,
Without cheating or being cheated,
Softly, silently, peacefully and calm.

What it is that is moving through the grass, Ross does not tell us, but the mystery is reinforced by the inversion in the first line, repeated in the fifth and final ones. Joan, eleven, writes, "Out of the stillness comes a voice"; Herbert, "Only in the daytime the world is awake," and "Like ripples on the water,/ Blow the leaves forward and backward." Sometimes as in Katy's poem, the inversion may be used to break the monotony of subject and predicate order, sometimes to achieve a more cadential rendering as in the lines of Herbert. Needless to say, none of this is a conscious choice, but that makes it nonetheless valid and effective.

Personification, that device of speaking of inanimate objects as though they were persons, occurs in the younger as in the older children. Martha, at six, dictates:

> Candles, do you talk to somebody on the table
> When it's supper time?
> Red balloon, would you pop
> If I gave you a hit?
> Do you talk to anybody
> When you pop?
> You get a little hole in you
> When you pop, too.
> Do you know anybody who lives around the village
> When you go flying through the air
> And people try to catch you?
> What store did the people buy in
> That lost you, red balloon?

Rose, at eleven, writes:

> I have a plant of violets,
> And when I go to water them,
> They look at me with their yellow little eyes,
> They look so stern and serious,
> They make me take a step back,
> And say, "Oh!"

Joan, eleven, writes:

> "Day," said the sun, "we welcome you every morning
> With a friendly greeting.
> The flowers and trees bow and curtsy,
> The winds kiss you gently, and sometimes savagely,
> But always there is a welcome for you.
> Why do you not answer?
> Are you rude and have no manners?
> Please tell us why."
> The day did not answer,
> But smirked and walked on.

Emily, thirteen, writes:

DARKNESS

Night slowly takes day into its arms.
It also wishes to take me, I think—
The way it says,
"Please come and see me meet day."

As earlier mentioned, when the children employ rhyme they are driven into the most absurd ineptitudes. Too often the mere ability to concoct a set of rhyming lines is acclaimed by adults as something of a feat. Actually many children have great facility in spinning off rhymes, but the poems in which these occur are invariably trivial—a rehash of old ideas and subject matter generally unrelated to the child writing.

A few illustrations will suffice. An eight-year-old girl has an easy hand at rhyme, but note what she writes:

RAIN

The rain is good for the flowers,
  It makes them grow.
I like to stand in the rain
  And run about to and fro.
I like to hear the sound
  Of the pitter-patter on the ground.
Out of my window I always look
  To see if the water has made a brook.

While this contains no absurdities, it contains the trite phrases "to and fro" and "pitter-patter" and presents no fresh vision. Again she writes:

Little children playing in the night
  Are like little fireflies
With their sparkling lights.
  Playing on the side-walk,
  Playing in the street,
  But the nicest part
  Is when new neighbors meet.

Running, skipping, jumping,
Playing to and fro,
Smelling pretty flowers,
Playing in the snow.

Here we have the "to and fro" again and the incongruity of smelling
pretty flowers in the snow. Both absurdity and/or incongruity are
present in most of the younger children's rhymed poems, and the older
ones are caught up in the same trap; there is no need for further illustrations. These examples indicate why I believe it is advisable to direct
the children away from rhyming.

What they are able to write when they forego rhyme is evident in
poems in which they tellingly express certain moods, as does Rachel in
"Alone" quoted later, and Sean in "Night.'" Other instances of what
children write when they are able to tap their own resources follow:
Rhoda, eleven, writes:

There was no moon last night
As I walked into the garden.
In the silent darkness
Everything was different and queer.
The flowers were turned into goblins
Waiting to catch me.
I bumped into a tree whose long fingers grabbed,
And on whose branch was an owl—
Staring.
I ran away and saw a ghost
On Mother's clothes-line.
I went into the house
And turned on the lights.

Emily, thirteen, writes:

I am tired,
I walk slowly—
Everyone knows I am tired.

I am happy,
I walk fast,
Everyone knows I am happy.

Again she writes:

SLEEP

Sleep approaches me,
It lays warm soft hands on my eyes,
And makes the eyelids heavy.
First I am in a wakeful dream,
My eyes go blurry, I can't see straight.
My light I turn out,
And I lay my head on the soft smooth pillow.
Sleep's hands are stronger than my eyelids,
So I fall asleep.

This time I am in a true dream.
Nothing is blurry, but nothing is clear either.
Nothing stays in my mind.
I travel from one thought to another,
Yet each thought makes a firm impression on my mind.
Then I get terribly mixed up,
And I wake up.
I turn over and go to sleep,
And sleep quietly and soundly.

No one can question the authenticity of these experiences, and the dream sequence is one that everyone has shared; though not particularly poetically expressed, the poem is simple and genuine. Donna, too, writes of dreams:

I had a dream.
It was a wonderful dream of gladness.
I could hear it whisper
Soft words of joy in my ear.
It was like music coming in through my heart.
When I woke up I was sorry to leave it.

This, also, is authentic, but expressed with more poetic cadence than the previous poem.

Gary, eleven, writes:

PINE TREES

As a swift brisk wind sings through the tall stately pines,
A feeling of vastness comes over me . . .

Donna, twelve, writes:

Staring, staring at the endless sky
Makes you feel as though there were something else besides the blue—
That the universe could fit into.
But what would be beyond that?
When you think of it,
You have a feeling of emptiness and endlessness.

Kay, ten, writes:

LONELINESS

A still black shadow creeps over you at night
When you can't get to sleep—
   Loneliness.

The same black shadow crawls over you again
When you are alone in the room—
   Loneliness.

It happens to kings and queens,
It happens to beggar boys and beggar girls,
But it is always
   Loneliness.

Even children as young as eight demonstrate at times a sense of form
by the use of repeated lines or refrains. Katy, at eight, writes:

The old wooden chest
Stands in the corner of the house
Waiting to be used some day.
It is a lonely sight
And full of cobwebs.
Nobody knows what's in it,
Because the key has been lost.

It stands there with nothing in. it,
Or maybe full of some treasure.
But nobody knows,
And will never find out
What is in the old wooden chest
Standing full of cobwebs
In the corner of the house.

By the same child:

THE PLANT BY THE WINDOW

The plant by the window
Is a green plant,
And has long leaves
Sprouting out of the roots.
To me it looks as though it was staring out
At the view below it.
The plant by the window
Sits in a tall white pot
On the window-sill.
It is staring out
At the view below it.

Such repetitions of lines are very common, even among older children who frequently frame their poems by repetition of the opening line at the end. Rachel, twelve, writes:

ALONE

Being alone is a queer feeling.
It brings you happiness and wonder.
You look for something
And never seem to find it.
You reach for that one thing.

I seem to realize things about our world—
New things—
I get the feeling of love, gentleness.
My feeling of being alone is a queer thing.

I find new impressions of people, places and things.
I get the feeling of someone creeping up behind me.
I turn quickly—no one's there.
I feel as though I'm trapped in a cage.

I enjoy being alone,
But also I get scared and frightened.
Being alone is a queer feeling.

This poem ranges somewhat wide, but the repetition of the opening phrase in line nine and again at the end serves to unify it.

Rena, at twelve, writes:

THE SKY

The sky is gray, just gray—
Only cloudy.
Only one black speck breaking through the gray.

It's a bird. It passes swiftly on its way.
Is it going home or just flying?
It's gone.

The sky is gray, just gray—
Only clouds again.

The repetition of the first line here seems to reinforce the poem's mood, as does the repetition in the poem "Loneliness" quoted earlier.

But the poem evincing the most intricate and elaborate sense of form is Kent's written at eleven:

OUR NAVY

A shadow passing before the sun
Signifies the passing of a dirigible,
    A torpedo on wings,
Guardian of the Navy's airplanes,
Spy on the enemy's movements.

A swish of water and a heavy swell,
Signifies the descending of a submarine,
    A great gray shark,
A destroyer of battleships,
Battleship of the depths of the sea.

A roar of motors, a heavy drone,
Like hundreds of bees from their hive,
    Swift little insects,
Fast messengers of the fleet,
Swift grey hornets with a deadly sting.

> Like a piece of fog that has gone astray,
> Its guns smoking and bellowing forth
>   A whale basking in the sun—
> The Navy's floating fort.
> Faithful fighter of the seas.

This poem, when analyzed, evinces not only an extraordinary organic form but great subtleties as well. Note, first, the poem is composed of four five-line stanzas, the third line of each being shorter than the others and presenting a metaphor of the particular craft described. Then each first line indicates the motion of the craft; each fourth and fifth lines, the function. In the first two stanzas the form of the second line is repeated, but obviating monotony, in the third stanza a metaphor is substituted for the previous "signifies." In the fourth stanza there is another modification—instead of the form of the opening lines of the other stanzas, this begins with a simile. And a certain climax is suggested by the order of presentation of the craft.

Of course all of this—structure and modifications—is (as is the case of all the children's employment of poetic devices) not done deliberately. But that makes the achievement nonetheless remarkable. Inspiration is impossible to analyze, and that such a poem as the above is not created in full consciousness of the artistic devices employed cannot be argued. Had such a poem been deliberately planned there is little doubt but that the result would have been different—the spontaneity would have been lost, and the organic unity might not have been present. We have noted previously what too great self-consciousness on the part of children leads to in their writing, but that a certain consciousness does arrive "after the fact" will be evident in the following chapter, in which will be treated the standards children have deduced from their reading and from the practice of writing.

11

Learning through Growth

THE CLASS is sitting around our large library table. We are ready to begin a poetry session. Before each child is his book in which he enters the poems chosen at our previous meeting, also the booklet containing poems of his own writing. One child asks, "Can't we read our own poems today instead of having our regular lesson?" I welcome the request since one of the reasons for making the booklets was precisely that of affording the children the opportunity for rereading their own poems. Also, the rereading may bring forth comments, which I surmise will have some significance. And the comments *are* forthcoming. I take these down, and date them, then later go to my files to ascertain the dates when the poems commented upon had been written. Given the date of the comment and the time lapse between it and the writing of the poem, I may be able to draw some conclusions as to what has happened to the child in the interval.

Let us note some of these poems and the comments on them. Katherine, ten, has written:

THE FIRE BELL

Whenever anybody pulls the long chain on the fire bell
It goes "Gong, Gong" as if to say, "Fire, Fire!"
Then the people run out of the building
To get the fire engines,
And pretty soon they come,
Ding, dong, cling, clang down the street.
Then the men put the fire out.
Then ding, dong, home they go.
"The fire is out," I say.

Reading this later, she says, "Cut out the 'I say.'" The deletion here is no doubt because of the irrelevance of the phrase, since there has been no previous use of "I" in the poem.

Joyce, ten, has written:

> The daffodils and the chrysanthemums
> Were standing straight one day,
> When there came a little wind
> That blew them all away.
> They blew and blew for miles and miles
> And then they landed on the ground.

She comments, "Tear it up. I don't like it." When a child gives no reason for changing or discarding a poem, one can only guess what the motivation is. In the present case, perhaps, though Joyce may not be conscious of the fact, she may feel that the poem is not related to experience; obviously it is not, since chrysanthemums and daffodils do not bloom at the same time of year. Note the use of rhyme in the second and fourth lines only—which will be discussed below.

Barbara, eleven, has written:

ACACIA SEASON

> Acacia has such pretty stems,
> And little yellow flowers,
> And when acacia's season's over,
> I wait and wait again.

She comments later, "I don't like the last line," which is again an irrelevant intrusion.

Emily, at eight, has dictated:

> Silvery moon so bright, so bright,
> Over the ocean,
> It is a full moon,
> But it does not give enough light
> For the ship to go.
> The ocean is silent
> And everybody is asleep.
> The rushing of the waves
> Makes the most noise.

On copying this poem for submission to the yearbook, Emily asked to omit line three, no doubt because of the prosy direct statement, but in any case the change is for the better.

Fay, nine, writes:

> Down by the ocean,
> Down by the bay,
> That's where I used to play.
> Sometimes with sand,
> Sometimes with rock,
> And then I'd go in wading,
> And it wouldn't be so cold—
> Down by the ocean,
> Down by the bay.

On reading this Fay strikes through the sixth and seventh lines. Again one can only guess the reason she does so, but here too we find a rhyme, once used then immediately abandoned. This is a characteristic procedure in the children's use of rhyme: they never feel a commitment to continuing with it.

These examples of deletions, chosen from among many, were made shortly after the poems had been written. Irrelevancy then seems to be one of the first criteria children bring to bear on their writing, and redundancy is a close second. But even young children, as does Katy, at eight, amend for aesthetic reasons:

> When winter comes
> The snow falls
> Right outside my house.
> It's soft, white and fluffy.
> It looks like powdered sugar.
> As I step into it I fall down.
>
> There are little prints in the snow
> Beside my own.
> They are the prints of the deer.
> From that I know
> They came to drink at night
> From the cool rushing stream.

At the session after writing this Katy amends the line, "As I step into it I fall down," to "As I step into it I sink down into the soft drifts," which is not only an improvement in cadence, but also gives a more sensory picture.

In the process of growing older the children discard their more childish concepts and expressions at the same time as they evaluate their writing by more mature aesthetic criteria. Likewise, since they have become more articulate and specific in their statements, they no longer oblige me to guess the reasons for changes or deletions.

Rachel, at twelve, writes:

TIMID SKY

Oh, huge sky, do you ever end?
You stretch your wings across the earth,
Your colors are so timid.
If you rain your tears,
The whole world is sad.
If you are filled with glory and sunshine,
The world is happy.
The food shelter people live on you.
Oh, blue sky, do you ever end
With your helping hand.

Reading this poem a year after writing it, Rachel says, "The line about food and shelter doesn't make sense." She deletes it and the final line. The metaphor of "raining your tears" is a telling one, also the sky stretching its "wings." Later she writes:

SHH!

How funny the street looks so bare,
The long paved road, the high buildings,
The tall telephone poles
Reaching high in front of each house.
But the house looks warm, still and welcoming.
I wonder what's inside that house.
I wonder if there is a blazing fire,
And some people talking softly around it.
But everything is so quiet.

Shh! I don't want to break my dream.
Then if I wake, I wake to reality:
A dirty street, tall ugly buildings,
A ragged house,

An unfriendly look upon its face,
An electric stove to heat the house,
And a hot sound of laughter.
How sad!

Shh! Don't wake me from my dream,
For it is hard to wake
And think of what you meant by this dream—
If it resembles anything specific.
Shh! Don't wake me.

Reading this a week after writing it, Rachel says, "It's terrible," but when I press her to define what is wrong,[1] she says, "Well, I don't always think this way." I reassure her: "One often has moods or feelings that are not habitual—it is quite all right to express them." Then she adds, "I don't like the line, 'If it resembles anything specific,' and the word *specific*." This is a sound criticism—the line and the word are prosy. From her criticism of the first poem on the score of sense, to that of the second on aesthetic grounds a year later, I feel we are justified in concluding that a certain growth has taken place. "A hot sound of laughter" is an original formulation.

Joan at thirteen writes:

> The boat was standing still
> When the dock began to slide backwards,
> Until it was left behind.[2]

Of this she says, "It's not a very good poem. It just makes a statement." Joyce makes a similar remark about her poem:

WAR

> Why should such a thing as war
> Be brought into a civilized country?
> If we were helpless and nothing else
> Could settle our arguments,

[1] Ordinarily I never press the children to define their objections, but in this case since Rachel tends to take refuge behind inarticulateness, I feel she may be helped by being induced to try to define her feelings.

[2] From Flora J. Arnstein, *Adventure into Poetry* (Stanford, Calif.: Stanford University Press, 1951).

> If we were savages and lived long ago,
> I would not object—
> But now what good does it do us,
> Killing a thousand men,
> Taking them from their families,
> Killing a man you don't dislike.

Note that these children have discovered for themselves that mere statement of fact does not constitute poetry—that some transmutation has to occur in order that material may truly belong to the category of poetry. Also by the frequency of the remark "That sounds more like a story than a poem" the children are demonstrating their realization that uncadenced exposition is more in the province of prose than of poetry. At a very early age they sense the distinction, and the older children, although they may not make use of the word "story," often say, "It doesn't sound like a poem," as does one girl of her poem:

> The little vine tries to climb up the wall,
> Clinging to every little ledge that juts out,
> Struggling to the top.
> And when it gets to the top,
> It climbs down the other side.

She is, of course, correct: there is nothing to distinguish this from straight prose.

David, twelve, writes:

THE DOOR

> I know of a door, a singing door,
> That sings the whole night through.
> I know this door is fantasy,
> Like a ghost or fairy tales,
> Or a witch on a broom.
> And when I go to sleep at night,
> It sings and makes me fall asleep,
> And then I dream of things I love,
> That's why my door is so, so sweet.

Rereading this several months later, he says, "I don't like the last line," which obviously is out of key with the rest and also carries a sentimental aura which children almost invariably repudiate. He deletes this line and changes "I dream of things I love," to "I dream of what I love,"—which he may feel is more inclusive—extending *things* to *people*.

The consideration of certain words as being inappropriate to poetry—at least in certain contexts—dawns upon many children, as it did to Rachel with reference to the word *specific*. A girl of twelve has written:

LIFELESS

Fluffed is her hair in tight little curls,
Its softness has wandered far from life.
Her eyebrows are gone, a line takes their place,
Her lips are painted, unnatural they look,
Her cheeks are a soft fake pink.

Of this she says, "I don't like it," and a class member adds, "There shouldn't be *fake*. It's not a poetic word." The same girl writes:

Up the mountain by sunlight,
Trailing down in the pitch black night,
We waited for the moon.
But it came not that time.
So down the slopes we started,
Tumbling over one another,
Falling into hollows,
Till we reached our destination
Without the pale moon.

"I don't like it," she says, "especially the word 'destination'!"

Up to this point we have in the main been discussing the children's criticism of their own poems. We turn now to their comments on one another's. These comments rarely arose in the regular poetry sessions, but the following occurred when the children were engaged in selecting poems submitted for inclusion in their poetry yearbook. These "editorial" meetings brought forth a wealth of commentary, and it is from these occasions that most of the data relative to the development of criteria have been drawn.

The following poem was submitted by a twelve-year-old boy:

THOUGHTS

Looking across the mighty Pacific
With its vast waste of waters,
One thinks of Japan far off,
With its temples and palaces fair.
Then into your mind like a flash,
Comes the thought of the fighting between the
    Japanese and Chinese—
Their guns booming and flying like strong wind.
Suddenly your thoughts of far away
Cease with the loud noise of the surf.

One member of the editorial group comments (again): "It sounds like a story, not a poem"; another, "That line about the Japanese and Chinese is out of rhythm," noting even in the general nonrhythmic character of the poem the prosy awkwardness of the cadence.

A girl of twelve has submitted this poem:

FIRS

The firs hold their branches upward
Toward the sun and moon.
When the sun shines upon them.
The branches turn to a lighter, brilliant green,
And in the late afternoon
They give the rays of sunlight back to the sun,
And take on a new silver light from the moon.
In the morning they return the moonlight,
And receive the rays the sun has ready for them—
And this continues.

Hearing it read aloud she asks to withdraw it, without specific comment, but one member of the group says, "It sounds like a report." At another time the same girl is troubled about a poem she has written and asks for class comment.

From the light you cannot see to the dark
But from the dark you can see to the light.

If you have been in the light,
And try to find something in the dark,
You cannot find it.
But just the other way around,
If you have been in the dark,
You can find something in the light.[3]

"I don't like it," she says, "but I don't know why." "Well," says another girl, "it's just like *saying* things." Another comments, "It's too jerky." The writer then comes to her own evaluation: "I know. It's really not a poem at all."

Just as the children have arrived at a conception of the nature of poetry, so do they reach certain conclusions concerning infelicities, such as clichés, without ever having heard the concept formulated. Actually, in their own writing they make infrequent use of trite expressions. On one occasion a boy objects to a phrase descriptive of death: "No one can thwart its sting," by commenting, "It's not good—it's usual." One submission to the yearbook is the following:

This family is poor.
They have no fire in their fireplace
To give them cheery light.
They have no table in the room
On which to set their crusts of bread.
They have no bed
On which to rest their tired limbs.
This family is poor.

The above, by a boy of eleven, is scored by a girl: " 'Crusts of bread' and 'tired limbs' are too poetic," by which she undoubtedly means that they are clichés. Exception is taken to such poeticisms as "babe," and in one instance a girl discards her poem as being "too poemy," which probably means that she considers it spuriously poetic.

As with the case of clichés, so too the children without ever having heard of mixed metaphors criticize these as they appear in the following poem.

[3] The three poems above are from Arnstein, *Ibid.*

TWILIGHT

The twilight falls.
It cloaks the earth—
A grey and silent blanket,
And pushing through
Come tiny points of lights—
Showers of stars.[4]

One girl remarks: "The writer thought she ought to have images, but a *blanket* with *showers of stars!*"

Acclaim and appreciation of one another's poems are far more frequent than criticism. Of the poem "Our Navy" in the preceding chapter, one boy says, "It's a marvelous poem!" Another, "It has wonderful comparisons," which a girl amends with, "You mean images, don't you?" "I have only compliments for it," says another. Such commendations occur continuously—too many to quote.

Here, then, in this body of commentary by the children lies the answer to the question whether learning can take place without direct teaching. "How can the children learn if they are not told?" is the query frequently posed me. Can it be doubted that from the children's remarks we are being shown an emerging sense of what constitutes poetry, together with repudiation of prosy statement, clichés, inappropriate words, and, in cases of which I have not given illustrations, criticism of faulty rhythm? Surely this is evidence of growth. But such development does not take place in a vacuum. The children have derived their concepts through exposure to poetry, but mere exposure is not enough. Their attention has been constantly directed in the poems read them to the elements of poetry. Thus when they come to write their own poems, they unconsciously submit them to the concepts of poetry they have absorbed.

Still, it may be asked: Since the children are able to entertain such discrimination, why wait for them to arrive at it themselves? Why not tell them the good from the bad earlier? The question implies the fallacy of the assumption that telling presumes learning. Actually such telling frequently stands in the way of learning, for the reason that criteria presented to the children often serve to confuse rather than to illumi-

---

[4] The two poems above are from *Ibid.*

nate. Not having reached the stage in their own development at which they are able to assimilate criteria (and no one can know just at what time they are able to do so), they are more likely than not to misapply them.

Let us suppose that the teacher has defined the word. "prosy." It is in the nature of children to "latch onto" such a word because it carries with it an adult flavor, and then to apply it indiscriminately. But worse than this, they may be beset with the fear that what they write may be considered prosy, and in consequence they may suppress their spontaneous expression. Children are in such matters too prone to accept on authority. If the teacher designates something as good or bad they do not question; thus they are prevented from exercising their own judgment. And it is only by the exercise of judgment that they can arrive at valid evaluations—valid for them. By abdicating their genuine reactions they are losing touch with their inner source of aesthetic discrimination.

The acquiring of taste cannot be hurried; it can only be nourished and allowed to grow. It is, in any field, the product of exposure to works of superior quality over an expanse of time. Also by the wise and discriminating guidance of his teacher the young person is led through enjoyment and appreciation to the development of some measure of taste. The time element is important as well, for it takes time for certain values to become assimilated. One would not, for example, expect of a beginning student the response to poetic values that one would of a student who had been studying poetry for a year or so. Taste and discrimination are not matters of the mind alone. Poetry has its root not only in the intellect but in the emotions as well, and the young person in order to respond to it must have the experience of exploring (to a certain extent) his own emotions. He must, again through a period of time, have been in rapport with his own feelings in an atmosphere in which feelings are not only tolerated but valued. Taste requires time, guidance, and the proper environment in order to grow. Discrimination cannot be conferred by edict; it must be encouraged, and in order that such encouragement be not merely nominal the young people should even be permitted to express dislike of a poem the teacher may have brought to class. Nor should they be made to feel that this implies a criticism of him. They should have his sanction that there is room for preference in poetry as in everything else. Nor should the teacher insist that the children give reasons for their likes and dislikes. Formulation of values is too difficult (except as was the case with Rachel mentioned above). Our insistence upon formulation results frequently in rationalization, the children saying the first thing uppermost in their minds. By allowing a child to express his dislikes without censure, the teacher encourages in him the development of criteria which are available to him and valid for him at the given time.

This, then, is the case for growth. We adults too often err in not taking into account a child's potential; we need greater faith in him and in his inherent powers. In our eagerness to teach we sometimes encroach upon those areas of growth which offer the child the greatest opportunity for learning and the most lasting possibilities of enjoyment and appreciation.

12

To Speak for Oneself

THE TEACHER may at times be puzzled how to recognize authentic poetic expression in the children's poems. One of the earmarks is genuineness and a certain uniqueness: a child is speaking from himself, from his own feeling and observation. Of course this does not mean necessarily that the utterance is poetry, but at least it has that essential quality of poetry, the individual touch. As one boy put it, "Everyone writes about trees and rain and sky, but they should write about them differently." The difference lies in the fact that the writer has drawn upon his own experience, has not resorted to trite or derived expression, but has noted something distinctive, something to which he brings his own personal reaction. Joan, twelve, writes:

RUNNING RAIN

Watch the wind blowing the rain.
It looks as if each rain-drop
Is racing with the one ahead of it.
It seems to go straight across the sky.
It looks as if it's never falling,
Just racing on and on.

This, while not notably poetic, still draws upon individual observation, does not resort to the ready-made "pitter-patter" of rain.

Another mark of authenticity is unpretentiousness. When the children "go in for" *fancy* words, they are usually parroting something that they have read. Such parroting is especially evident when the children write in rhyme, as previously noted, and in their use of obsolete words and phrases. Often a truly felt experience seems to bring with it a poetic cadence, as is evident in the following two poems by Van, twelve:

A silence which is too quiet—
Then the rain.
It's raining—
With gusts of wind;

It's raining—
With sheets of water;
It's raining—
With dripping trees.

Then all is again still.
It has stopped.
A clearness settles—
Clear greens and blues,
And a dripping world
Is now outside.

The repetition of "It's raining" gives cadence to the poem while contributing to the sense of the continuing rain.

In the following poem the longer lines make for a quieter cadence, reinforced by the repetition of vowel sounds, the short "I" in *mist, dim,* and *thick* and the long "I" in *lightly, sky, whine, combines.*

The mist hangs lightly over the dim landscape,
The smoke blends with the soft sky.
Over where the mist is thick
The incessant whine of the fog horn
Combines with the early morning street sounds
Of the milkman's truck, and an occasional street car
To break noisily into the stillness.

Joyce, thirteen, writes:

I plunged into the silent pool—
The waters were silent and green,
And I pushed the water behind
Till I reached the other end.
Then I turned to look
At the silent green waters,

But the pool was in ripples—
My path could be seen,
And the silent green waters
Were no longer still.

The repetition of silent and green waters gives a cadential tone to the
poem.

Donna writes:

THE END OF THE WORLD

The end of the world is far away.
It is way beyond the forest lake,
It is over a hundred oceans.
The birds will show you the way some time,
Perhaps today! Who knows?
. . . .
The shadows glare at me from the wall.
I look back at them thinking,
Why do you glare at me so?
But the shadows never answer.
They are quiet and black as a jungle.

Here in these two poems we have a child's own thoughts and imaginings
not reminiscent of anything she may have read elsewhere.

A felt experience tends to bring with it a somewhat organic structure,
so that the poem holds together with a sort of inherent logic. This is
observable in many of the children's contemplative poems. Rena, thirteen, writes:

A tree strong and stalwart,
Leaning against a deep blue sky,   ·
All alone in a sea of greenness. . . .

Play around me, Children!
Come to me, I'll give you shade
On a hot summer's day.

This falls naturally, though the child may not have written it in that
way, into two clearly defined stanzas of three lines each.

Rachel, twelve, writes:

> Beauty is what?
> Is it the love for others,
> The tremendous rolling hills,
> The stars up above,
> The gentle faces,
> The wind-blown trees,
> The flowing stream?
>
> What is beauty?
> Did God create it,
> Or did it just come naturally?

Here structure may be said to reside in the unity of the poem—what has been said is complete, rounded off. The same is true of the following poem by the same girl:

> I took a trip to the sea shore.
> The wind was blowing harshly,
> And the waves were thumping,
> Pounding against the soft sandy earth's surface.
>
> The sky was so beautiful—
> The big shrilling streak of red and gray
> Mixed together so gracefully
> In front of the frosted blue sky.
>
> A cold spray from the ocean breeze
> Made me shiver from head to toe.
> I ran on the wet sand,
> The wind blowing my hair,
> I ran faster and faster,
> And jumped and fell into a sand pile,
> And rolled and rolled in the soft cool sand.
>
> I went back to the hot fire,
> And listened to the sounds of the beach—
> Ah, yes, all the sounds of the beach.

This is unmistakably authentic, rising into poetry in phrases such as "the frosted blue sky" and "the shrilling streak of red and gray."

David, aged twelve, writes the following:

THE OCEAN

The ocean is a funny thing.
The tide comes in, the tide goes out.
No one will ever know the deep mist mysteries
Of the white coral reef
That is beyond mankind's ideal.

The ocean is a mysterious thing,
Where its powerful hand
Hits its enemy, the land.
And at night time it goes to rest
And then starts a new mystery:
A mystery in death.

Here each stanza begins with a literal observation about the ocean but goes on to an imaginative and evocative conception that seems to have a symbolic connotation. This does not mean that the boy necessarily consciously recognizes any symbolic intent, but that there is often more involved in creative work than what is consciously planned is too evident to need argument.

Rachel writes:

DEATH

Death is the most frightening thing in the world to me.
You say to yourself that people manage to go on living,
But to me I feel as if the day will stop
When the people I love die.

I probably will go on living,
But to think that I'll never see them again!
I'm scared to think maybe some morning
I won't wake up to see the sun rise and fall,
Or to see my loved ones again.

To me it's hard to realize
How life is arranged in such a pattern.
Why does there have to be an end?

I never want to die or to leave the ones I love and hate.
I wonder why, Oh, why there is such a thing!
I'm very scared of death.

Here in this poem we have a child daring to plumb her thoughts and feelings concerning the problem of life and death. It takes courage to bring into words every man's deepest concern. But that the children have this courage and that they grapple with thoughts that adults do not usually credit them with having is abundantly proved by their poems.

Here are some poems in point. Carol at twelve writes:

> The wind is like a sudden thought:
> It blows wildly for a moment,
> Then settles down into itself
> And decides it is wrong.

Sean, twelve, writes:

DESIGN

> Design is a written form of man's wondering,
> Which leaves an abstract idea on the paper,
> But a real impression on a man's mind.

Design as a "written form of man's wondering" is surely an original conception. Teachers will be astonished at the depth and range of children's thinking, once the setting has been established in which the children venture into their private world and have the courage to reveal it.

Readers of this book may be inclined to think that too much space has been accorded to the children's writing, but this has been done with deliberate intent. In the writing is shown the children's own engagement with the aesthetic act, and it is through this engagement that they seem to make the surest step in the direction of appreciation. By creative writing they parallel the impulse that moves the adult poet to expression; they are introduced to the source of poetic utterance, which, in the case of any one child may not merit the term *inspiration*, but which at least allows him a glimpse of what takes place in the mind of the poet. And through his own effort he learns what goes into the making of poetry—the cadence, the imagery, the "feeling-thought," and perhaps something of the proportion and balance that make of a poem a memorable utterance.

What children themselves think of poetry is best expressed in their own words. Sean asks:

> What is poetry?
> A written form of man's thoughts,
> Or a man's version of imagination?
> No one can really know except one . . .
> The poet.

Emily, ten, asks:

> What is poetry?
> Poetry is like the stars
> Left undiscovered . . .[1]

She touches here upon the limitless sweep of the poetic imagination. Donna, ten, gives her definition of poetry:

> Sunbeams are poems—
> All kinds of poems—
> They fill the air.
> Rain is poems, too—
> Diamond jets of poems.
> Fog is poems, too—
> Like a creeping tiger
> Ready to catch its prey.[2]

Donna realizes that poetry lies everywhere—"it fills the air," and she shares the poet's sensitive vision in her designation of rain as "diamond jets."

May we hope that by now this book has fulfilled its purpose: to demonstrate that poetry can be meaningful to children. By the references to poetry in the poems quoted above, and by the children's own poems, have they not shown that there exists a natural affinity between

[1] From Flora J. Arnstein, *Adventure into Poetry* (Stanford, Calif.: Stanford University Press, 1951).
[2] From *Ibid.*

them and poetry? If this is true, then it remains for us teachers to provide the setting in which such an affinity may be discovered and enjoyed by the children. It rests with us to throw open the doors, to provide the welcome, and to play the gracious hosts, offering to share the bounty of poetry with our willing guests. Let us never be the ones to erect barriers to poetry enjoyment. Let us never be among those who strip children of their wings, who give justification for the sorry question posed by one frustrated child:

THE CANYON

Deep in the canyon all gray and green,
With a soft blue tint to the tops of the redwoods,
I would like so much to spread my wings,
And fly over you and listen to the roaring of the water.
Who took away my wings?[3]

---

[3] From *Ibid.*

INDEX OF FIRST LINES OF POETRY[1]

[1] For poems by children, the numeral after the name indicates the age of the child at the time the poem was written.

121

T H E
Passersby

Arikha tells:

"In the light of falling night, I paint my bookcase. The backs of the books. Those which stand out when the light sinks."

He adds:

"Where I live I am unknown. Indifference is good for work."

I transpose:

"In the light of falling night, I paint my life. Those who have crossed it. What stands out when memory fails."

I would like it to be people, but at this moment what I see, in the light of the heart—what remains of it—are doors.

To Arikha's words, "Indifference is good for work," answer the flickering stars that black holes lie in wait for.

To the stars' words, triumphant—for a moment more—my trembling and my praise respond.

First Door
and
First Praise

To paint, even with words, it's necessary first to see, and I, tonight, I see only doors.

Those of my house open, but onto empty passages. I mean: only I live there. Those of our houses, where our friends came. The one where I left you. The one where I had been left. I don't even want to remember your first name. You no longer have a voice or a face. Like a scar, you did not disappear but you no longer cause pain.

The most dangerous desert is the one that we become ourselves. The beings that one has loved can no longer come, even in thought, and if they come, they can neither breathe nor remain.

That is probably why, in the light of my eyes, which I had to put out so that I could love, and of my heart, which I had to stop from beating so I could no longer be tortured, I see only doors.

Starvation — of the flesh — of the heart — of the spirit — of the soul.

* * *

That is not new.

I am seated on the floor, on a landing, against a door. It is dark.

I am nine or ten years old. I have been thrown out. I sing wrong and I intrude.

Suddenly, I'm no longer breathing. My friends are singing. Through the door, their singing, which a little while ago I didn't like, reaches me—apart, a good distance away. I'm struck by its manifest and hidden beauty, and I love it.

It is again the end of day in my empty house.

I speak from afar and I see no one.

"Indifference is good for work," says Arikha.

I call work this passion to paint (with words) beings, so that they will live again, a good distance away—to be the one who will reveal their manifest beauty and their hidden beauty.

Second Door
and
Second Praise

In a rich house, in Marseille, at the end of a war, a young girl is starving herself to death.

She is fourteen years old, or fifteen. Her name is No—her first name. *But I'll get out of it* is her last name.

She goes to high school, she studies furiously, she goes on long mad walks in the coves, but for months she has not been eating. People see her bones. She's beginning to lose her memory.

The meals are torture for the whole family. *Me I live,* the maid of the house—she has a wooden leg; she doesn't wear bloomers and she brags about it—passes the dishes. The mother, *I'm dying,* the father, *God does a bad job, I'll take over,* and the four sisters, *Yes, YesNo, NoNo,* and *YesYes,* pretend not to look when *No* serves herself. *No* puts two or three ends of something on her plate. She cuts and recuts it up into a hundred tiny bits. She doesn't touch it.

They all concentrate on their plates, on their forks, on the pieces of meat and fried potatoes that they are about to chew. They all act as if *No* doesn't exist, but each one looks at *No* and suffers.

No also suffers, from the suffering of her father, from her sisters, from her mother. She would eat so that they wouldn't suffer anymore, if she could.

"But really!" cries *I'm dying*. She controls herself because of a look from *God does a bad job*—they had resolved to try not to say anything, on advice from the doctor, *Leave it to me*.

"But how can you do without eating?" cries the grandmother, *Give me a discount* (implying: you owe it to me because I am Mrs. *But I'll get out of it* from Main Street in Montpellier). She had made the journey, she had made the sacrifice of closing up her shop, to help *God does a bad job* and *I'm dying* make *No* eat.

"It's so good to eat," pleads *God does a bad job*, *I'll take over*. He can no longer hold back the words.

The cook, *Above all no man*, comes into the dining room to lend a hand: "My little *No*, you who are so intelligent, you must understand: a motor needs oil. I made you *pets-de-nonne*."

The only one who hasn't said anything during the entire meal is *I speak alone but I still am sound of mind*, the nurse of the two youngest children, *NoNo* and *YesYes*.

She watches for the moment when *No* leaves the house to go to school. She is near the open door. She hands *No* a very thin slice of bread and butter. *No* would like to please her. She cannot. *I speak alone* says nothing. She has tears in her eyes. She remains for a moment on the doorstep with her very thin slice of bread and butter, hoping that *No* will come back to take it.

After school, *No* buys some chocolate. She eats it while running so that she doesn't see it, so that it doesn't exist.

In the light of the years, *No*, aged, suddenly sees the profound understanding in *I speak alone*'s love.

I speak alone will be eighty-five years old in a few days. She is still sound of mind, and she knows to rejoice in being alive, although she lives alone.

With the little money that is left to her, *No* will send — by telex — some flowers.

Some flowers for you — to say without words — delayed too long: "Thank you."

Third Door
and
Third Praise

No's condition worsens.

Even her friend *I will make myself tubercular* worries.

That *No* has become bony to the point of fainting is right: the great poets have always been great invalids, therefore to become a poet one must first fall ill; that's why *I will make myself tubercular* lies naked on the ground in the middle of winter. But *No* can no longer translate the *Odyssey*. She can no longer read. She, who wills herself all spirit, thinks only of not eating. She madly counts, recounts, what she has swallowed down: huge chunks of bread—well, almost; one olive. No, three. One in the morning, one at noon, one in the evening. She is nauseated. *I will make myself tubercular* recites a poem to her about sublime desperation by a fervent poet, but *No* doesn't hear. She remembers only extra chunks of bread. She ate chocolates, with cream in them. Eight. No, twelve. Maybe sixteen. She stole them from the bookcase in the living room. Why does her mother hide them there? Doesn't she have any respect for books? "She has no respect for books," cries *No* from deep inside herself, which provokes murderous rage, a terrible nervous fit that no one understands the reason for.

Let's say: this young girl, delicate, sensitive, has begun, lately, to work herself up into nervous attacks that are outlandish, uncontrollable.

The two youngest girls, *NoNo* and *YesYes*, escape to the garden. If it's cold they shut themselves in their playroom. *I am dying* starts to die again: she closes all the curtains in her room; she buries herself in the darkness, in her bed, a cold compress on her forehead, and begins to groan. This woman is an artist of groaning. Her moans, furious, rhythmic, accusing, make the house shake. She forbids living.

In their room next to their mother's, *No* cannot calm down. *Yes* reasons with her. *Yes* is the oldest. She is the only one who can patiently accept *No*. *No* would love her if she wasn't, with all her being, a yes without reservation to what she herself hates with all her being.

Yes is beautiful and most of all she wants to love. She sews her red dress to go dancing in. This ball and this red dress pain *No* so terribly that she starts her insane cries again.

＊　＊　＊

YesNo will tell her later how she had been afraid of her—she will tell her when her own daughter will have to be taken care of.

There are moments of such grief that it seems the story cannot continue.

I see *No* from the back, seated on her bed, so contorted, and the daughter of *YesNo* thirty years later seated in the same way on a bed in a mental hospital, where *No* has taken her.

YesNo and *No* cry, in their high heels, on the damp earth in the private garden of *YesNo*, they cry against their mother, dead many years. They cry like two children—they are old women but two children all the same. They cry against their mother, who mutilated them, forever, by her melancholy.

Our mother herself recovered from it only on her deathbed. We keep vigil, in the cold room of a hospital, the last of a long series.

Suddenly—she has been dead only a few hours— here she is white, relaxed, childlike, invaded by something that one rightly could call by the name "happiness."

*　　*　　*

A happiness stronger than herself, stronger than her history, that finally comes at the end of her long and stubborn and mad resistance.

Even under the white sheet her body radiates a supreme happiness, which makes her beautiful and unforgettable.

Fourth Door
and
Fourth Praise

The light of falling night is the most beautiful. It gives itself lavishly to what it loves and what remains has already disappeared.

Suddenly I see — instead of the beings who were important to me — the supervisor from the Mongrand School. She enters the classroom, breathless, interrupting the lesson:

The principal wants to see Miss *But I'll get out of it* immediately.

"She can't already want to congratulate you, the semester has barely started," she reasons, trotting ahead of *No* in the corridor.

The principal is a woman whose face is nondescript. She exudes grayness. Her skin, her voice, her hands, her words are gray.

"I asked you to come . . . I would like . . . Your parents asked me . . ."

Here we go.

It's going to start again.

* * *

She's going to cry, like the others:

"Why don't you eat? You want your parents to die of grief? You want to kill yourself?" Et cetera?

But the principal does not continue. She has this delicacy characteristic of people who live only in books, fed by thought, by poetry contained in books.

"My dear child, we are all very worried about you."

She invokes the necessity to eat, to have the strength to study, the necessity to eat even to study.

What puts No's life in danger, she does not see. No would like to tell her, but this woman lives in her library without seeing that around her everything burns in a fire that leaves the trees whole, and the sky, but that consumes individuals, a fire that comes from the heart, against which even books . . .

"I don't want to tell you," concludes the principal, discouraged.

No remembers her with tenderness forty years later. She remembers the excessive refinement, the blindness of a woman who had enclosed her life in the splendor contained in books.

Fifth Door
and
Fifth Praise

Yes shouts throughout the whole house:

"*I will create myself* will be here tonight!"

I will create myself is nineteen years old and he is returning from Auschwitz. There, he lost his father, his mother, his sister.

As soon as he arrives at the house, *I am dying* and *Give me a discount* feed him until he is stuffed.

Later, he will tell *No*, laughingly, about the story of the pears.

"Your grandmother had given me one. I had the bad luck of mentioning that it was good. She was convinced that I loved them and couldn't resist them. As soon as I arrived she gave me at least four—to please me!"

"You ate them?"

"To please her! But since then I haven't touched even one!"

Then, as soon as he arrives, *I am dying* requests that *Above all no man* prepare her best dishes in great quantities so that after eating, her guest can take some with him.

The Passersby

* * *

Give me a discount hurries over, with her delicious jams, her wine, which is barely drinkable—she makes it herself—the figs and the grapes of her country, all that she can carry, the best of all that she has.

This young man had starved: one cannot give him back his family, one cannot heal him of having lived through what he had lived, but one can refresh him, dote on him, embrace him, love him.

When we adopt him, he will keep his last name, *And I'll get out of it.* It is not that he scorns the *"But."*
He wants to render homage to his father, to his mother, to his sister, who disappeared in smoke.

Yes calms him, *No* listens to him.
He needs to tell, she needs to listen.
They walk beside the lake, or in the meadows, all summer long. Each day he tells, for hours. Each day she listens, for hours.

He recounts the meals, the train, the song, the *kapo*, the tin can, the bursting laughter, the danger of being killed at every instant, the forced marches, the doors—to enter the camp? not to enter? if you made a mistake, you were dead—the rope. He tells how, at the moment of the rope, he had been, yes, a superman. Years later, he will add to the telling; for the young girl, the wound remains hidden but always raw.

"As soon as I see a being, I see him down there. I wonder who he would have been down there. He would have been like us, an animal, at feeding time. The most distinguished professors, the most helpful doctors, the most fervent rabbis, the most refined individuals became, in a few seconds, when the soup came, animals, savages — it's a feeble word."

This voice that he has in telling, he will lose it later; it will grow softer, it will smolder like a contained hidden fire.

At night, No cries secretly: "God! that the sound of the horn is mournful in the depths of the forest," all the poems that she knows and that she loves, as if poetry was possible after such accounts.

At the time of the walks, beside the lake or in the meadows, No still eats. She eats a great deal. She eats, like *I will create myself*, the delicious sustenance that the family strives to increase, and she can be healed no more by poetry than by food of the tales of the one who will become her brother.

*   *   *

29

He, on the other hand, he loves to eat. He loves to tell, he loves to laugh, he loves to love.

Much later, in his white and lively house that he designed himself, he tells the one who had become his sister long ago:

"In Auschwitz, I had a friend. He was a Freemason. One day, he said to me: 'Listen carefully. God is everywhere. In you also. If you want something desperately, with all the divine strength that is within you, you will receive it, because you are a part of God.' I wanted to live—I wanted it very much. I told myself: 'I will create myself and I'll get out of it, as I am a part of God.'"

Since then, each time that he is in danger of death, he re-creates himself, and he lives.

Sixth Door
and
Sixth Praise

He is there, in Marseille. He had left his *sana* to come to see *No*. He had come to tell her:

"Listen carefully: nothing is more beautiful than to live. I, I can tell you, nothing is more beautiful than to live."

No believes it since he says it: nothing is more beautiful than to live. But me, I cannot. I cannot.

Dr. *Leave it to me* prescribes injections for her. He talks about morning fatigue that occurs at eleven o'clock. He talks and he believes he's saying something.

Finally, an idea comes to him: "My dear little one, in the state that you are in, I believe that it will be in your interest . . . to separate . . . for a while from your family, I mean, to go to Switzerland, in a . . . clinic."

"And my studies?"

"In the state that you are in . . ."

"I study, Doctor."

"Oh, well, you can study down there also!"

*   *   *

And *No* feels lighthearted, pleased. She is going away. *I am dying* packs her suitcase. Down there she will have friends, she will study, she will create her life, she will be able to say, with all her heart, with her whole being, with *I will create myself*: "Nothing is more beautiful, more important, than to live."

Seventh Door
and
Seventh Praise

God does a bad job, I'll take over accompanies his daughter to Prangins, in Switzerland.

They walk a few steps, in a wood, near a station, while waiting for a transfer.

God does a bad job is nervous. He speaks as if he might still be able to find the words that would heal his daughter, that would make it unnecessary to put her in a mental hospital.

No doesn't hear him. She has not been able to follow him. She is livid. He becomes aware of it. He shouts. His suffering worsens, whatever she says. Then she no longer says anything.

Suddenly—she believes she is speaking in a loud voice, but her mouth is shut—"If you were not my father, you would be able to help me, as you were able to help *I will create myself.*" *I will create myself* has told her, he tells often, how he and *God does a bad job* had met and helped each other.

*   *   *

37

"I was dying of hunger in a hotel room in Paris. It was so ridiculous, to die of hunger after having been liberated. But I didn't want help from an organization. I had survived thanks to my will. A divine superhuman will. I did not have to beg. They had only to come and bring me my due. Evidently, the idea hadn't occurred to them. But your father came. He came to a shabby hotel room to help a proud boy he didn't know. He looked at me as one looks at a human being. He cried. He told me about himself. He apologized for his grief over the suffering of others, to the extent of needing, selfishly, to help them. He had truly convinced me that I could help him, *God does a bad job but I'll get out of it*, by accepting his help.

Long after, at the moment of death of *God does a bad job*, his son, *I will create myself*, says to his sisters:
    "Thanks to him I could not be driven mad. That a man like him can exist, that is what healed me of hate, that is what permitted me to respond to Auschwitz with the decision to be happy."

Eighth Door
and
Eighth Praise

The head doctor—*Deranged* is his first name, *My money above all* is his last name—invites Mr. and Miss *But I'll get out of it* to dinner as soon as they arrive.

Again I see this long oval table, this ill-assorted family like a creature without a spine, presided over and guarded by a living masthead, erect, massive, crowned in white: it is the hair of the doctor on duty—*Out of control* is his first name, *Danger* is his last name.

God does a bad job does not eat this evening either. He looks at the people who will live with his daughter. They do not seem so very disturbed, or dangerous, but Dr. *Out of control* watches them closely.

It will be the same apparent benevolence, the same artificial ease, less luxurious, thirty years later.

Little No does not eat.

The patients ask her why. They persist in order that she eat, especially the one who smears himself with his meat.

After the meal, *No* and *Little No* go to the park.

They avoid the patients.

They sit down. *Little No* is so weak, so frail, and dressed all in black.

She says it is comfortable here, that she wants to stay, that she wants to go away.

No repeats for the umpteenth time:

"You will be fine here. Dr. *I make men run* knows how to talk to you. The park is beautiful. You will be able to breathe. If you want to go away, you can—the doors are open, and you have money. But, please, stay at least one week. I will come to visit you next week."

No gets in the hospital van to leave. She sees the look on *Little No*'s face. Again she sees her father, when he had left her in Prangins.

He had told her also:

"You will be fine here. Dr. *Out of control* doesn't seem bad. He will know how to talk to you. The park is splendid. Have you seen the lake? The deer? You will be able to breathe. Next month, I will come to see you."

The motor of the van is running. *Little No* waves a final small good-bye. She looks like a bird. She, used to luxury, is going to live here, in this . . . , with these. . . . *No* wants to get out of the van, then she remembers: *Little No* tried to kill herself last night, and nearly succeeded. She really needs to be looked after. Only the doctors can do it.

Liliane Atlan

Then, in the train, and afterward in her home—the house is empty, *Holiday* has not returned—she does not cry, she does not think.

She is cold.

A coldness of stone.

Again she sees her father. She feels what he feels when he leaves her. He cannot leave her there, with people who are really insane. He is going to take her out, but she really needs to be looked after. Only the doctors can do it.

He has been dead for a long time and his suffering remains. Sometimes, the grief is such that it becomes indestructible.

The story can no longer continue.

But it continues, and it is perhaps the most wonderful praise.

Ninth Door
and
Ninth Praise

No's room is in the castle—that is where the convalescents live, she was told, before they closed the door.

From her bed, she sees the door.
    There is no knob.
    But she can ring a bell.

She sees, through the window, trees a hundred years old, dense, thick. They reverberate with thousands and thousands of songs. How can the birds dare to sing?
    She notices that the window does not have a handle.

But there is a mirror.
    She looks at herself in it, naked, every morning.
    Too much flesh.
    One does not see enough ribs.

Every morning, she calculates her weight with a look. The judgment does not change: still too much flesh.

About eleven o'clock, Dr. *Out of control* knocks at the door. He opens it. He sits down. He looks at her. He says to her kindly:
    "Is it your mother that you want to kill? your father?

The two of them?" *No* is truly amazed. She is silent. "I see, it is your sister. My child, the crimes that we do not commit, we can admit. If we admit them, they cease to torture us."

He will come back tomorrow. He will say the same thing again. He will try the books: a treatise on morals by Gobineau, *The Fruits of the Earth* by Gide. From among them she remembers this:
"Families, I hate you."
Out of boredom, she waits for the plates.
She does not touch them.

She is weighed once a week, and is allowed to take a little walk in the corridors.
Afterward, Dr. *Out of control* comes back to discuss crimes with her.
One day he becomes angry:
"Your silence is a terrible weapon."

Dr. *Out of control's* idea of genius is Miss *If I could, I would grant myself the luxury of being sick.*
Like *No*, she dreams of writing.
She writes, every night, in the cottage of the dangerous ones, where she is housed.
During the day, her work is this young girl who began killing everybody by ceasing to eat.

*   *   *

They sun themselves on the porch, take a few steps outside, go to the tearoom beside the lake.

Miss *If I could* tells *No* what she knows about the patients that they meet.

For two people who will write, this hospital is a gold mine.

There is this lady with fat jowls and garbled speech. She is the niece of Verhaeren, whom she has not read. She specializes in depression. This one in black silk, stuffed like a sausage, pasty, worldly, eager to please even chairs, she is slightly hunchbacked because of the pink pigs that are accustomed to living in her stomach. "During the day, they remain calm," relates Miss *If I could*, "but at night, she rings us endlessly. We give her a placebo to calm them."

There is this handsome young Englishman, dark haired and green eyed. He is stooped forward. He never says anything: "He still suffers from the pieces of shrapnel in his head, which he received during the war."

And this Pope's guard, stiff, mute, absent: His existence diminishes a little more each day. That is what he wants.

And this gentle and beautiful young woman paralyzed on the right side: "A bad marriage. Half of her no longer functions. She can afford that luxury because she is rich. Me, I must work."

* * *

"Where does this music, so beautiful and sad, come from?" *No* asks, lying down again.

"From the Princess. She lives above you."

"What does she suffer from?"

"From her heirs. Dr. *My money above all* is their accomplice."

"Do you mean that she is not sick?"

"She becomes sick and is lost in music."

It happens that one night *No* is awakened by screams of relentless anguish, coming from an actor locked in the emergency room next door.

"I no longer hear him. Has he been cured already?"

Miss *If I could* lowers her eyes and *No* understands that he has not been cured, but removed.

Added to *No*'s sickness is the suffering of strangers near her, for whom she cannot do anything. "Unless you become a doctor one day, to create from your failings a system and a profession?" And with this answer, which escaped her, Miss *If I could* becomes *No*'s friend.

I will create myself and *God does a bad job* are there.

"But you're not so thin! Compared to us, in the camp, you are even a bit fat."

He laughs, then he adds:

"Your father never should have let me become a part

of your family. I never should have spoken to you like that."

I will answer you forty years later, with the books that I will write, with the words that I will say to you in your garden when finally we find each other again. For the moment I'm thinking of only one thing:

"You are not so thin. You are even a bit fat."

It is possible that my real name is *I will kill myself.* Or *I will kill.*

"You make me fat. What do you do to make me fat?"

"I add a little sugar to your banana in the morning. Dr. *Out of control* prescribed it. I can't trick you. But you can lose the couple of ounces, if we go on some outings."

The forced marches begin: in the park, in the countryside—Swiss, calm, exasperating, except for the pathetic light of the sky, when the sun is hidden. The most boring, the most exhausting day was the day they spent in the catacombs of Lausanne.

A new inmate just arrived, *I need poison.* He doesn't look sick. He jokes without losing his aura of being under a curse—he slept with his sister, he takes morphine, it's still far from being fashionable. He lives in the cottage of pleasure. They go there often, for tea.

*   *   *

No is glad to go downstairs at mealtime. From afar she will see *I need poison*. She will feign the most desperate look to seduce him, from afar, in the tearoom.

Thanks to time away from the clinic to go to the movies, she will end up approaching him. A fragile little unstable group forms Tuesday evenings.

The Princess, languid, abnormally beautiful, says a few polite words. What sets her apart is not that she is foreign, but that she observes the others.

A film actress with a lion's-mane head of hair smokes several cigarettes at the same time. She speaks or rather groans in a language all her own, which no one can comprehend. But the language of her eyes is clear:
"Help me. A few seconds more and it will be too late."

I need poison, the Don Juan of Tuesday evenings, says to *No* in a stage whisper, in a muffled, caressing tone:
"A prince is journeying. He lost his way. He walks. He walks. He sees a house with lights. He enters. Nothing. There is nothing but a long corridor without any door. He goes as far as the end of this corridor, which turns, just at the last moment, into another corridor. It doesn't have any doors either. He goes as far as the end of this second corridor, which turns, just at the last moment, into another corridor. It doesn't have any

doors either. At last he finds a staircase, or rather a
stepladder. He climbs up. He climbs up. He enters
another corridor without doors, which turns into a
corridor without doors. But there, in the last corridor, is
a pedestal table. And on the pedestal table . . ." His
voice breaks. He controls himself, and ends by saying
dryly: "On the pedestal table, there are some pills. He
doesn't touch them. He wants to go down but the
staircase has disappeared. There is nothing more than
this pedestal table, and on this pedestal table, these
pills. With a glass of water. He takes them."

If I could loses her wits:
"No, what do you think? He would like me to go to
bed with him, but I'm engaged. He says that it will cure
him. My fiancé is far away, in Indochina, in the war. He
still has three more years there. If that would cure him,
tell me, should I do it?"

The eyes of *No*—two black daggers—answer:
"My poor Miss *If I could*, you are only a *Yes*."

Yes of Prangins beams:
"I did it! He is! But his wife, it's she who did him
wrong. She arrives this evening."
And this fool cries.

Another fresh idea that these gentlemen or their
nurse have is boating. With a young acne-covered

English schizophrenic. *No,* to lose weight, does the rowing.

Suddenly, the splashing of the water in the silence opens a door in her. There is there, somewhere, a hidden mirth, involuntary, unchangeable. But the nurse tries to encourage a flirtation. *No* feels regret. She does not eat but she is healthy.

When she has the time to fall in love, it will not be with an acne-covered young man in pleated pants.

No appears at commencement in Marseille, all dressed up with Miss *If I could.*

This young woman makes a good impression—who would doubt her participation? She accompanies *No* to the door, and picks her up again at the exit. *No* has been able to respond, but the wooden benches hurt her bones.

At the house nothing has changed. *If I could* is charming them, then they stuff her. She eats with great pleasure, which makes her exasperating. *Yes* utters trivialities, overexcited: she is getting engaged; she talks only about her clothes and her fiancé.

I am dying, this woman obsessed with cleanliness, always dribbles oil on her chin when she eats salad. As for *God does a bad job,* his suffering makes him intolerable.

They go to the ocean.

The light reflected on the ocean revives for a moment this wellspring of joy without cause.

Then it dies, in the house.

No has received her bachelor's degree and has had a relapse.

Dr. *Out of control* no longer hesitates.

To the insulin.

It is in a room where neither the door nor the window has a handle that she writes her first poem, and it is called "Rage."

Her father comes to see her. She shows it to him. He complains, without crying—he can no longer cry:

"Why 'Rage'? Why not a poem of love?"

It is the month of August, a Swiss national holiday. They hold a ball in the dining room. No one dances.

The chairs are pushed up against the walls, a good distance apart from one another. Suddenly, the niece of Verhaeren cries, distraught. A nurse in her Sunday best leads her out, with much respect, included in the cost.

No has succeeded in stitching a wallet in leather. She alone does not see any reason for pride. She has pity on the deer that sometimes come into view on the walk. They also make up part of the cost.

If I could has invited her to her house. She wants to show her the photo of her fiancé, to read her short stories.

No goes then to her house, the cottage of the dangerous ones.

On every floor, she hears cries and she sees chains.

She says no to everything, no indeed to madness, or to death, or to remaining shut up in sterile revolt.

She was born for something else.

What, she does not know.

She informs Dr. *Out of control* that she is going away.

"But you are a borderline case . . . you can never . . ."

"It's not you that I'm promising. I will eat and I'm going away."

Did *If I could* know that by inviting *No* she would save her? *No* says good-bye to her; she has pity for her because she is staying here. *If I could* has pity for *No* because, obviously, she will have to return.

No will come back, but much later. From outside she will point out the park and the castle to her husband, *I will discover the secret of life.*

Certain places are black holes. Nothing can be said for them.

The only praise possible is that one exits from them.

Tenth Door
and
Tenth Praise

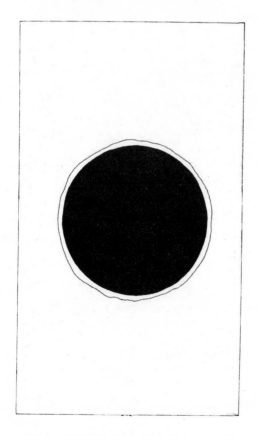

No has not been able to keep her promise. Her whole body refuses it.

In the formal dining room of a luxury hotel in Paris—the family "settles down," to quote *I am dying*—the waiters in uniform pass the plates. *No* cannot serve herself. No one says anything because she is going to die. She herself acknowledges it. They avoid facing it.

Her parents ask her to come with them to Place Vendôme, to the home of Mr. *I love beauty so much*—this is his first name; *She refused me* is his last name.

He is small, hunchbacked; he lives alone, in luxury.

Like *God does a bad job, I'll take over*, he sells textiles.

He gives them to theater people.

One day, he will give money to *No* for a play.

The meal, even more than usual, is torture.

No is no longer blinded by rage: she sees her parents. Her mother, still young, so beautiful, in mourning for her second daughter, the one who had set herself to hate her. Her father with his excessive sickening kindness, already legendary, who had not been able to prevent his daughter from dying. *Yes*, in red, her wild beauty. And the little ones—she had forgotten, for years, to speak to them, to know them.

To make the air breathable, a friend of her father—*I believe in fairy tales* is his first name, *I fight so that they become true* is his last name—begins to tell a story.

He speaks of his school, I Study, on two levels: The Future, the Past. It bears the name of a young man who had the idea, in the underground, before being killed.

"He dreamed of a school of very high standards, where one would study the most modern thought, but also our traditional and esoteric thought. We had blown up a train. *I study* had been killed. I had been wounded in the spinal column. I remained in bed lying down for six months. I decided to create this school as soon as the war ended. It has already been in existence for three years. Every year, about twenty boys and girls—I choose them from among the best of our movement—come, from all corners of France and Africa, to study, to reflect together. We want to respond to the war by inventing a new way to live. When we are strong, we will change the world."

He speaks simply.

His cheeks are lined with two enormous folds; they are accentuated when he smiles—his smile must have etched them in. *No* observes him, although she works hard not to lift her eyes from her plate. She looks stubborn, insensitive, but the words pronounced make her heart beat again.

After the meal, *I believe in fairy tales* suggests that *Yes* and *No* come visit *I Study*.
  Yes accepts. *No* hears herself say:
  "To visit, no. But, if I was accepted . . ."

Then, *I believe in fairy tales* accompanies her, in the car, as far as the door of Dr. *I say nothing and I take*. He speaks a long time; what he is talking about *No* no longer remembers. He overflowed, one day when he was cheerful—it was his habit, his cheerfulness; he created it, it radiated, it emanated, in a natural, physical way.

Dr. *I say nothing and I take* admits her into his silent office.
  She stretches out on the couch. She is quiet. *I believe in fairy tales* has warned her that, in spite of the time devoted to studies, it is the life in the house that counts above all. And *No* is frightened, not of having to do housework, or wash the dishes, nor even of eating, but of not being able to devote all of her time to her studies. She has already forgotten that she has to interrupt them, because she is going to die.

*   *   *

Suddenly, she stands up. She announces:

"I will come to see you from time to time to please my father, but I'm going away to I Study." Astonished by her own decision, she finds the strength to walk down to the hotel.

She says to her mother:

"Tomorrow I'm going to I Study."

"You will come back for lunch?"

"I'm telling you that I'm going away."

"But, my angel, a young girl leaves her home only when she marries."

To the pain of having a daughter who set herself to hate her is added now the shame of allowing her to leave for something other than marrying. *I am dying,* who does not cease to sacrifice herself and to point it out, "prefers rather," she insists, she "prefers rather" to bear the shame than to be in mourning for her daughter. To thank her for it, *No* will call her Mama at the moment of departure.

She arrives at I Study in the evening.

No, used to luxury, which she loathes, notices the bareness of the rooms, the ugliness of the chairs, the dubious color of the walls—at home, *I am dying* rises at night to remove, with a bit of cotton, the least spot.

*   *   *

She lies down on the bed that they prepared for her. Suddenly, someone speaks to her, in a low voice: "My name is *Nylon*; I come from Nice. And you?"

"My name is *No*; I come from . . . Paris."

"I wanted to come to I Study for a long time, but I'm the one who helps my mother to earn money. There are eight of us at home; my father has been deported. I didn't want to leave her alone, but she herself told me: 'My daughter, you must go there. What we need to raise your brothers is an ideal.' "

No, who has not spoken to anyone for a long time, gives herself to this young girl, whom she only knows by her voice:

"I haven't been eating for a long time. They had to carry me so that I could come here, but I'm not going to die. This ideal that you speak of, I'm not going to die without having helped to find it."

Then at peace, they go to sleep.

Dreamer skinned alive bursts into laughter as soon as he sees her.

They are seated face-to-face at the table. It is a table shaped like a horseshoe, loaded with huge pieces of bread, pitchers of coffee with milk, bowls of cereal, around which are crowded together boys and girls, noisy and hungry.

"You don't take milk? Or bread? I see! You came to I Study to launch a new trend, the art of rattling bones! What is your name?"

"No."

"That is the name of a princess. Me, my name is *Dreamer skinned alive*. So is his. So is his. As you probably know, we are scouts, leaders, the best. But the best have sinned. We are all miserable. We have fathered children without marrying. They are there, with their wet nurses, dispersed in the village. As soon as we have a minute, we run to make them smile. *I believe in fairy tales* had taken us in order to regenerate us."

Dreamer skinned II and *Dreamer skinned III* confirm what he says. They assume tragic looks, which does not prevent them from asking for more helpings. They have already devoured several loaves of bread.

"Let's go, Princess, don't be sad. We are virtuous. We have pulled your leg."

She bursts out laughing, and she swallows down, without being aware of it, a big piece of bread.

I know everything and I am unhappy waits for them in the classroom. *No* recognizes him. He came to the house in Montpellier just after the end of the war. *God does a bad job*, this unbeliever who could not do without going to the synagogue, had brought him back. "He made a speech! A speech! Even more beautiful than those of Rabbi *I love to walk!*"

When *I know everything and I am unhappy* was returning from the war, his truck had been blown up by a mine. He carried his right arm in a sling; he suffered from a head injury.

He observed the ritual laws of purity, and he had a pressing need to get married.

God does a bad job saw to it. He was trying to convince *I am in mourning for my mother and my brother* to marry him, immediately. *I know everything* pressed her to accept, without looking at her, without seeing in her something other than a remedy to be applied in extreme haste. She refused. He felt a longing, on the balcony of *God does a bad job* where one saw the sea. He asked *No* if they had Arabic music. He had a need to listen to it—he was romantic, he wrote poems. He had not said that he knew everything. He did not know all. It was at I Study that he became aware of it. He came there as a pupil, and he began to teach. He smiles—he remembers her. The wink of his eye means:

"You are the only one who knows that I write poems, and I am the only one who knows that you were a chubby little girl in love with life."

Once a week, her father's chauffeur, *I drink my two pints a day*, comes to pick her up.

He parks in front of the entrance and waits.

This black limousine still astonishes, thirty years later, *I wonder what I did to remain loyal to our ideal*, and *No* is ashamed, thirty years later, of this luxurious sedan. *Dreamer I, II, III*, et cetera, rush toward it; they pretend to be princes during the entire trip.

No hardly looks at *I say nothing and I take*. She settles herself on the couch. She speaks:

"Last Friday, just before the Sabbath, a new student arrived. As soon as we saw each other, in the bathroom, we burst into laughter: we were wearing the same yellow sweater, the same maroon skirt, we were bony in the same way, and we are both named *No*. We became sisters immediately. We asked to be put in the same room. They agreed to it. Through the door, we eavesdrop on our two neighbors, *I talk a lot and I have much charm* and *I do not have genius and I do not know it*. *No* of Rabat is already dying for the love of *I talk a lot* . . ."

At the end of three quarters of an hour, which is rather expensive for *God does a bad job, I drink my two pints a day* drives *No* of Montpellier to *I Study*.

The following week, *I say nothing and I take* has the honor of hearing, through *No*, a class given by *I know everything*:

"Here is how the world began. . . ."

"Why did God create it?" asks *No.*

To this question, even *I know everything* cannot respond. But he explains, in a luminous way, how every night the Creator would consider what he had done, understanding that it was good.

After the coming of man, he had to stop.

I know everything tells why:

"He made us capable of hearing the pulsations of His thought."

I have genius and I know it concludes:

"All that is very good. If God really created us!"

I know everything and I am unhappy slams the door.

For six days, he no longer speaks to us. We hear only his furious footsteps in the corridors.

"Even the footsteps of a master are a lesson," comments *I do not marry.*

"*I know everything* is sick," *No* announces, even before lying down on the couch. "He no longer leaves his apartment. *I have genius* and *I do not marry* live in front of his door. As soon as he goes to the lavatory, they escort him, hoping to draw from him an ultimate teaching, the secret of secrets. He told us that he knows it—he cannot die without revealing it to them! He gives them morsels of one or two difficult verses to interpret, then he returns to his suffering."

* * *

"You no longer talk about yourself," complains *I take*.

"Oh! I could tell you how I shamed *I am dying*. I had discovered, in the attic, a poncho worn at sports events, much too large for me, very dirty. I found it splendid. I put it on, and in this outfit, with *No* of Rabat, I went to see my parents—they still 'camp' at the Continental. At the front desk, people looked at me as if I came out of a sewer, but they overlooked it because my father gives big tips. My mother, when she recognized me, cried out—she had forgotten to notice that I had gained some weight. Sir, I'm not coming back anymore. What I need, I find at I Study: an ideal, a purpose, friends."

"You will miss me," predicts *I take*. He repeats it several times while escorting her back.

"One day, you told us that you didn't want to go there anymore," says *I have a tender heart and I hide it*, the wife of *I believe in fairy tales*. She also repeats it several times. The older she became, the more she looked like what she was, a very great lady. *No* asks her if *I believe in fairy tales* had lunched with them by chance at Place Vendôme.

"It is Rabbi *I love to walk* who called on us. Your father implored him for his help. He thought of us."

"You knew my father?"

"Yes. During the war he helped us."

It is not then the philosophy of *I know everything and*

I am unhappy that saved me, but those individuals who helped each other to be better able to help the others.

I cannot continue.
I'm crying.
I'm crying for *God does a bad job, I love to walk, I believe in fairy tales*, those beings who diminish the horror of things by the sole fact that they exist.
I see them.
Almost alive.
Absent.

I control myself, to bring them forth.

No trembles. With fear. With rage.
"My father is going to come. He will make me ashamed."
No of Rabat laments, but she will be the first to betray—in other words, to let herself be bribed by *God does a bad job*.
He has just arrived and already he pleases everyone. He holds court at the foot of the stairs—even there he radiates joy next to his daughter in white in the photos of her marriage. He laughs, and he makes everyone laugh, even *No*. Before going away, he tells her:
"There are four possible husbands for you here: *Dreamer skinned alive, I brown myself in the sun, I will*

discover the secret of life. Which was the fourth? I do not remember."

The light of falling day casts a glow, forever, on what it touches before vanishing. Our house no longer exists, but in the light of the heart it sparkles, like a queen.

I see us again, standing in the halls, throughout the nights, making and remaking the world. The rising day and we are arguing: "Your hospital is only a dismal ward." "Your 'ideal' city is only a trap!" *I do not marry,* endowed with a formidable sense of reality, concludes:
"We have remade the world and it does not work."

Our show, we had titled it *The Forsaken Men.*

Dreamer was putting his hand in an imaginary paste and could not withdraw it.
Dreamer II was cutting a block of imaginary stone and could not separate himself from it.
My mouth is twisted was bending like a tree and could not stand up again.
I do not marry was analyzing the situation to make it acceptable, but the words could not make her lips open.
No could no longer walk—she was in Prangins.

*   *   *

Then she saw *I will discover the secret of life.* He was accompanying them in their madness by playing the piano. He was as beautiful as his name.

No is in love with *Dreamer,* but *I will discover the secret of life* follows her everywhere, to speak of happiness.

He laughs a lot and *No* finds him crazy.
     He claims that one lives to be happy.
     "You were not in Europe during the war."
     "And so?"

One day, he tells her that he has an ache in the knee.
     That means that he is in love with her.
     In those times, she understood the language of bones.

One holiday evening, they are both serving. There are so many guests that they must wash the dishes between courses. In the very small room which serves as an office, *No* washes the plates; *I will discover* dries them. He sings for her the melodies of the seder. This evening, he does not have theories about happiness. He is beautiful and he is vulnerable and she is afraid.

After the meal, they walk. They go as far as the lake. They sit down on a bench. They become engaged without being aware of it.

The Passersby

* * *

No pays a visit to her parents in their new house, or rather in their new palace. *I am dying* is dying more than ever. *No* wonders why her mother is unhappy. She finally has the courage to tell her:

"I am engaged. He is called *I will discover the secret of life.*"

The dressmakers circle, armed with pins, around *No*, standing, in an unfinished lace gown, reading her book of logic. She complains that they disturb her. She has her exam the day after her marriage.

God does a bad job, proud of himself, shows *No* and *I will discover* the apartment that he bought for them, furnished. She complains, exasperated at having to give her opinion about colors of curtains, about trifles. Really, marrying is wasting a lot of her time.

I have a tender heart and *I believe in fairy tales* come from their kibbutz for the marriage. "Your father offered us, in addition to the voyage, a car—he rented it for us for a whole month!" says *I have a tender heart*, much later, still amazed.

I see them again, running toward City Hall. Their plane was delayed. They arrived just the same, in time for the scandal.

*   *   *

The judge, decorated, corpulent, imbued with the prestige of his district, the sixteenth, delivers his speech in a tone that is both routine and solemn:

"Mr. *I will discover the secret of life* — your first name; *Pinched and superior* is your last name — do you take for your lawful wedded wife Miss *No, Moon* . . ."

Moon! This first name, concealed like a defect, unleashes hilarious laughter from *No* and *I will discover*.

The judge, infuriated, scolds:

"Mister, Miss, marriage is a serious matter!"

And he repeats, in a tone even more routine and solemn:

"Miss *No, Moon* . . ."

They are overcome with wild, irrepressible laughter. His Honor, the judge, offended for City Hall, for Decency, for the Country, is going to make a speech, but *God does a bad job*, like a lion, rises up:

"Your Honor, my children know better than you, marriage is a sacred matter, true marriage, the one that we will celebrate Sunday, at *I Study*, with the distinguished rabbi *I love to walk!*"

His Honor, the judge, purple with rage, does not explode, aware of the large amount of money these illmannered people will leave.

*   *   *

No, in her room, writes.
All night long.
The notes of marriage.

At I Study, the family is gathered in the apartment of *I know everything*. He has lent it for the great day.
No has tried on her wedding gown. She shows it off.
God does a bad job cries out:
"Even on her wedding day, my daughter's hair is badly combed!" Quickly, two or three pins here, there, and the rebellious mass of hair ends up caught in the lace. *No* feels disguised.

Give me a discount, having come from Montpellier to marry off her granddaughter, winks at her, takes her aside:
"*Nonny*—still a godsend of the family, this diminutive!—listen carefully. You are descended from a line of princes. In Salonika, we were princes among the princes. From *But I'll get out of it*, and, in addition, *Marked with genius of unity*. Your husband ought to wash your feet."

And *No*, in her gown of lace, truly has the look of a princess when she descends, slowly, on the arm of her father, beaming with pride, the two floors of this staircase so simple and legendary, where so many loves were formed. The two little ones, *NoNo* and *YesYes*, hold the train in white satin. A hundred friends, at least, are there, at the foot of the staircase, in the halls, in the great drawing room, around the huppah where *I will discover the secret of life* waits for his fiancée.

Here she is.

She crosses the great drawing room, accompanied by her procession, and everyone is singing, until the moment when finally she sits down under the huppah.

Rabbi *I love to walk* marries them.

He is an unpretentious man.

He does not make long speeches.

He is radiant.

She feels blessed.

Like everyone, she has an ideal, a husband, friends, and especially, symbolized by the wedding huppah, a crown.

It is said that there flies above beings, when they are pure, like a bird, a crown, and that it is the soul of their soul.

"You had relegated us into the second dining room. You did not want us," *Do not talk about me,* the husband of *Yes,* complained for a long time.

"I needed to be surrounded by my friends, by their singing, by all that formed my life."

"Still, we were your family."

The Passersby

At the end of the meal, *I believe in fairy tales* had admitted it, he believed in fairy tales, on the condition that one fights to make them come true. This *No* they had married off—he, *God does a bad job*, and Rabbi *I love to walk*—they had truly fought to save her.

I see her, seated, in her gown of lace, under the trees in the park. The boys circle around her while dancing and singing, seven times, as is the custom. I have forgotten its meaning.

No and *I will discover the secret of life* will remain married a long time. They will have two children, *Little No* and a boy, *Little Yes*. People will take them for the ideal couple even after they are separated.

How *No* will end up by saying no to madness and to death is a long story that is not finished.

Again, I see only doors.

Starvation, of the flesh, of the heart, of the spirit, of the soul.

No poisoned herself, without knowing it, with copper residue.

"But how did you do it?" ask *Yes* and *NoNo*.

"I was bored. I put gadgets in my teakettle. I had the impression that I was disintegrating."

"Come to my house in the country. You will get well there," offers *Yes*.

No drives without paying attention to the route, and by a miracle she arrives at Dangers.

Her sister welcomes her, comforts her. They chat late into the night.

Their friendship is precious to them.

It is born the day of their mother's death.

No gained strength after she began to say yes.

Yes to meat, to wine, to lovers. *Little lamp held in secret, Holiday, Better than nothing, Spare tire*— she noted their passing, as one notices the speedometer.

The Passersby is the name of a people who have passed through the ages and empires; they have survived and they have awakened to say: "We are born for something else." *The Passersby* is no longer only the generic name of the lovers of a woman who has begun—she believes it—to live.

Starvation, of the soul, of the spirit, of the heart, and finally, of the flesh itself.

The day falls, very slowly.

No marvels at the beauty of the trees, of the sky, of the flowers, of the smell of the earth, at still being alive.

The Passersby

She circles with the sun around the house. She watches the changing of the light. She feels, in the place where she is, the precarious and sovereign movement that one calls the universe.

She knows how to love, the wife of *I will create myself*, comes to call for her.

They have known each other for years, but this evening they see each other, they speak to each other.

Here they are truly sisters.

Why this night? Why so late?

She knows how to love shows *No* her house.

She designed it for *I will create myself*, and he, he designed it for her.

In their house, even the stones express tenderness.

I will create myself is there.

He has aged: he has wrinkles, white hair.

And he has not aged: his hidden inner strength is the same. Intact.

Since their marriages, they had seen each other often. They were brother and sister in the past and not in the present.

They are again—they feel it right away—but it takes time to learn to speak to each other again.

✻   ✻   ✻

He suffers the pain of people who are killed, now. He has forgotten nothing of the extermination of his own people, of his own family, and it is why he feels in his own flesh the grief of those individuals against whom genocides are now committed.

The weather is beautiful. They enjoy the sunshine in the garden.

She has given all, the mother of *She knows how to love,* asks *No* the ritual question:

"And the children?"

"The children! *Little Yes* resembles *God does a bad job.* Like him, he gets angry suddenly, terribly, which does not last, and he gives, more than he has."

"And *Little No,* what is she doing?"

"*Little No!* In two and a half years, she had three babies: *God of joy, Joy of God,* and *Endowed for friendship.* They are monsters! Do you know what they said about me? 'Grandma made the room a mess.' "

"*Endowed for friendship* speaks already? At three weeks?"

"Not really. *God of joy* serves as spokesman for his little sisters. The other day, he was flirting with a young girl of a year and a half. I was waiting, near a stone. I thought that he had forgotten me. Not at all. He passes close by and says to me with a protecting look: 'Grandma, come.' And he returns home, with his fiancée and his grandmother. This young man is two and a half years old."

"And *I will discover*, have you seen him again?"

"I left him precisely not to see him anymore," says *No*, with spirit.

"Admit that you loved him," says *I will create myself.*

"That is the legend."

"But you married him."

"It is he who married me! First, he took me to *Dreamer*. He saved his life—no connection with me—while holding him, by his shirt collar, above a precipice. At the end of an engagement of a few years, I said to him: 'For one year, we will not see each other.' And I fall in love with a red-haired man, *I have three first names and two thousand women. I talk a lot* was spying on me. He warns *I will discover*, who crosses through all of Paris on his scooter to tell me: 'I'm marrying you.' 'I want to write.' 'The one does not prevent the other.' He was good-looking as always. I then said yes. One hour after his departure, I write him a sublime letter of farewell. He receives it. He recrosses all of Paris on his scooter to come to tell me: 'You change your mind every two minutes. From now on, what you say no longer counts. We have something to do together. We will do it. A date in a month. Under the huppah.' I must say that this decisive spirit pleased me. A few days later, I fall in love with a newcomer at I Study—*I'm sick of living* was his first name, *To respond to Auschwitz* his last name. I go to see my mother. I hint to her that I am in love: still a little with *Dreamer*, more with *I have three first names*, and out of my mind with *I'm sick of living*. She did not want to hear. She and my father were very much reassured that a lunatic was there to marry me!"

"A lunatic!"

"A lunatic. Of genius. Extraordinary. Exceptional. I still dream about him, every night."

"But why did you leave him?" asks *She has given all*.

"If I knew!"

I will create myself and *No* go for a little walk in a field.

At a moment's end, as before, he speaks.

He has lost the habit; people cannot stand him.

He says that man is first and above all an animal, that we must not forget it.

Then he tells the promise that he had made, in Auschwitz, to his best friend:

"He gave me his piece of bread. I did not want to take it, the bread, it was life. He said to me: 'You must take it. I'm going to die. You, you will live and you will tell the story.' I have told. A little to your father, a little to *She knows how to love*. But especially to you."

"To me!"

"To you."

He is quiet, then he says, several times:

"To my children, I have not been able. *Frivolous* cannot bear it."

Let people help me find the words that will pass on your testimony to your children.

I interrupted myself.

Your testimony, I had forgotten it.

It had formed all my books and yet I had forgotten it.

I had forgotten it as one forgets one's own childhood, one's own history, as if one has no need to be aware of the code that makes our flesh live.

And they are there. How alive memory is, in the least atom of our flesh.

Here is The Rope.

"At the end, they were evacuating the camps. We had to walk, we were almost naked, it was winter, the snow. Among us were some who had only the ends of cartons for shoes. Twenty-five miles a day on foot. Without eating. If you fell, they shot you. I was going to fall. Some comrades formed a circle around me, held me, carried me, they were walking, and me, in the middle of them, standing, I was sleeping. Then it was your turn to walk and to carry. Down there they could kill you for a scrap of bread and they could carry you in the snow at a time when you yourself no longer had the strength to go ahead. Yes, I saw what a man is. A savage and cruel beast, and all of a sudden a friend. A friend, and all of a sudden a savage and cruel beast. We were walking on the dying, on the dead. We had to stop. Selection. Two SS men held a rope. If you jump, you live. If you touch it, they kill you. It is my turn. I jumped. They had not looked. I had to do it again. I no longer had any strength. In the camp, all night, instead of sleeping, I recharged my will, in order to want to live. Here, I had only a minute, only one. I could never. And I had been able to. I had jumped. It was something superhuman, I swear it, superhuman. And I was proud. It is true. I was proud."

I appeal to *Frivolous*, the son, to *frivolous*, the daughter.

Nothing resembles the testimony of your father, *I will create myself.*

It is unique.

Like a crystal containing all—destruction, creation, the divine will of passing through all.

Why had this story been put in the hands of an obscure little girl who had hardly suffered during the war?

"I have often thought that I did you much harm in telling you," her brother told her.

"I was not born for myself. I have just come to understand it," she answers him.

I was badly prepared for happiness from my childhood. I see at last that this was luck.

Because otherwise I would have quickly forgotten your story. Perhaps I would not have even listened. I would not have put all my passion into the words. The words give life, eternity.

Thanks to the sickness of his daughter, *God does a bad job*, amazed that people had healed her, gave during the years, until his death, the necessary funds so that I Study could exist. Thanks to what the mind and the soul of a people half murdered had been able to revive.

It is said that in front of black holes a disk forms. It circles around; it does not fall into the hole but it cannot tear itself away from it. Does it know, in its panic, that it signals to others, that it permits them, perhaps, to avoid it?

I was not born for myself—such is my name from now on, as it is without doubt for many people.

Thus, what does harm becomes praise.

Glossary

page 3 **Arikha:** Contemporary Israeli artist who was sent to a concentration camp when he was fourteen years old. He survived because an SS soldier admired his drawings.

page 12 *pets-de-nonne:* Pastries.

page 28 *kapo:* Prisoner who served as a guard in the concentration camps.

page 29 **"God! that the sound..."**: Line from a poem by the French poet Alfred de Vigny (1797–1863).

page 33 *sana:* Sanitarium.

page 48 **Joseph-Arthur Gobineau (1816–82):** French advocate of social determinism.

page 48 **André Gide (1869–1951):** French writer, humanist, and moralist, whose *The Fruits of the Earth* reflected his personal liberation from the fear of sin and his acceptance of the need to follow his own impulses, however unconventional.

page 49 **Émile Verhaeren (1855–1916):** Belgian poet.

page 53 **Indochina** refers to the three states of Vietnam, Laos, and Cambodia formerly associated with France, first within its empire and later within the French Union. From 1946 to 1954, the French fought the Indochina War, which ended in Vietnamese independence.

page 71 **seder:** The ritual service celebrating the Jewish holiday Passover.

page 72 **kibbutz:** Israeli collective settlement, usually agricultural and often also industrial, in which all wealth is held in common.

page 75 **huppah:** In a Jewish wedding, the portable canopy beneath which the couple stands while the ceremony is performed. In popular usage, the term huppah may refer to the wedding ceremony itself.

THE CASE OF THE
MISSING CAT

THE CASE OF THE MISSING CAT

John R. Erickson

Illustrations by Gerald L. Holmes

Maverick Books
Published by Gulf Publishing Company
Houston, Texas

Maverick Books
Published by Gulf Publishing Company
P.O. Box 2608   Houston, TX 77252-2608

A   B   C   D   E   F   G   H

Library of Congress Cataloging-in-Publication Data
Erickson, John R., 1943–
    Hank the cowdog and the case of the missing cat/
John R. Erickson; illustrations by Gerald L. Holmes.
      p.   cm.
    Summary: Pete the barncat swindles the intrepid
cowdog out of his job as Head of Ranch Security.
    ISBN 0-87719-186-7 (cl)—ISBN 0-87719-185-9 (pb)—
ISBN 0-87719-187-5 (cassettes)
    1. Dogs—Fiction. [1. Dogs—Fiction. 2. Cats—Fiction.
3. Ranch life—Fiction. 4. West (U.S.)—Fiction. 5. Humorous stories.] I. Holmes, Gerald L., ill. II. Title.
PS3555.R428H2866   1990
813'.54—dc20
[Fic]   90-1104
                                            CIP
                                            AC

Printed in the United States of America.

Dedicated to the memory of my father,
Joseph W. Erickson

CONTENTS

C H A P T E R
1

PETE'S CON GAME

It's me again, Hank the Cowdog. Have I ever mentioned that I don't like cats? I don't like cats.

And the cat I don't like the most, the cat I dislike with my whole entire body and soul, is a certain selfish, sneaking, lazy, never-sweat character on my ranch named Pete the Barncat.

You see, it was Pete who lured me into the Case of the Lumber Pile Bunny. That was the straw that broke the camel's tooth and set my wicked mind to plotting ways of . . .

Hmmm. How can I say this so that it doesn't sound crude and tacky? I decided, don't you see, that our ranch would be a happier and more wholesome place if Pete were suddenly to . . . well, vanish, you might say. Without a trace.

No clues. No suspects. No way that Sally May could connect me with the, uh, tragedy.

But I'm getting ahead of myself. Better start at the beginning.

It was mid-morning, fall of the year, as I recall. I was making my way around the yard fence, heading towards the front of the house, when I encountered Pete the Barncat and my assistant, Mister Half-Stepper, Mister Sleep-Till-Noon, Mister Look-At-The-Clouds. Drover.

They were sitting across from one another, looking down at the ground between them. Their behavior struck me as suspicious. I mean, at a distance of ten or twelve feet I could see nothing on the ground between them—nothing but dirt, that is—so why were they looking at dirt?

I put my primary mission on temporary hold, altered course, and went over to check this thing out.

"Number One, what's going on around here? Number Two, you're supposed to be resting up for night patrol, Drover. Number Three, mingling with cats is against regulations."

Drover's head came up and he gave me his patented silly grin. "Oh, hi Hank, we're play-

ing checkers.''

''Playing checkers?'' I moved closer. ''It's odd that you should say that, Drover, because I don't see either a checkerboard or checkers.''

''That's because we're playing Checkerless Checkers, aren't we, Pete?''

The cat grinned and nodded. ''That's right, Hankie. We're playing Checkerless Checkers. Want to play?''

3

"Negative. Not only do I not want to play Checkerless Checkers, I don't believe there's any such game. And if there's no such game, I refuse to play it, period."

Pete shrugged and turned his attention to the ground. He moved his paw across the phoney so-called "checkerboard," tapping it in three different places.

"Sorry, Drover, but I just jumped three of your men."

Drover squinted at the ground. "Oh darn. I guess I shouldn't have made that move. Did I lose another game?"

Pete nodded and grinned. "Um hmmm, you did, but you're getting better all the time. You sure you don't want to play the winner, Hankie?"

I pushed Drover aside and moved in closer. "Okay, I've seen enough to know that there's something fishy going on here. Drover, where did you learn this so-called game?"

"Well, let's see. Right here on the ranch."

"From who or whom did you learn it?"

"Well, let's see. From Pete."

"In other words, your only knowledge of the rules of this so-called game came from Pete, is that correct?"

"Well, let's see." He squinted one eye and

4

rolled the other one around. "I guess that's right."

I began pacing. "Very good. Next question. Are you telling me that you can remember every move in a checker game?"

"Well, I can't but Pete can."

"How do you know that?"

"He told me so."

"I see." I glanced from one face to the other. The pieces of the puzzle began falling into place. "One more question, Drover, and I'll have this thing wrapped up. Which of you has won more games?"

Drover looked at the sky. "Let's see. Pete won the first one. And Pete won the second one. But Pete won the fourth one. And then Pete won the fifth one."

"Hold it right there. You failed to mention who won the crucial third game."

"I think Pete won that one."

"Hm, yes."

I paced around the two of them. Drover watched me until his head went as far to the south as it could go without coming unscrewed, and at that point he fell over backwards.

"Get up, Drover, and listen carefully. I've found a pattern here."

He struggled back to a sitting position. "Oh good."

"Does it strike you as odd that Pete has won five out of five games? Did it ever occur to you that Pete might be cheating?"

"Oh heck no. We promised that we wouldn't cheat."

Pete was still grinning and had begun to purr. "That's right, Hankie. We both promised not to cheat, because cheating isn't nice."

Suddenly I stopped pacing and whirled around. "It's all clear now, Drover, and I can tell you what's been going on. You've been duped. This cat lured you into a game you couldn't possibly win, and he has cheated you."

"But he promised. . . ."

"Never mind what he promised. Cats always cheat. You can write that down in your little book."

"I don't have a little book."

"Get one. I'm ashamed of you, Drover. Only a chump would play Checkerless Checkers with a cat."

"Well . . . we had fun."

"Exactly, and having fun is one of the many things we're not allowed to do in the Security Business. Speaking of which, since you've

6

spent most of the morning goofing off, why don't you go down to the corrals and check things out."

"We can't play another game?"

"That's correct, because I'm closing it down. This cat is through, finished."

"Oh drat. I was just catching on."

"Go! And I'll expect a full report in twenty minutes."

Little Drover went padding down towards the gas tanks. When he was gone, I turned to Pete. He was doodling around on the so-called checkerboard with his left front paw. His tail stuck straight up in the air and the end of it was twitching back and forth.

"Pete, you ought to be ashamed of yourself, taking advantage of a dunce."

"It's hard to fool you, Hankie."

"Not just hard, Pete. Impossible. I had your con game figgered out the minute I walked up here. Playing checkers without checkers! I can't believe you talked the poor little mutt into that."

"You never know until you try."

I studied the cat for a long time. "Pete, there's a certain understanding between creeps like you and a dog like me. It's like cops and robbers. Only the cops know how good the robbers are in their shabby work, and only the robbers know how good the cops are."

"That's right, Hankie. You understand me and I understand you."

"Exactly. We're on opposite sides of the law, we're sworn enemies, and yet we can't help admiring each other's work."

"Um hm. I learned long ago that I couldn't put anything over on the Head of Ranch Security."

"Exactly. We'll never be friends, Pete. Fate has taken care of that. But in a crazy sort of way . . . what are you doing?"

He had swept his paw over the so-called checkerboard, and now he appeared to be . . . I wasn't sure what he was doing.

"Oh, I'm through with the checker game. I know it won't work on you."

"That's correct, but what are you doing?"

After clearing the board of so-called checkers, he appeared to be . . . setting it up again?

He looked at me with his lazy cattish eyes. "I thought I might play a game of chess—with myself."

"Chess?"

"That's right. You've probably never heard of it. It's a very complicated game that requires concentration and . . ."

I couldn't help smiling. "Pete, is it possible that you think I don't know about chess? The ancient game of war, invented thousands of years ago by the Balonians? Which requires cunning and intelligence? Hey, I've got bad news for you, cat. I know ALL about chess. Ask me anything."

"Black or white?"

"Huh?"

"Would you rather play black or white?"

"Oh. Black, I suppose. It matches the color of my heart."

"All right. I'll open with pawn to king four."

"Oh yeah?" I hunkered down and studied the board. "Well, that doesn't scare me at all, cat, and I'll move this little fawn out here."

"It's a *pawn,* Hankie, not a fawn."

"Whatever. There's my move. Weed it and reap."

Five minutes later, I was in deep trouble. I had lost three bishops, one knight, and my castle was in check. And at that very moment, I realized Drover was standing beside me.

He stared at us. "What are you doing?"

I looked at Drover. I looked at Pete. I looked down at the empty space of dirt between us. It occurred to me that . . . I swept my paw

9

across the so-called chessboard, erasing all traces of the so-called game.

"We were studying the dirt, Drover, talking soil samples, you might say, and what are you doing back so soon?"

"I just wanted to tell you that I saw a cotton-tail rabbit. He was eating grass right in front of our gunnysack beds."

"You're bothering me with a report about a rabbit? I'm a busy dog, Drover, and I have no time for . . ."

It was then that I realized that Pete had disappeared. I glanced around and saw him—creeping down the hill TOWARDS MY COTTONTAIL RABBIT!

C H A P T E R
2

PETE MAKES A
FOOLISH WAGER

It didn't take me long to catch up with Pete. "Hold it right there, cat. It appears to me that you're moving towards a certain cottontail rabbit. Before you get yourself into some serious trouble, I should point out that the alleged rabbit belongs to me."

"Oh really? I thought you were too busy for rabbits, Hankie."

"I was misquoted. What I meant to say was that the rabbit belongs to me and you can keep your paws off of him."

"Now Hankie, be reasonable. You don't have any use for a rabbit."

"Oh yeah? Says who?"

"In the first place, he's not bothering anyone. He's just a cute, innocent little bunny who's eating grass."

"Yeah, but it's MY grass, see, and he's down there by MY gunnysack and he doesn't have a permit to eat my grass in the vicinity of my gunnysack."

Pete grinned and licked his front paw with a long stroke of his tongue. "And in the second place, it's a well-known fact that a dog can't catch a rabbit."

I stared at the cat and began laughing. "*A dog can't catch a rabbit*? Is that what you just said?"

"Um hmm, because a dog goes about it the wrong way. Instead of being patient and stalking the rabbit, as a cat would do, a dog just blunders in and starts chasing."

"Blunders in and starts chasing, huh? Go on, cat, I'm dying to hear the rest of this."

"Mmmm, all right. And once the rabbit starts running, the game is over because a dog can't catch a rabbit on the run. That's a well-known fact."

"No, Pete, that's well-known garbage, just the sort of half-truth and gossip that a cat would spread around. What you're saying is so outrageous that I refuse to discuss it any more."

"Whatever you think, Hankie."

"Except to repeat what I've already said: Leave my rabbit alone. Now, if you'll excuse me, I've got . . ."

"I'll bet you can't catch him."

". . . two weeks' work lined up for . . . what did you just say?"

"I'll bet you can't catch him."

I lowered my nose until it was only inches away from the cat's face. "You want to bet me

that I can't catch a sniveling little cottontail rabbit? On my ranch? When I'm Head of Ranch Security?''

"Um hmmm.''

My first thought was to meet his challenge head-on, take him up on his foolish bet, and settle the matter once and for all time. However . . .

It was too easy. Something was wrong here.

See, when you've worked around cats as much as I have, you develop a certain degree of caution. They're stupid animals, but they're stupid in a cunning sort of way.

They have a talent for twisting things around. It's a minor talent, it doesn't compare at all with the larger and grander talents you'll find in even your average breed of dogs, and I'm talking about, oh, just to mention a few: good looks, high intelligence, courage, tremendous physical strength, good looks, speed, quickness, determination, endurance, and devilish good looks.

I must give Beulah the Collie most of the credit for spotting those qualities in . . . well, ME, you might say. Otherwise I might never have known they were there, which would have been a real shame.

Where was I?

Funny how Beulah seems to creep into my thoughts, but I was talking about something else, seems to me, and . . .

Oh yes, cats. They have this minor talent for twisting things around, and over the years I've learned that when a cat makes a simple statement or says something that appears on the surface to make sense, it's time to pull back and study the deal from a different prospectus.

I walked a short distance away and switched over into Heavy Duty Analysis Mode.

Pete had just offered to make a foolish wager with me, one which he had no chance of winning. Now, why would a cat do such a thing?

Answer #1: The cat is just dumb, and you must expect a dumb cat to make dumb mistakes.

Answer #2: The cat is dumb, but not quite as dumb as he appears to be, in which case he should be approached with caution.

Answer #3: The cat is actually pretty smart and . . . I didn't need to follow this one out any further because it was too outrageous to consider. I mean, this was the same cat who had invented a nonexistent game called "Checkerless Checkers," right? Nothing more needed to be said.

And so, having dismissed Answer #3 in record time, I ran Answer #1 and Answer #2 through my data banks. What the printout revealed was a confirmation of Answer #1, which I had suspected all along.

Pete had made a dumb mistake and had thrown down the goblet, so to speak, and challenged me to enter into a foolish wager. Foolish for Pete, that is.

Okay, the only question left to ask was, "Would Hank the Cowdog consider taking unfair advantage of a dumb cat?" And I didn't need to run that one through the data banks.

In a word YES. I would, with all my heart and soul.

Stealing glances as I paced back and forth, I studied the cat, measured him, sized him up, and prepared my next move. A strategy began to take shape in my mind, and at that point I was ready to respond.

I swaggered back over to him. "Okay, I'll take you up on your bet, kitty, but only if there's something at stake."

He looked up at me with his big cattish eyes. "Hmmm. You mean something valuable?"

"Exactly. I don't enter into bets with cats for my health. If you can't put up something that makes this deal worth my time and trouble, I'm not interested."

"My goodness, Hankie, you get pretty serious about these things, don't you?"

"You got that right, cat. I'm a very busy dog and the nickel-and-dime stuff doesn't interest me."

"Well, let me think. I'll bet you tonight's supper scraps."

"Not enough."

"Well, then I'll throw in tomorrow's breakfast scraps too."

"To be real blunt about it, Pete, scraps don't excite me right now. If we're going to bet, I want to bet something that really matters—something that, if lost, will hurt BAD."

"Ummm! That kind of bet!"

I smirked and gave him a wordly, sideways glance. "Now you understand, Pete. No penny ante here. This is go-for-broke. Do you want into the deal or do you want out?"

He studied his claws for a moment, I mean, the cat was obviously scared and stalling for time. "All right, Hankie, if that's the way you want it."

"That's the way I want it."

His eyes came up. "I'll bet you your job as Head of Ranch Security."

"HUH? My job as . . . now wait just a minute.''

"You wanted big stakes, right? You wanted to go for broke, right?"

"Yeah, but . . ."

"There's the bet," he grinned, "if you're dog enough to take it."

My eyes narrowed and a growl began to rumble deep in my throat. "Watch what you say, cat. Your words could come back to honk you. And if your words don't honk you loud enough, I might consider doing a little honking of my own. Repeat the bet."

"I'm betting your job as Head of Ranch Security that you can't catch that rabbit."

My data banks whirred. "Let me get this straight. If I lose, you get my job as Head of Ranch Security. But what are you putting up? What happens if you lose?"

"Well, if I lose, you win the job as Head of Ranch Security. We'll both be playing for the same prize, and if the prize is the same for both of us, it has to be a fair bet."

I didn't like the way he was grinning, so I took the time to study the deal from every possible angle. It checked out. For the first time in years, this cat had offered a deal that was equal, fair, square, level, and plumb.

"All right, cat, you've got yourself a bet. It's

a done deal and there will be no backing out."

"You only get three tries."

"Sure, fine, don't bore me with details."

"But what if you lose, Hankie? Will you pay off?"

I laughed. "That's not likely to happen, kitty, but if it does, I'll pay off. You've got my Solemn Cowdog Oath on it."

"Mmmm. And a cowdog never goes against his oath, right?"

"Exactly. And now that you've committed yourself to the deal, I can reveal that you've made a very foolish blunder. Pete, old buddy, old pal, you're fixing to lose it all on one roll of the dice."

He gasped! Yes, he tried to hide it but I saw him gasp. Hey, that cat was beginning to feel the jaws of my trap closing around him.

All that remained was for me to lumber down and catch the rabbit, which would be a piece of cake for this old dog. I mean, catching rabbits was no big deal for me—just by George run 'em down and snatch 'em up in the old iron jaws.

Yes sir, and when that happened, fellers, Pete the Barncat would be out of luck and out of business.

CHAPTER
3

THE CASE OF THE
LUMBER-PILE BUNNY

As you might expect, old Pete was shaking in his tracks, and we're talking about worried sick and scared to death.

I guess he'd finally figgered out that he'd bet his entire future on this deal and that his chances of winning had come down to Slim and None.

Slim Chances, not Slim the Cowboy. There are several Slims around here, don't you see.

Anyways, I headed down to the gas tanks to find the Lumber-pile Bunny.

Did I mention where he got his name? Maybe not. Okay, here we go.

One of my jobs on the ranch was to identify and track the movements of every rabbit within the perimeter of ranch headquarters. At that particular time, I was following the movements of three alleged rabbits: the one we called the Cakehouse Bunny, who stayed under the cakehouse; the Cattleguard Bunny, who lived in the cattleguard just north of headquarters; and the Lumber-pile Bunny.

I knew them all on sight, had memorized their markings and habits, and had been keeping all of them under pretty close surveillance for months and months.

"How could one dog keep track of three rabbits at the same time?" you ask. Good question. All I can say is that I did it. A lot of dogs would have found it difficult, it not impossible, but for me, it was just part of the job.

The next thing you're probably asking yourself is, "Where did the Lumber-pile Bunny get his name?" Another good question.

I had assigned the code name "Lumber-pile Bunny" to this particular rabbit because . . . well, because he lived in a lumber pile, and maybe that was fairly obvious. But there was nothing obvious about where the lumber pile came from.

Here's the scoop on that. Back in the spring, the cowboys became so embarrassed by the appearance of their corral fence that they took the drastic step of replacing twenty or thirty rotten, warped, moth-eaten boards with new lumber.

Any time those guys give up on using a baling wire patch the action can be regarded as drastic. Yes, they did in fact replace the old boards with new boards, but did they *haul off the old boards*?

No sir. Throwed 'em in a pile on the west side and drove away, saying, "We'll haul that lumber off when we get caught up with some of this other work." But did they? No sir.

That's a pretty sorry way to run a ranch, seems to me, but did anyone ask the opinion of the Head of Ranch Security? Again, NO. I'll say no more about it.

Except that lumber piles attract rattlesnakes and skunks and provide a place of refuse for sniveling little rabbits, speaking of whom . . .

Would you care to guess who took up residence in the lumber pile? That's correct, a certain cottontail rabbit, to who or whom I assigned the code name "Lumber-pile Bunny." This was the guy I was after.

Okay. Some ten feet north of the gas tanks, I throttled back to a slow gliding walk, switched my ears over to Manual Liftup, began testing the air with full nosetory equipment, and directed my VSD's (Visual Scanning Devices; in ordinary dogs also referred to as "eyes") towards a patch of grass directly west of the gas tanks.

This procedure soon bored fruit . . . bared fruit . . . produced results, as my instruments began picking up the telltale sounds of a rabbit munching grass.

It was the Lumber-pile Bunny.

He was munching tender shoots of grass some 25 or 30 feet to the west of my bedroom. The foolish rabbit seemed unaware that he had entered a Secured Area and that the Dark Shadow of Doom was slipping towards him like a dark shadow in the night.

Well, maybe not in the night. You wouldn't be able to see a dark shadow in the . . .

Even though I had switched over to Silent Mode, the bunny heard me coming. They have pretty good ears, don't you know, and it's hard to slip up on one.

But get this. Instead of running away, he stood up on his back legs, looked straight at me, and wiggled his nose in what I would describe as "a provocatory gesture."

Okay, what we had here was a rabbit who had never been taught his place on the ranch. Or else one that had lost his mind. He wanted to play with fire, so he was fixing to learn about fire.

Well, this was it. I glanced back to be sure that Pete was watching (he was), took a deep breath, and rolled my shoulders several times to loosen up the enormous muscles that would soon propel me at speeds unknown to ordinary dogs.

I turned back to the rabbit, locked in all guidance systems, and began the countdown procedure, which goes something like this, in case you're not familiar with technical stuff:

"Five! Four! Three! Two! One! Launch, liftoff, charge, bonzai!!"

And in a puff of smoke and a cloud of dust, I went streaking towards the target.

Rabbits are famous for their speed, right? What many people don't know is that your better grades of cowdog are every bit as fast as a rabbit, and in a few rare cases (me, for example) are even faster.

I'm not one to boast, but speed was just built into my bloodline.

In other words, the Lumber-pile Bunny was in big trouble from the very beginning. I closed in on him fast and was only inches away from snapping him up in my jaws when . . .

Let's call it luck. He got lucky, that's all. And why not? After all, he was carrying around

24

four lucky rabbit's feet.

Luck kept him a couple of feet ahead of me as we went streaking out into the home pasture. Inches, actually. We made a wide loop, some 25 yards in front of the corrals, and then I realized that Bunny had changed directions and was high-balling it straight to the lumber pile.

It was an old rabbit trick. I recognized it right away and took appropriate measures. I went to Incredible Speed and . . . like I said, he was carrying four lucky rabbit's feet.

I never denied that rabbits are pretty swift and, okay, maybe he beat me to the lumber pile, but not by much. If the chase had gone another ten feet, I would have nailed him.

I returned to the gas tanks to wait for him to come out again, as I knew he would. Off to the north, I heard a familiar whiney voice say, "Mmmm, that's one, Hankie."

"Don't worry about it, kitty, that was just a warmup."

I waited. And waited. The minutes dragged by. Perhaps I dozed. Then . . . the munching of grass reached my ears. He was back, same place. Munching grass right in front of my bedroom. Foolish rabbit.

Within seconds I had gone through the

launch procedure and was back on the chase. You should have seen me! Made that loop out into the pasture and virtually destroyed three acres of good buffalo grass and virtually had that bunny trapped in the deadly vice of my jaws, and if the chase had gone another five feet, that little feller would have been a stasstistic.

Stasstisstic.

History.

Real close race, almost got him, a huge improvement over the first run, and as long as a guy can see improvement, he knows that he has won a moral victory. And so, with a victory hanging in the trophy room of my mind, I returned, triumphant and victorious, to the gas tanks.

A little winded, yes, but beneath the huffing and puffing was the warm glow of satisfaction that comes when a dog knows he's done his job right.

"Mmmm, that's two, Hankie," said the cat. "Only one shot left."

I chuckled and didn't bother to reply. I knew what the cat was trying to do—put pressure on me so that I would choke. What he didn't know was that some dogs *thrive* on pressure, I mean, it's like throwing gasoline into a . . .

CHOKE! GASP! ARG!

On the other hand, I was beginning to feel a small amount of . . . I mean, my job, my position, my entire career was riding on the next . . .

WHEEZE! ARG! GASP!

Holy smokes, if I didn't catch the rabbit on the next run, *Pete the Barncat would be the next Head of Ranch Security*! Not only would that be a personal disaster for me personally, but it would be disaster for the entire ranch.

Gulp.

Pressure. It weighs heavy on the mind, smashes creative impulses, crushes the little flowers of courage that try to bloom in the warm soil of . . . something.

I was curled up in a ball, in the process of pretending that I was a puppy again, back in the sweet days before I had assumed all the crushing responsibilities of running a ranch, when all of a sudden . . .

I lifted my eyes and narrowed my head . . . lifted my head and narrowed my eyes, I should say, and there sat the Lumber-pile Bunny, not ten feet in front of me.

Okay, this was it. My whole career had come down to this moment, this last chase.

I arose from my gunnysack bed and prepared myself for what was sure to be the most important mission of my life.

CHAPTER
4

THE BUNNY CHEATS
AND LIES

"Good luck, Hankie. Is there anything I should be doing to prepare for my new position?"

That was Pete the Barncat, trying to use underhanded sneaky tricks to shake my confidence. I tried to ignore him, which is the second-best thing you can do with a cat.

The first-best thing you can do with a cat is to beat the snot out of him and run him up a tree, which I sincerely wanted to do but couldn't, for the simple reason that I had an appointment with Destiny.

This was my last chance, fellers, and I had to put everything into it. Hence, instead of rushing off and wasting my last shot, I decided to analyze the two previous attempts and try to learn from my . . .

I wouldn't exactly call them *mistakes*. Errors might be a better word.

Bad luck.

Difficulties.

Unfortunate circumstances.

Tiny miscalculations.

Windows of opportunity that had been slammed shut by the winds of Life.

Circumstances beyond the control of myself or any other dog on earth.

I decided to learn from the past, shall we say.

For you see, I had detected a certain pattern in the bunny's response to my missions against him. Here, look at this map. Oh well, you can't see it.

Okay, imagine a map. The gas tanks form Point A, right here. The lumber pile becomes Point B, over here. Point C is the point in the home pasture to which the bunny had run on the two previous encounters.

As you can see, the three points, if joined together by imaginary lines A Prime, B Prime, and Prime Rib, would form a triangle.

Pretty suspicious, huh? How did that rabbit know about triangles? How could he have known that if you connect any three points in the universe with straight lines, you get a triangle?

I mean, we're talking about geometry—the kind of heavy duty math we use all the time in the Security Business, but not the sort of thing you'd expect a bunny rabbit to understand.

This was my first hint that perhaps I had underestimated the intelligence of the alleged rabbit. Not only had he won the first two outings against me, but there appeared to be more than a slim chance *that his victories could be traced to something other than dumb luck.*

In other words, I was staring right into the jaws of a conspiracy. This rabbit had been using strategy against me, and to explain what I mean, let's go back to the map.

I'm here at Point A. The rabbit is right in front of me. He takes off towards Point B. I follow him, pursuing a course described by line A Prime.

You still with me? I know this is pretty complicated stuff but just hang on.

Okay, Bunny reaches Point B in the pasture. What does he do then? He changes directions and goes streaking towards Point C, the lumber pile, following line B Prime.

Here's the startling conclusion of all this. It was beginning to appear that the rabbit had led

me to Point B, KNOWING ALL THE TIME
THAT HE WOULD END UP RUNNING BACK
TO THE LUMBER PILE!

Now, if that's not cheating, tell me what is.
It's the kind of backhanded, underhanded,
lefthanded, sneaking approach you'd expect
from a cat—but from an innocent little rabbit?
No sir.

Hey, if you can't trust a rabbit anymore,
what kind of world are we living in? What are
we coming to?

I mean, once the rabbits turn to lying and
cheating, who's next? The kids? Mothers?
Baby birds? Puppy dogs and fawns? Apple pie?
Christmas carols?

Is there anything sacred left in a world
where bunny rabbits lie and cheat and steal
and rob and spit at their grandmothers?

Just when I think I've seen it all, I see something else. Just when I think I've hardened myself as hard as I can harden, I find fresh evidence of something new and awful. Just when
I think this soiled world has no more shocks
and surprises, I see something like this, and it
just about breaks my heart.

Rabbits cheating. Rabbits lying.

Well . . . a guy can't just quit or resign from
Life or crawl under his gunnysack and hide

from all the meanness and ugliness. He's got to come back and strike a few blows for Honesty and Decency.

And that's where I found myself, after going through several minutes of spiritual heartburn and moral agony. I couldn't change the world, fellers, or put all the bad guys out of business or spare the little children from the mess we'd made of the world.

All I could do was catch that stupid, stinking, sniveling, sneaking, counterfeit little rabbit who had made a fool out of me, not once but twice, and teach him an important lesson about lying and cheating.

What a fool I'd been! I'd played the role of Mister Nice Dog and what had it gotten me? Okay, he wanted to play games with me, so we'd play games. But we were fixing to play MY game.

Here's the crutch of the whole matter. I'll reveal it if you promise not to blab it around. See, that rabbit was more devious than I'd ever supposed. He'd made that loop out into the pasture, knowing all along that I would follow him.

Heh heh, but just suppose that I didn't follow him. Just suppose that instead of running my legs off out in the pasture, I took a short cut through the corrals and was standing in front of the lumber pile when he came hopping up. Heh heh.

Pretty awesome, huh? Let me tell you something. I hadn't been named Head of Ranch Security strictly on my good looks, although that had been a big factor.

A dog's mind is a scary thing, and moral indigestion is a powerful force. Put 'em together and you have something that is truly awesome.

Okay, here we go. I rose from my gunnysack bed, just as I had done before, and began the Pursuit Phase of the procedure. The bunny ran. I chased. We headed out into the pasture and began the Sucker Phase.

I was watching the rabbit very carefully this time, don't you see, and when he stopped looking back over his shoulder, I altered my compass heading, veered off hard to the right, and went zooming straight for the corral fence.

As I approached the fence, I did one last instrument check. Allowing for wind and so forth, I would arrive at the lumber pile three seconds before the victim.

All systems were go. All I had to do now was perform what we call an Under-The-Bottom-Board Maneuver, a fairly simple and routine

G.I.Holmes

procedure in which your cowdog approaches
a corral fence at top speed and darts under
your bottom 2 × 6 board without

CRUNCH!!

Uh.

Uhhh.

Uhhhhhhh!

Lorkin @#$%&*?%$#@ murgle porkchop
snicklefritz aimed a wee bit high on that one.
Swimming in molasses, the stars came out gork
murg snork and I gathered myself up off of

the . . .

I became aware of a throbbing pain in my head. My neck was badly cricked and someone had removed my legs and installed a new set made of soft rubber. The earth was turning in an odd direction and I found it hard to stand in one spot.

It appeared that I had, or shall we say that my instruments had failed me at a very crucial point in the maneuver, and once your entire guidance system has gone on the fritz . . .

Laughter? Did I hear . . . yes, the cowboys. Laughing. Howling. Leaning against the saddle shed. Doubled over. Slapping their thighs.

They had been spying on me, had watched the entire incident. Did they rush out with ice packs or bandages or even an encouraging word? Oh no. Everything's a big joke with them.

"Go get that little rabbit, Hankie!" one of them yelled. I don't remember which one, it doesn't matter, I don't care, one's as bad as the other and neither one shows much sensitivity to tragic situations.

"Sic 'im, boy!" said the other, as he was brought to his knees by a convulsion of childish laughter.

So there I was—not only badly injured from

wounds received on a combat mission, not only wrecked and deformed and partly crippled, but also mocked and scorned by the very people I had sworn my Cowdog Oath to protect.

Maybe you think I had hit the absolute bottom, that I couldn't stink any deeper, sink any deeper, I should say; maybe you think that everything bad that could have happened to me had happened to me.

If that's what you think, then you've forgotten that I had wagered my job as Head of Ranch Security and HAD LOST THE WAGER.

In other words, fellers, not only had I lost my job but it had been won by Pete the Barncat.

That's what I'd call a pretty scary thought.

CHAPTER
5
HUMBLE PIE STINKS

Well, the cowboys got a real lift out of my disaster. I mean, it just about made their whole day.

After howling and chuckling and slapping their knees and rolling around in the dirt, they finally ran out of excuses for loafing and had to go back to work. I know that broke their hearts.

And don't forget that if they had hauled off that pile of junk lumber in the first place, there would have been no lumber pile and therefore no Lumber-pile Bunny.

Hence, by simple logic, we see that the cowboys were actually to blame for the entire incident—which didn't make my broken neck or damaged head feel one bit better, but it's always nice to share the blame with someone else.

I mean, sharing is a very important thing in this old life. Furthermore, there is a wise old saying about people who laugh at the misfortunes of others: "He who laughs first . . . he who laughs last . . . he who laughs in the middle . . ."

There is this wonderful wise old saying about people laughing but I think we'll skip it for now. It's a real good wise old . . . never mind.

I went limping back to the gas tanks. I mean, I'd just suffered one of the worst setbacks of my career and had lost just about everything that was dear to me, but I still had my old gunnysack bed.

That was the one thing they couldn't take away from me. It was my place of refuse, the spot from whence I could launch myself into the sweet dreams about Beulah and feats of greatness. No matter what happened to me, that old gunnysack would always be there to welcome me home.

I dragged myself towards the gas tanks, hoping with all my heart that Pete wouldn't see me. I'm never anxious to see Pete, but this time I was even less anxious than usual.

Luck was with me for a change, and Pete did

not appear.

At last I could see it: my gunnysack, my friend. It was waiting for me, calling my name, ready to embrance the folds of my tired and worn body, ready to launch me into . . .

A cat in my bed?

A grinning face with partially hooded eyes rose from my gunnysack. "Mmmmm, it's Hankie the Cowdog, and isn't this a wonderful coincidence!"

I summoned up just enough energy to issue a short growl. "Out of my bed, cat, before I . . ."

"Ah, ah, ah. Don't say anything you'll regret, Hankie. You haven't forgotten our little wager, have you?"

"I, uh . . . did I think to mention that, down deep in my heart, I don't approve of betting or wagering or gambling of any kind? I mean, I might have forgotten to . . ."

"You forgot to mention that, Hankie."

"Yes, well, it just slipped my . . ."

"It must have slipped your mind, Hankie."

"Exactly, and I'm sure the same thing has happened to you a time or two, you get caught up in something, excited and so forth, and before you realize it . . ."

"You've made a stupid mistake, hmmm?"

"Right. Well, stupid is pretty harsh . . ."

"A dumb mistake?"

"Yes, right, exactly. A dumb mistake. Or call it a hasty decision, or it could be that you misunderstood my true meaning, see, and you might have thought that I was making a foolish wager . . ."

"Um hmmm, I did, Hankie, I certainly did."

". . . when in fact the record will show that I was . . . only words. Really. Honest."

Pete stretched out on my gunnysack and made himself right at home. I could hear him purring. Oh, and that tail of his was sticking straight up in the air.

"Mmmm, so you're saying that you didn't intend to make the bet, is that right, Hankie?"

"Right. Yes, and I'll be the first to admit it, Pete. I was misquoted and I'll have to take full responsibility for my actions. If I hadn't opened my big mouth, I never would have been misquoted in the first place."

"Um hmmm."

"And as far as I'm concerned, we can chalk the whole thing up to experience. I mean, it's been a painful lesson for me, and why are you shaking your head?"

"No deal, Hankie."

"By 'no deal' do you mean . . . no deal?"

"I mean, Hankie, that we made a bet and you lost."

"Oh, I see, yes, well, let me hasten to . . ."

"And I'm ready to collect, Hankie."

"Huh? Collect? You mean . . . now wait a minute, Pete, you can't do this to me."

"Fair is fair, Hankie."

"I know that fair is fair, I've said that many times myself, but YOU CAN'T DO THIS TO ME!"

He grinned and purred and flicked his tail back and forth.

"Oh yes I can, Hankie. I won. You lost. I'm ready for you to pronounce me Head of Ranch Security."

"I won't! I can't! I . . ." I began pacing. "Listen, Pete, we can cut a deal, just you and me, right now. How about this: you'll be my First Assistant. Hey, wouldn't that be great?"

"Mmmm, and what about Drover?"

"Ha! He's out, through, finished, fired. It's just me and you, Pete, just the two of us, a team for the future!"

"No thank you."

"Huh? Okay, listen to this. Dog food, all you can eat for three days!"

"I'll pass on the dog food, Hankie."

"Good thinking, pal, I don't blame you, but

here comes the killer deal of the century." I winked and leaned forward. "Bones, Pete. You give me a number and I'll deliver the goods."

He yawned. "I don't think so, Hankie, because bones hurt my teeth."

"Good point, hadn't thought of that, okay, we'll dig a little deeper in the old . . ."

"Hankie, had you thought of *begging* for your job?"

"Huh? Begging? Well, I . . . no, actually I hadn't thought of . . . begging. It sort of goes against my grains. Don't you see."

"Well, you might try it and see what happens." He studied his claws. "I've never been tested before, and who knows? It just might be my weak spot."

"I see. Begging. Could you give me some odds and percentages? I mean, I wouldn't want to go into a begging situation without knowing the . . . I'm sure you understand."

"Mmmm, yes, I understand, Hankie."

"I mean, it would be very painful."

"Oh, I know, it would hurt so bad!"

"Right, which is why I'd like to know . . ."

"Fifty-fifty."

"Fifty-fifty, which is only slightly better than average."

"That's the best I can offer, Hankie."

"Okay, well, fifty-fifty beats forty-forty, and uh . . . you said beg?"

"Umm hmmm. Just hop on your back legs and beg, and we'll see what happens."

I coughed and cleared my throat, paced back and forth, scratched my ear, paced some more, and wrestled with this heavy decision.

"This is very difficult for me, Pete, I hope you understand that, and I mean VERY difficult and painful, but if this is what it takes to . . . I don't look forward to this, Pete. It's going to be very humiliating and I've never . . ."

"My patience is wearing thin, Hankie."

"Right, okay, and so the best thing for me to do is just . . . only for you would I do this, Pete, so watch carefully."

Against all my cowdog instincts, I hopped up on my back legs and brought my front paws into the Begging Position.

"There we go! What do you think of this, Pete?"

His smile went sour. "Mmmm, something's missing, Hankie. It just doesn't move me."

"Okay, what's missing is this little flourish which we call Moving The Paws While Begging. You'll love it, Pete, it's going to knock

44

your socks off. Watch close!"

I did the maneuver, which is very difficult, by the way, and very few of your ordinary dogs have the muscle tone and coordination to pull it off.

"There you are, Pete, that's the whole show. Pretty impressive, huh? You ever see anything quite . . . you're shaking your head again, Pete, and I'm wondering what that means."

"Oh, Hankie, I'm afraid it didn't work, and just drat the luck!"

"Drat the . . . didn't . . . wait a minute. Are you saying that you're not going to call off the bet? After I lowered myself and humbled myself and made myself look like an idiot?"

The grin spread all the way across his mouth and his eyes brightened. "Mmmm yes, I'm afraid so, Hankie, but nice try anyway. Now, you may pronounce me Head of Ranch Security."

At last the pieces of the puzzle began falling into place. I had been duped and humiliated, and now I was fixing to be stripped of my rank.

I lowered my front paws to the ground and glared at him. "I should have known better than to do business with a cat." He nodded his

G.L.Holmes

head. "You'll regret this, Pete."

"Fair is fair, Hankie."

I took a gulp of air and plunged into the terrible unknown. "Very well. I pronounce you Head of Ranch Security, and I hope you get a big ringworm right where you sit down."

"Thank you, Hankie. Your unhappiness means more to me than I can possibly express."

"Fine. Now get out of my bed."

"Ah, ah, ah! MY bed. It goes with the job."

My mind was reeling, my head was pounding, my body was begging for rest. I didn't have the energy to argue.

"All right, Pete. You've got it all: my job, my pride, and now my bed. You win. I'm whipped. The ranch is yours."

And with that, I turned and limped away from my bedroom, my home, and the gunnysack that had been my last friend in the world.

CHAPTER
6

THE CASE OF THE DISHEARTENED CHICKEN

I dragged myself up to the machine shed. Drover was there, sleeping on the cement pad in front of the big double doors.

I needed a friend to talk to, fellers, I mean I was at the bottom of my luck. On another occasion, I might have chosen a friend with more wealth, influence, and brains than Mister Stub-Tail, but this wasn't another occasion.

Yes, Drover had his flaws and his shortcomings, but after working beside the little mutt for years, I knew in my heart that if he were the only dog available, I would chose him to be my best friend.

This was his lucky day.

"Drover, I don't want to alarm you, but the very worst thing that could possibly happen has just happened."

"Skonk snort zzzzzzzzzzzzz."

"Please don't panic. Screaming and running in circles won't help the situation."

"Snork glorg rumple ricky tattoo."

"I've come to inform you that I have gambled away my future and ruined my life. I'll be leaving soon to spend the rest of my miserable years living in ditches and gutters. I know this must come as a terrible shock."

"Skaw shurtling snort zzzzzzz."

"All I ask is that . . . wake up, you idiot! Can't you see that I'm pouring out my heart to you?"

He raised up and stared at me. His eyes were crossed, his ears were on crooked, and his tongue was hanging out the left side of his mouth.

"Oh my gosh, who's going to clean up all the blood?"

"Blood? What blood?"

He staggered to his feet. "I can't stand the sight of blood, where am I?" His eyes began to focus. "Oh, hi Hank, I must have dozed off. Did you hear about the murder?"

"Murder? No, what happened?"

"Gosh, I'm not sure, I just heard about it, but somebody got murdered, maybe it was a

G. L. Holmes

chicken, and they busted into the chicken house and cut her heart out and chopped it up into little pieces!''

''Chopped up her heart!''

''Yeah, it was awful. And then they poured out the pieces of heart all over the ground! And then they chopped up her lizzard and giver and . . .''

''Hold it. Do you mean gizzard and liver?''

"Yeah, did you hear about it too? Oh my gosh, I guess it's true, Hank, and there was blood everywhere, I saw it with my own eyes!"

"You witnessed this unspeakable murder with your own eyes?"

"I think they were mine. Yeah, they must have been."

"Holy smokes, Drover, why wasn't I informed?"

"Well, I never would have thought you'd be interested."

I glared at him. "You didn't think I'd be interested in a ghastly murder?"

"No, I meant my eyes."

"I don't care about your eyes!"

"That's why I didn't tell you."

"I'm talking about the . . ." Then I remembered. "But never mind all that, Drover. I've just lost my post, so it doesn't matter anyway."

"Well, there's a whole bunch of them over in the post pile, and I think there's a rabbit over there too."

"Don't mention that word in my presence, Drover."

"You mean post?"

"No, I mean rabbit. A rabbit has just ruined

51

my life."

"I'll be derned."

"Because of that lying, cheating rabbit, I have lost my post."

"Ate the whole thing, huh?"

"Exactly, and I'd appreciate it if you'd never speak of rabbits again."

"I guess they'll eat anything."

"It just breaks my heart to think about this terrible loss."

"Oh, you can always find another post. Digging the hole's the big problem."

"Yes, it's an enormous hole, Drover, and I'm wondering if I'll ever be able to fill it."

"Well, you might try dirt. That works sometimes."

"A whole lifetime down the drain, Drover, and I have no one to blame but myself."

"I'd blame the cowboys."

"No, it was my fault. All the cowboys did was laugh at my stupidity."

"Yeah, but if they'd feed these rabbits once in a while, maybe they wouldn't have to eat fence posts."

My eyes swung around and focused on him. "WHAT?"

"I said . . . well, let's see, what did I say? I think I've already forgot."

"Out with it! Something about fence posts."

"Oh yeah. I said, if they'd feed these fence posts once in a while, they wouldn't have to eat so many rabbits."

"The cowboys are eating rabbits?"

"No, the fence posts."

"*The cowboys are eating fence posts?*"

"No, the fence posts are eating . . . you said the rabbits were eating . . . fence posts?"

I looked into the huge emptiness of his eyes. "Drover, has it ever occurred to you that you might be going insane?"

"I've wondered about that."

"It has already happened. The post to which I was referring was not a fence post, but rather my post as Head of Ranch Security."

"I'll be derned."

"I lost it in a bet with the cat. I bet Pete that I could catch the Lumber-pile Bunny and I failed. Which means that Pete is now Head of Ranch Security and I am Head of the Broken Heart Society."

"Yeah, but the chicken doesn't have a heart at all."

"It was a rabbit, and yes, he was utterly heartless."

"No, I mean the chicken that was murdered and disheartened."

"Oh yes, I'd almost forgotten that. You witnessed the crime yourself?"

"I think it was me."

I looked up at the sky and heaved a sigh. "Drover, there was a time, not so very long ago, when the mention of such a crime would have gotten my full attention. I would have jumped right into the middle of the case and begun a thorough investigation.

"But now, because of my own foolish mistakes, I've lost my job and therefore my authority to press an investigation. I suggest you take your repeat to Port . . . your report to Pete, that is, and let him handle it. He's in charge now."

"Oh my gosh!"

"Well said, Drover. I think we both know what'll come of this."

"Yeah, the chicken'll never get her heart back and the ranch'll go to pot."

"Exactly. But it can't be helped, Drover. I'm afraid that I'm leaving this old ranch in quite a mess."

"Leaving!"

"Yes, Drover, I'm leaving. There's nothing left for me here except the sad memory of how things used to be, and that is nothing but a sad memory. I have failed my ranch, my hundreds of friends, my profession, myself. I'll spend the rest of my days wandering Life's ditches and gutters—a dog without a home."

"Boy, that's tough," he said, as he gnawed at a flea on his left flank. "If you put your job up in that bet, what did Pete put up against it?"

"I . . . that's a foolish question, Drover. Obviously, since I risked something dear and precious to me, the cat put up something of equal worth."

"Yeah, but he doesn't have anything of equal worth."

"Of course he does."

"Such as?"

"Such as . . . well, he . . . that is . . . what are you driving at, Drover? Are you suggesting that I might have been suckered into a stupid bet?"

"I wondered."

"Because if that's what you're suggesting, let me intrude into your little world of fantasy and point out . . ." I began pacing, as I often do to stimulate my thought processes. "Your whole house is an argument of cards, Drover, and all I have to do to send it tumbling down is to remove one single card."

"Yeah, and I've got a feeling that it's a joker."

Suddenly I stopped pacing and whirled around. "Because, Drover, there was a joker in the deck."

"I knew it."

"Don't you see what's happened here? It was a rigged game, Drover, a phony bet, a put-up deal. You thought Pete had won it fair and square, but what you overlooked was the obvious fact that HE CHEATED!"

"I think that's what I was driving at."

"Maybe you were droving, Driver, but you ran out of gas before you solved the mystery."

"My name's Drover."

"Exactly. You were close, Drover, and I know perfectly well what your name is and don't interrupt my presentation again, but not close enough. For you see, Pete risked nothing in our wager and therefore the entire bet is cancelled. And as of this moment, I am reclaiming my title as Head of Ranch Security."

"Boy, that's a relief."

"Exactly. And my first action will be to throw all units into the investigation of this gruesome murder you witnessed with your own eyes."

"Either that or I dreamed it."

"And my second action will be to settle all accounts with Pete the Barncat, who has become a minutes to society. Come on, Drover, to the chicken house!''

And with that, we went streaking to the chicken house to investigate one of the most chilling crimes I had encountered in my whole career.

CHAPTER
7

BLOODY WRITING ON THE WALL

We reached the chicken house only seconds after I had sounded the alarm.

The first thing we did upon reaching the scene of the crime was to plow into the middle of seven hens who were loitering outside. They were pecking around in the dirt and clucking to each other and performing the usual absurd rituals you expect to find among chickens, who are stupid beyond belief.

Since they were blocking our path, we seized the opportunity to mix pleasure with business. We just by George bulldozed 'em and sent 'em squawking in all directions.

I love doing that.

We sent them pecking . . . eh, packing, that is, and once again I experienced that feeling of exhilaration and well-being and mental health and so forth. That done, we plunged into the murder house and went to work.

As my eyes adjusted to the gloomy light, I did a visual sweep of the walls and ceiling, using my photogenic memory to record even the smallest details.

"Well, Drover, do you notice anything unusual?"

"Yeah, it stinks in here."

"Exactly. And does that tell you anything?"

"I'm glad we're not chickens."

I gave him a stern glare. "Let's not dwell upon the obvious. We're looking for clues, the tiny details that form the signature of the criminal."

"Well, let's see. Wait, hold it! What's that over there?"

I rushed "over there," following the angle of Drover's nose. It led me to the west wall, in the very gloomiest corner of the room. There, my eyes fell upon some mysterious form of writing.

"This is some mysterious form of writing, Drover."

"Yeah, and it's written in red! Could it be . . ."

"I'll take it from here, Drover. Red writing.

Does that ring any bells with you?"

He lifted one ear. "Not really."

"Here's a hint: Grandma's house."

"Uh . . . dinner bell?"

"Forget the bells, Drover, and concentrate on the hints. Here's another one: wolf."

"Arf?"

"No."

"Bow wow?"

"Wolf, the animal, a ferocious beast waiting to eat someone."

"Oh. Well, let's see here. What was the first thing you said?"

"Red writing."

The huge blank of his face suddenly filled with signs of recognition. "I've got it, I've got it! Little Red . . . oh my gosh, you don't think the killer was Little Red Writing Hood, do you?"

"Yes, Drover, either Little Write Redding Hood or someone in her disguise. She left a clue behind, as they always do, never dreaming that we would put 'red' and 'writing' together and come up with her true identity."

"What made her do such an awful thing?"

"We don't have the answer to that one yet, but I have an idea that it's just a matter of time until we come up with a motive."

"It makes me sad."

"Snap out of it, Drover, because there's still more to come. The mysterious message was written in red, correct?"

"Yeah, I already said that."

"But I said it first."

"But I saw it first."

"But I entered the chicken house first."

"But I was the first one up this morning."

61

"Yes, Drover, but I never went to bed, so your claim to being the first one up just doesn't hold water."

Suddenly, his eyes popped open. "Oh my gosh, speaking of water, I've got to GO!"

"We're in the middle of a very important investigation."

"Yeah, but we're fixing to be in the middle of a flood." He was hopping up and down and biting his lip.

"Very well, Drover, you may be excused, but this will have to go into your record."

He scrambled out the door. I waited inside, tapping my toe and counting off the seconds. I hate wasting time. He returned moments later, wearing a big smile.

"I'm ready for anything now."

"Where were we?"

"Let's see. I was the first one up this morning."

"No, you weren't, and why were we talking about that in the first place?"

"Well, let's see." He thought. I waited. "I don't remember. Something about water."

"Yes, of course. Water is very important to all life on earth. Without water, there would be no watermelons and . . . I've lost my train of thought."

"I've always wanted to ride in a caboose."

"Wait, I've got it. We were discussing the mysterious red writing, and I was about to point out a very important detail that escaped your attention."

"You mean that it might have been written in blood?"

I narrowed my eyes and glared at the runt. "Who's in charge of this investigation, you or me?"

"Well, you, I guess."

"That's correct. I am in charge of the investigation, and if there are any new and startling revelations to be made, I will be the one to make them. Is that clear?"

"Okay, but I was the first one up this morning."

"Fine. You were the first one up, and now you will be the first one to shut your little trap while I reveal that this mysterious message on the wall *was probably written in BLOOD*."

"Oh my gosh!"

"Yes indeed. Now we are only one step away from wrapping this case up. The only question left unanswered is, what does the mysterious message say?

"I will now move closer to the wall and try to uncrypt and decipher the message."

I moved closer to the wall and studied the message. It appeared to consist of a single word.

"All right, Drover, stand by. The first letter is A."

"Oh, that's awful!"

"The second letter appears to be an L."

"Okay, I got it, Hank. That makes A-L."

"Exactly. The third letter is F, followed by an R."

"A-L-F-R. That doesn't make any sense to me."

"Patience, son. The next letter is an E. And, stand by, the final letter is a D. There we are, Drover. Now read them all back to me."

"A-L-F-R-E-D."

"There must be some mistake. That doesn't spell Little Red Writing Hood."

"Maybe she couldn't spell."

"Very possible, Drover."

"Wait! It sounds kind of like . . . Alfred . . . doesn't it?"

"Alfred?"

"Little Alfred?"

"HUH?" I whirled around and took a closer look at the . . . "Drover, if you had studied the clues more carefully, you would have realized that this word was written in RED

CRAYON, not blood."

"Oh my gosh, it's getting worse and worse! You think Little Alfred was the killer?"

"No."

"The chicken bled crayon instead of blood?"

"No."

"I'm all confused."

"Yes." I paced back and forth in front of him. "Drover, in your report of the ghastly murder, you mentioned that the killer had cut up the chicken's heart and poured the pieces out on the ground. Do you see any signs of a chicken heart?"

"Well . . . not really."

"Your report went on to say that 'blood was everywhere,' to use your exact words. Do you see any signs of blood?"

"Well . . ."

"There is no blood, Drover, and there are no pieces of a chicken's heart. That means there was no murder. It means that Little Alfred wrote his name on the chicken house wall with a red crayon. It means that you have led us on a fool's errand."

"Well, I'll be derned. I sure thought . . . you don't reckon I dreamed all that, do you?"

I stopped pacing and stabbed him with a

gaze of solid steel. "I reckon you did, you dunce. I had just told you that I was pouring my heart out to you."

"Oh, is that what it was?"

"Yes. But instead of listening to a friend in need, you concocted an outraageous story about blood and murder."

"I knew it had something to do with hearts."

"Drover, you have just brought the Security Division to its lowest point in history. Do you realize that if someone had been watching us for the past half hour, he might very well think that we are a couple of fools?"

"Boy, that's wrong."

"Of course it is, but mere facts can lead to a false impression. Hence, you and I will take a vow of secrecy and swear never to reveal the deep, dark stupidity of what we've just done."

"My lips are sealed."

I put my paw on his shoulder. "And remember, Drover. Even though it's unpleasant to lie and cover up, we're doing this for our own good."

"Yeah, and somebody had to do it."

"Exactly. Now we will sneak out of here and forget this ever happened and hope that no one was watching."

And with that, we backed out the door and erased the entire incident from the memory of the world.

(NOTE: At this point in the story, I would appreciate it if you would remove this chapter from your book, since it contains very sensitive information that could damage the future work of the Security Division. Thanks.)

CHAPTER
8

THE HEALING WATERS
OF EMERALD POND

Once outside the chicken house, we made some fast tracks and got the heck away from there.

It had suddenly occurred to me that if Sally May saw me coming out of the chicken house, or even standing close to it, she might leap to some false conclusions.

I mean, on more than one occasion she had accused me of committing unthinkable crimes against her chickens—such as eating them and/or their eggs.

Crazy, huh? It's common knowledge that cowdogs, and especially Heads of Ranch Security, NEVER eat chickens or suck eggs. I mean, we protect the stupid birds and their equally stupid eggs, so it would make no sense at all for us to turn right around and eat them—although I must admit that . . . hmm.

What I mean is that all charges against me had been false and outrageous and unfair and unfoundered, but in the Security Business we must guard ourselves against even the slightest appearance of naughty behavior.

And fellers, two dogs backing out of the chicken house in the middle of a normal work day might have been . . . I think you get the point. And so did I, which explains why I got away from there just as fast as I could travel.

Well, we had dodged that particular bullet and made our way down to Emerald Pond—my own private name, by the way, for one of my very favorite spots on the ranch, the lovely green pool of water formed by the overflow of the septic tank.

That investigation of the chicken house had pretty muchly worn me out and I still had a slight headache from my encounter with the corral fence and I was ready to dive into the warm embrace, so to speak, of Emerald Pond, whose waters are known to have curative and healing powers.

I can also reveal that those same green waters can provide a dog with a very impressive "calling card," you might say—a deep manly aroma that has been known to steal the hearts of the ladies and just by George sweep them off their feet.

Pretty impressive, huh? And it's MY pond.

Well, I sprang right into the middle of Emerald Pond, filled my nostrils with its sweet perfume, rolled around, kicked my legs in the air, climbed out, and gave myself a good shake.

Say, that little dip had left me feeling like a million bucks!

Drover had watched all this from dry land.

"Son, one of these days you're going to realize what you've been missing."

"Yeah, I know. But I don't like water."

"This isn't just water. It's tonic, a magic elixir that's full of vitamins and minerals. I'd almost be willing to bet that if you stuck your stub tail into these waters, it would grow out to normal size."

"No fooling?"

"Yup. It's powerful stuff."

"But I kind of like my tail the way it is."

"Well, to each his own, Drover. If you're happy with a chopped-off, deformed stub, I guess that's all that matters."

"I never thought of it as deformed."

"Then forget I said anything about it."

"Okay."

"Your happiness is the most important thing."

"Thanks, Hank."

"And the fact that everyone else laughs at your ridiculous tail is irrevelent. Irreverent. Ir-reffluent."

"Irrelevent?"

"I'll speak for myself, Drover, but thanks anyway. The word is IRREFFLUENT."

"Okay. But do you really think my tail's deformed?"

I sat down and scratched a troublesome spot just behind my left ear. "Are you asking for an honest answer or one that sugarcoats the truth?"

"Whichever one makes my tail look better."

"All right, you have a magnificent stub of a tail."

"You're just saying that so I won't think it's deformed!"

"That's what you wanted, wasn't it?"

"No," he began to sniffle and cry, "I want a tail that the other dogs won't laugh at! All my life I've wanted a tail that wasn't handicapped! How can I ever find happiness with a deformed tail?"

"That's a tough question, son."

"I'm so miserable and unhappy! I hate my

71

tail! Why can't I have a normal tail like a normal dog? All I ever wanted to be was normal."

"Drover, your tail can be fixed."

"You really think so? You mean there's hope?"

"Son, the cure for your condition has been right here all along. You just haven't used it."

"You mean . . . "

"Exactly. You must sit in Emerald Pond for two hours."

"That's all?"

"Sit with your tail under the healing waters for two hour and repeat these words over and over."

"What words?"

"I haven't said them yet."

"Oh."

" 'Lizards, spiders, warts and scales,

Give this dog a normal tail.' "

A smile bloomed on his face. "I think I can do it, Hank, and boy howdy, I'm sure excited!"

"I'm happy for you, Drover. If you follow those directions to the letter, I can almost guarantee that you'll come out with a normal tail."

His smile slipped. "What's an 'almost guarantee?' "

"I, uh . . . it's just one peg below a Gold Plated Guarantee."

"I'd rather have the Gold Plated, if it's okay."

"We're out of those, Drover."

"Oh rats."

I stood up and stretched. "So get your little fanny into the water and begin your therapy. I'll be back in a couple of hours to check things out."

"Where you going?"

I couldn't help smirking. "If you recall, Drover, I have a little score to settle with the cat. While your tail is growing, Pete's tail just might get shortened by a few inches," I gave him a wink, "if you know what I mean."

"Something's wrong with your eye."

"What?"

"I said, THERE'S SOMETHING WRONG WITH YOUR EYE!"

"Don't yell at me, there's nothing wrong with my ears!"

"I know. It's your eye."

"What are you talking about?"

"Your eye was twitching. I saw it myself."

I positioned my nose right in front of his face. "I was winking, you brick, to show that I had let you in on a little secret."

"Oh. Well, I'll be derned. I thought . . ."

"Yes, I heard what you thought, and it's obvious that sharing my secret with you was a waste of time. I'm sorry I bothered."

"That's okay, you couldn't help it."

"Thanks."

"You're welcome, and I hope it gets better."

"What?"

"Your eye."

"Drover?"

"What?"

"HUSH."

I left the runt sitting in Emerald Pond and went looking for the cat. My first stop was the gas tanks, to see if Pete was still occupying my gunnysack bed. Much to my disappointment, he had left.

So I went padding up to the yard gate to check out his usual loafing spots, the main one being right beside the back door where he often lolled around in the shade, waiting for someone to come outside. Any time the door opened, you see, he would try to weasel his way into the house.

That's a cat for you, always trying to weasel his way into something or other.

I didn't see him on the back step and was about to check out the machine shed when I heard a voice that caused my bodily parts to freeze in place and the hair to rise on my back.

It was the cat. "Mmmm, hello, Hankie. I bet you wish you were still Head of Ranch Security."

Ho ho! Kitty Kitty had just set himself up for a rude surprise.

CHAPTER
9

PETE'S MINDLESS
SENSELESS VANDALISM
OF A SHEET

That voice does something to me, causes my hair to rise and my ears to jump to the Full Alert position.

A growl begins to rumble in my throat, my eyes narrow to slits and my lips begin to twitch and my teeth expose themselves in all their frightening glory.

I turned towards the sound of the voice and saw him, sitting beneath the clothesline and looking up at a clean sheet that was flapping in the wind. Now and then he would lift his front paw and bat the sheet.

"Did you just say something, cat?"

"Mmm hmmm. I said, I'll bet you wish you were still Head of Ranch Security."

76

"Is that what you bet? Well, this is turning out to be a bad day for your bets, kitty. I don't wish I was still Head of Ranch Security, because I AM Head of Ranch Security."

He turned his head around and smirked at me. "No you're not. You lost your job in a gambling accident."

"Ha, ha, ha. Ho, ho, ho. Hee, hee, hee. You make me laugh, Pete. And lest you get the wrong impression, let me emphasize that I'm laughing at YOU."

"Mmm, isn't that interesting." He slapped at the sheet. "I'm the new Head of Ranch Security and you don't have a job, but you're laughing at me? That's very interesting, Hankie."

I marched down the fence. "I can see that you still haven't figgered it out, cat. I have cancelled that bet."

"You can't cancel what's already happened, Hankie. Even you should know that."

"I have cancelled the bet. It's off, it's over, it's suspended, it's null and void. It's history and it never happened."

"Mmmm! It's history and it never happened. What an interesting idea."

"That's correct, kitty. On this ranch, history is whatever I say it is."

"But you're forgetting one small detail,

Hankie." He hit the switchblade in his paw and his claws suddenly appeared. He admired them while he spoke. "Your bet was backed up by your Solemn Cowdog Oath. You can't take that back."

"Oh yeah? I'm afraid you overlooked one small detail, kitty. The Solemn Cowdog Oath doesn't apply to cheating situations or crooked deals. You see, I analyzed our wager and found that we were both betting on the same thing: my job."

He fluttered his eyelids. "That seems fair."

"That seems *crooked,* and you know it. You almost pulled it off, Pete, but I'm afraid you've been caught in the web of your own spider."

"You're so clever, Hankie." He yawned and came slinking over to the fence. He sat down, stared at me with his big cat eyes, and began twitching the end of his tail. "If you'll lean a little closer to the fence, I'll tell you a secret."

I caught myself just in time and pulled my face away. "Lean closer to the fence, so that you can slap me across the nose with your claws? As you've done before on several occasions? Sorry, Pete, your sneaky tricks are getting threadbare. That one isn't going to fly."

He glared at me. Then he drew himself up, threw an arch in his back, and hissed at me.

Before I knew it, a ferocious growl was thundering in my throat and I was seized by a powerful instinct to destroy the fence between us.

But iron discipline saved me just in time. I sat down and laughed at him.

"I guess you thought you could hiss and throw me into a frenzy of irrational behaviour, right? Then I'd tear down the fence between us and chase you around the yard, right? And then Sally May would come running to save you, and I'd get pounded with the broom, right?"

He glared daggers at me through the fence.

"Sorry, Pete. I've made a few mistakes in the past, but it happens that I learn from my mistakes. Your cheap tricks just aren't working anymore. Sorry."

Oh, you should have seen his icy glare when I told him that! It killed him, just by George ruined his day.

By this time his ears were pinned down on his head and the pupils of his eyes had grown to the size of quarters. "You're making me angry, Hankie, and when I get angry it makes me want to use my claws and tear something up."

"Oh yeah? Well, if it gets too overwhelming for you, kitty, I'll be glad to meet you down along the creek, but if you think I'm going to get suckered into a fight on Sally May's doorstep, you're very muchly mistaken."

"I'm getting angrier and angrier."

"And I'm loving every second of it, Pete. Keep it up. Here, try this on for size." I stuck my tongue out at him.

"I can't control myself much longer, Hankie."

"Oh, yeah? Well, see how you like this." I crossed my eyes AND stuck out my tongue, all at the same time, see, and oh my, that really ripped him.

He was yowling now, the way cats do when they're so mad they could spit, only they can't spit so they yowl. "Just for that, I'm going to tear up a sheet!"

"Oh really? Tear up one of Sally May's clean sheets? You'd better not."

"I will, you'll see!"

And with that, the stupid cat dashed back to the clothesline and climbed the sheet. I could hear his claws ripping into the cloth.

"UMMMMMMMMMMMMMM!! You're ripping the sheet!"

"I don't even care, it's all your fault, you've made me so angry I just can't control myself!"

Well, as you might imagine, I was almost beside myself with joy and happiness. At last I had pushed Pete over the edge of the brink. Now all I had to do was sound the alarm, alert Sally May to what her precious kitty was doing, and then sit back to watch the fur fly.

I barked the alarm. "Attention please! Hank calling Sally May, come in Sally May. Red Alert at the clothesline, repeat Red Alert at the clothesline! We have spotted a deranged cat who is destroying one of your clean sheets. Report to the clothesline at once, and bring broom."

That would do it.

I sat back and prepared to enjoy the show. In a matter of seconds, Sally May would come flying out that door—her eyes filled with sheer meanness and . . .

I kept waiting. I frowned and began pacing. My eyes were riveted on the screen door. The seconds passed. No sign of Sally May.

That was odd.

And in the meantime, kitty continued to climb the sheet and perform mindless acts of vandalism. Mindless vandalism has always bothered me. I mean, there's no reason for it. It's just . . .

Still no sign of Sally May. Could she have gone to town? No, but she might have been taking a bath, in which case . . .

Senseless destruction of ranch property—that's what I was forced to watch, and before I knew it, a ferocious growl was thundering in my throat and I was seized by a powerful instinct to destroy the fence between us.

But, of course, this was Sally May's deal, not . . .

My hair began to rise and my ears jumped to the Full Alert position. My eyes narrowed to slits and my lips began to twitch and my teeth exposed themselves in all their frightening glory.

I heard a loud R-I-P! This was intolerable, unbearable. How much longer could I sit there, an idle speculator to mindless vandalism and the senseless destruction of ranch property? At what point did an idle speculator become a part of the crime?

I mean, there's such a thing as moral outrage. Some dogs have it and some dogs don't, and those of us who . . .

All at once I was finding it very hard to . . . that cat was not only defacing Sally May's sheet, but in a deeper sense he was committing a senseless act of senseless vandalism against MY RANCH!

Well, you know me. I take that stuff pretty

serious. Nobody messes with my . . .

Okay, that was it.

Red Alert, full throttle, all systems go, open fire, launch all torpedoes, charge, bonzai! THIS WAS WAR!!

I leaped over the fence like a buck deer, crossed the yard with three huge leaps, and flew right into the middle of that sheet, wrapped up old Pete in a nice little package, and was was well on my way to . . . screen door?

Ah ha, Sally May had finally answered the call and was coming to the rescue. And yes, her eyes were flaming and smoke was curling out of her nostrils and she was definitely armed with the broom, and I could see that she was ready to do some serious damage to her precious, perfect, sniveling little weasel of a cat.

I sat up straight, held my head at a proud angle, and wagged my tail as if to say, "Welcome to the war, Sally May. As you can see, I have just arrested this . . ."

HUH?

He'd been right there in the sheet.

Just moments before.

Wrapped up in a nice little package from which he couldn't possibly . . .

Sally May was standing over me. She looked very angry, very angry indeed. I began to develop a funny feeling about this deal.

I lifted my eyes and tried to smile and, uh, thumped my tail on the, uh, ground.

"Uh, Sally May," I tried to say, "I think I can explain everything."

"*You nasty dog, you've ruined my sheet!*"

"Me? No, it was the . . ." WHAP! ". . . . cat, don't you see, I caught Pete . . ." WHAP! ". . . honest, no kidding, I'm being very serious about . . .'' WHAP!

"*You get out of my yard and don't you ever come back.!*"

I never argue with a loaded broom. I ran in a tight circle for a moment, dodging that deadly killer broom, and then broke away and went zooming towards the machine shed . . .

. . . forgetting for the moment that the fence was still there, which caused a slight pile-up beside the foot scraper and actually hurt worse than the broom itself, but eventually we . . .

I ran for my life and hid in the darkest corner of the machine shed. It was there that I straightened my neck and licked my wounds.

And began plotting my final revenge against the cat.

CHAPTER
10

THE INFAMOUS BLACK HOLE OF MUSTARD

I just didn't understand.

Everything had been going my way. I had sniffed out all of Pete's sneaky tricks and had made the appropriate countermoves. I had held my temper, resisted the temptation to make hash of him, had maintained Iron Discipline throughout.

I had even laughed at him.

I had known from the start what he was trying to do, and yet he had somehow managed to do it anyway.

How could one cat be so lucky, so often?

It strained my concept of luck. It strained my concept of who I was and who I had always wanted to be. It strained my . . .

My eyes were rolling around in circles and,

hmmm, I appeared to be banging my head against the northwest leg of the work bench.

Something bad was happening to me, fellers. I was losing control of my control. My instruments were shorting out. I felt myself spiraling towards the Infamous Black Hole of Mustard.

In one last desperate effort to save myself, I took a firm grip on the cement floor with all four paws and fought against the tremendous swirling vacuum sweeper that threatened to swallow me up.

And—you won't believe this—I saved myself from vacuumization by singing a song. Why not? "Music hath charms to soothe the savage beast," says the old saying, and here's how the song went:

I Must Dispose of the Cat

I don't understand what's going on here.
It makes me have questions about my career.
I used to have pride, I thought I was shrewd,
So how come my game plan is coming
    unglued?

My countermoves backfire, my plots go
    awry,
I've got indigestion from Pete's humble pie.

It's happened so often, I'm starting to think
This cat will eventually drive me to drink.

So to save the dignity of my ranch,
To stop this mental avalanche
I hereby burn the olive branch.
I must dispose of the cat!

It's not that I'm bitter or violent or mean.
I'm not in the habit of making a scene.
I don't take positions from which I won't
    budge,
Yet now I perceive that I'm holding a
    grudge.

There's nothing too personal in this, I
    submit.
Well, maybe I'm bothered by cats, I admit,
Their hissing and yowling and humping
    their backs.
I hate them, that's all, it's as simple as that.

So to save the dignity of my ranch,
To stop this mental avalanche
I hereby burn the olive branch.
I must dispose of the cat!

El Gato is rumored to have several lives,

Nine, I believe, which is four more than five.
But gato and gravy, served up on a plate
Will get the grand total down closer to eight.

A kitty for supper, a kitty for lunch,
A kitty *con queso,* a kitty with punch.
A kitty for snacks, oh my this is fun!
And shortly the total will shrink down to
   none.

> So to save the dignity of my ranch,
> To stop this mental avalanche
> I hereby burn the olive branch.
> I must consider the pros and cons
> Of bumping off the cat!

When I had finished the song, I looked around. I was standing in the middle of the machine shed. The bells and whistles had vanished. My mind had cleared.

Best of all, the Infamous Black Hole of Mustard had swallowed itself and returned to the ethers of the vapor, or wherever it is that Black Holes come from.

But the important thing was that I had snatched myself back from the edge of dispair and had survived one of the most dangerous moments of my career.

And, all at once, it was clear what I had to do. Heh, heh. Oh, a few details still had to be worked out, but those were small matters of procedure.

I wondered why I hadn't thought of this sooner. Surely it was a testimony to my sweet nature and gentle disposition—and yes, to a certain dread of consequences. Sally May, for example.

I had a suspicion that she would not think kindly of my plots and schemes, and that fact pretty muchly determined the method I finally chose for the job.

Here's what I did. I left the machine shed and, on silent feet, went hunting for the villain. I checked out the yard. He wasn't there, which was good. I checked those tall weeds around the water well, and he wasn't there too.

I was on my way down to the corrals when I happened to glance to my left and saw something that brought bubbles of joy bubbling to the surface of my . . . something. *Pete was asleep on my gunnysack bed beneath the gas tanks.*

This cat, who had been so cunning and shrewd only hours before, had made the incredibly dumb mistake of taking an afternoon nap—away from the house and on my bed! He was making it easy for me, which I appreciated.

There are several ways of catnapping a kid . . . kidnapping a cat, I should say, and also several ways of getting your eyebrows torn off your face by a hissing, spitting, clawing little buzz saw—unless you happen to pick the cat up by the loose skin behind his neck, in which case he will hang as limp as a sock.

You see, I had watched Little Alfred in action on many occasions and had observed him dragging Pete all over the ranch in this manner.

Pete never suspected a thing. I slipped up to the gas tanks, scooped him up in my jaws, and was well on my way to the wild canyon country north of headquarters before he knew what was happening.

"Mmmm, you're taking me somewhere, Hankie." I couldn't respond because my mouth was full of cat, don't you see, and I didn't have anything to say to him anyway. "It's a nice evening for a walk in the pasture, Hankie, but I think we've gone far enough."

Silence.

"Hankie, I'm wondering where we're going. Are you listening?"

I was listening but my heart had turned to cement. I continued on a northward course until I reached the base of the caprock. There, I stopped and released the cat.

"Here we are, kitty. This is where you get off. It's called Coyote City."

Pete had his ears pinned back. He humped up his back and hissed at me, also took a swipe at me with his paw but I managed to dodge it.

"You know, cat, if you'd ever shown any signs of wanting to get along with me, things never would have gotten to this point. But you're so greedy and spiteful, you've forced me to take drastic measures."

He yowled and hissed.

"You've driven me to this. What happens is your own fault."

He yowled and hissed.

"Nobody ever deserved this more than you, Pete, but on second thought it does seem a little severe, and if you approached me just right, I might consider accepting an apology."

"I'll give you an apology, Hankie. Just take two steps this way and I'll give you an apology you'll never forget."

"There, you see? You cats won't compromise. You don't even try to get along. But after considering the finality of what we're do-

ing here, I'm willing to give you one last chance to apologize and start all over with a clean slate."

"Cats don't compromise, Hankie, and we don't ever apologize for anything. If we can't run the show, we don't play."

I shook my head. "Hey Pete, you might think we're playing games here, but let me point out that when I leave, you're going to be all alone in the middle of coyote country."

He continued to glare at me. "Cats enjoy being alone, Hankie, because when we're by ourselves, we're in the very best of company."

This was hopeless! I began pacing. "Listen, cat, you don't know what you're talking about. Maybe you've never had any experience with coyotes but I have, and I can tell you that their very favorite meal is fresh cat. Now, if you'll just . . ."

"I can take care of myself, Hankie. I don't need the help of a bungling dog."

I stopped pacing and our glares met. "Okay, Pete, let's lay all the cards on the table. I brought you up here because I wanted to bump you off. Now that we're here, I find myself having second thoughts about it. If you'll just make a small apology . . ."

"Not interested, Hankie."

"Okay. If you'll promise to make a small apology within the next three days . . ."

"Apology is a word cats don't understand, Hankie."

"All right, this is absolutely your last chance. If you'll promise *to consider thinking about* making a small apology . . ."

He grinned and shook his head.

"Very well, Pete, in that case I have no choice but to order you to return to the ranch with me—immediately. And that's a direct order."

"But Hankie, I don't take orders—not from you, not from anyone. Cats are very independent and we take care of ourselves."

"Will you listen to reason?" I yelled at him. "This place is crawling with wild hungry coyotes. If I leave you here, you won't have a chance to take care of yourself because you'll be a kitty sandwich."

He studied his claws. "I'll go back with you, Hankie."

"That's better."

"IF you'll make a full and complete apology to me, and IF you'll agree to let me be Head of Ranch Security forever and ever."

HUH?

I stared at him. "Are you crazy? You want me to . . . okay, fine, I should have known better than to talk sense to a cat. Have it your way, Pete, I'm washing my paws of the whole mess. Goodbye and good riddance!"

And with that, I whirled around and headed back to headquarters, satisfied that I had done the world a tremendous service.

CHAPTER

11

TOTAL HAPPINESS
WITHOUT PETE

Trotting back to headquarters, I felt great. Wonderful. Tremendous. At last, peace and quiet. At last, total happiness. At last . . .

The dumb cat! How could he . . . can you imagine him thinking that he could . . . well, that was just fine, everything had turned out for the . . . and furthermore, I didn't give a rip.

And even if I did give a rip, it was a very small rip.

I put it out of my mind, just by George wiped it out of my memory and forgot that I had . . . never mind.

I made it back to headquarters an hour or so before sundown and headed straight to Emerald Pond. It was time to check up on Mister

Stub Tail.

Sure enough, there he was, sitting in the water and looking up at the clouds. I was glad to have something to take my mind off of . . . well, other matters, shall we say.

"All right, Drover, you can come out of the water now."

"Hank, did you hear the news? Pete's gone! They can't find him anywhere."

"Oh really? My goodness, that's . . ."

"Sally May and Little Alfred looked all over for him. I'm kind of worried."

"Worry about growing a new tail, Drover, and leave the cats to take care of themselves."

"Yeah, but what if he wanders away and the coyotes get him?"

I put my nose in his face. "I don't want to

talk about cats or think about cats, do you understand?"

"Gosh, you're kind of touchy."

"I'm not touchy! The subject bores me, that's all."

"You didn't see Pete while you were gone, did you?"

"I, uh, no, of course not, and why would you ask such a ridiculous question?"

"Just wondered. Where'd you go?"

"I went for a little walk, Pete."

"I'm Drover. You called me Pete."

"Yes, of course, how silly of me. I went for a walk."

He looked at me and twisted his head to the side. "You're acting kind of funny. Is anything wrong?"

"Wrong? Why, heavens no. Everything's great. Wonderful. Terrific. Now get your little self out of the water, Pete, and let's take a look at your tail."

"You just called me Pete again."

"Get out of the water!"

"Gosh, you don't have to yell and scream."

"I'M NOT YELLING AND SCREAMING!!!"

"You are too yelling and screaming, and I don't understand why you're acting so funny all of a sudden, and my tail didn't grow one little bit."

"How do you know that?"

"Well . . . I checked on it . . . a couple of times."

"*You checked on it!* You mean, you got up out of the water?"

"Yeah, I got bored. And tired of sitting."

"What about the magic words? Did you say the magic words over and over for two solid hours?"

"Well . . . they weren't very solid."

"What are you saying?"

"Well . . . I forgot the words after a while, and they were kind of boring too."

I shook my head. "I should have known. Well, stand up and let's have a look. I hope that your foolish behavior didn't cause a reversal of the growing process."

His eyes flew open. "A reversal! You mean . . ."

"Exactly. Sometimes when you fool around with powerful medicine, it has bad side effects. It's possible, Pete, that you might have no tail at all."

"Oh my gosh! What would everyone say?"

"They'd point at you and laugh and call you Little Mister Lost-His-Tail."

"Don't say that, Hank! I don't think I could

stand it."

"It'll be tough, Pete."

"You called me Pete again."

I gave him a withering glare. "Will you stop talking about that cat? That's the third time you've brought him up."

"Yeah, but that's the third time you've called me Pete."

"I did no such thing. Your name is Drover, you may have just lost your tail, and you have more important problems to think about than a sniveling, troublesome cat."

"Okay, I'll try."

"We're lucky to be rid of him, and whatever happened to him, I'm sure he deserved it."

"You're still talking about the cat."

"And besides, you can't expect a cat to live forever. Even if he hadn't been eaten by coyotes, he probably would have died of gluttony."

"What's gluttony?"

"Eating too much. You might recall that every evening at Scrap Time, Pete would go streaking to the yard gate and eat himself into a stupor of gluttony."

"I guess you're right."

"So, as you can see . . ." At that very moment I heard the screen door slam up at the house. My ears shot up. So did Drover's. "What's that?"

"Scrap Time!"

"Holy Smokes, we've got all the scraps to ourselves tonight! Come on, Drover, to the yard gate!"

"What about my tail?"

"Bring it along, we'll look at it later!"

We went streaking past the gas tanks and up the hill, and sure enough we got there first and beat . . .well, actually there was no one to beat, now that . . . we had all the scraps to ourselves, which sort of took a little of the challenge . . .

I slowed down and walked the last ten yards, I sat down in front of the yard gate and Drover joined me.

"Hank, I've got my stub tail back, I'm so happy!"

"Great, glad to hear it. And I'm happy too, for slightly different reasons. With both of us happy, this should be a very happy evening."

Sally May was standing out on the porch, holding a plate of wonderful scraps and gazing off in the distance. All at once she began calling . . . Pete. She called his name over and over.

And on every calling of his name, I . . . well,

flinched with happiness, you might say. And wished she would change the subject.

The back door opened again and out came Little Alfred. "Did you find Petie?"

"I'm afraid he's gone," she said combing the boy's hair with her fingers. "Sometimes cats wander off and don't come back."

"I miss old Pete. I hope he comes back."

"I know, so do I. And maybe he will."

Then both of them began calling Pete's name. And as if that wasn't bad enough, Little Mister Moan-and-Groan chimed in.

"Gosh, I never thought I'd miss old Pete, but I do."

"Think about all the extra scraps you'll get. Think about your new stub tail. Think about the clouds."

"Okay, I'll try."

After a bit, Sally May stopped calling and gave a big sigh and came over to the yard gate where we were waiting. She scraped the fork over the plate and deposited a delicious-smelling pile of roast beef scraps on the ground in front of us.

"I guess you dogs get it all tonight," she said, then turned and went back into the house. Little Alfred followed her, with his chin down on his chest.

I turned to Drover. "Well, this is True Happiness, son. At last we have all the scraps to ourselves. Now, before you get any big ideas, let me point out that I get the larger portion."

He sniffed the fragrant vapors that were rising from the scraps and . . . hmm, very strange . . . he shook his head. "You can have 'em all, Hank. I'm not very hungry."

"How could you not be very hungry?"

"I don't know. Somehow food doesn't seem as interesting when we can't fight over it . . . with Pete."

"Well, you just sit there and watch, and I'll . . ."

Funny, I'd kind of lost my appetite too. I stood over the scraps, sniffed 'em, licked 'em, took a bite and rolled it around in my mouth. The exciting taste I'd expected to find just wasn't there.

"It's not the same, is it, Hank?"

"What?" He'd been watching me. "I don't know what you're talking about."

A tear rolled down his cheek and dripped off the end of his nose. "I wish old Pete would come back and fight with us. Gosh, we might starve to death without him."

I heaved a sigh and pushed myself up to my feet. "All right, Drover, let's go see if we can find the stupid cat.''

All at once he was jumping up and down. ''Really, Hank, honest? You mean that?''

''I'm doing it as a special favor for you, I want that understood right now. Let's move out. I figger we've got one hour of daylight left.''

And with that, we headed north towards the caprock and launched a rescue mission to save . . .

I was still having a little trouble believing this was happening.

CHAPTER
12

HAPPY ENDINGS AREN'T AS SIMPLE AS YOU MIGHT THINK

We zoomed past the mailbox and headed north. Drover broke the silence. "You don't reckon we might see any coyotes, do you?"

"Are you joking?"

He started laughing. "Yeah, I was just joking."

"That was a good joke, Drover, because up in that rough country, the coyotes are as thick as fleas."

All at once it appeared that Drover suffered a blowout on his left front paw. "Boy howdy, this old leg just went out on me, Hank! I was afraid that might happen, I never should have pushed it so hard."

"Hurry up, son, this is a race against time."

He was falling farther behind. "You'd better go one without me, Hank, I don't want to hold you back. I'll see you guys back at the house."

I didn't have time to mess with Drover. The seconds were ticking away, and with every tick of the tock, uh clock, Pete the Barncat was coming closer to . . .

I still couldn't believe I was doing this.

I hit that big sand draw just east of the prairie dog town and followed it north to the base of the caprock. Up ahead, I could see the lone hackberry tree where I'd dumped him off . . . uh, left him . . . delivered him, shall we say.

Since I didn't know what I'd find there, I approached it with maximum caution. Some twenty-five yards out, I slowed to a walk and shifted into Stealthy Crouch Mode. I eased up to a bluff and glanced around in all directions. I peered over the top and saw . . .

Pete the Barncat, surrounded by two hungry-looking coyotes who reminded me very much of two long-limbed, yellow-eyed, slack-jawed, utterly humorless cannibal brothers named Rip and Snort.

Yes, it WAS Rip and Snort, and it had certainly been nice knowing old Pete and I kind of regretted losing him after I had gone to the trouble of running all the way to the caprock, because *nobody takes cats away from Rip and Snort.*

I mean, you talk about guys who love to fight and eat and belch! Those two were champs.

Tough. Double-tough.

So I just lay there on top of the bluff and watched and listened. Hmmm. Pete was sitting and he appeared to be studying the same thing. Staring at the ground.

Snort stood nearby, looking over Rip's shoulder.

That was odd.

All at once Pete extended his right paw and tapped it on the ground, three times, and said, "Mmmm, sorry, Rip, but you sure let that one slip up on you."

Snort began to laugh. "Huh, huh, huh! Brother lose again! Brother got great big dumbness in head. Maybe now we stop and eat," his gaze drifted to Pete, "cat supper!"

"Uh!" said Rip.

"Mmm, let's not rush into anything," said Pete—and you'll notice that he didn't hump up and hiss at those two guys, since that would have made him an instant meatball. "Now let

me see. I played Rip and won. I played Snort and won. But Rip and Snort haven't played each other."

"Huh!" said Short. "Snort not waste time play Chesterless Chester with brother, 'cause brother just big dummy."

Rip scowled and said, "Uh!"

"Oh, I'm not so sure about that," Pete said, flicking the end of his tail, "and if you'll just watch the tail going back and forth, back and forth, to and fro, lull-a-bye and good . . ."

BLAM!

Snort clubbed kitty over the head with his paw. "Not try funny cat trick on Rip and Snort."

Pete scraped himself off the ground, straightened his ears, and spit dirt out of his mouth. "I'm sure I don't know what you're talking about."

"Talking about cat try to cheat, but Rip and Snort not fall for funny cheating cat trick, huh! Now cat move back and let Rip and Snort play Chesterless Chester, oh boy!" Snort swatted Pete out of the way and sat down at the so-called board. "Brother go first move."

"Uh!" said Rip, and suddenly we had two cannibals staring down at a blank area of dirt and giving total concentration to . . .

Total concentration? Hey, if they were so wrapped up in their . . .

Creeping over the edge of the bluff and extending my body to its fully extended position, I closed my jaws around Pete's head and snatched him into the air. He did a flip and landed on the ground—on MY side of the bluff.

The second he landed, he humped up and bristled and drew back his paw to deliver his usual swat to my nose. Lucky for him, he caught himself just in the nicker of time.

"Mmmm, my goodness, the cops are here!"

"That's right, kitty. I've come to save your worthless carcass, don't ask me why, but before I do any life saving, I want to hear you say 'calf rope.' "

"Calf rope? Well now, ordinarily cats don't . . ."

"Say it, Pete, or I'll throw you back with the cannibals."

"Mmmm, I'm liking it better all the time. Calf rope, and let's get out of here."

"Hop on my back and hang on!"

He sprang up on my back and we went zooming down the sand draw. We hadn't gone far when I heard a riot starting behind us. No doubt Rip and Snort had looked up from their Checkerless Checker game and had figgered out that they'd been conned by their supper.

And they didn't sound too happy about it. "Uh, stop thief! Not leave with cat! Ranch dog in berry big trouble now!"

Yes, "berry big trouble" indeed, which was a powerful incentive for me to stretch out my legs and use my incredible speed to move our deal from the caprocks down to headquarters.

I had just begun to pull away from them when Pete turned around in the saddle, so to speak, and faced the back and began talking trash to the brothers.

"Mmmm, you big galoots couldn't catch a flea on a grandpa's knee, and ha ha ha and ho ho ho and hee hee hee, and I'll bet your momma wears old tow sack drawers."

Seemed to me that Pete had a real short memory and real poor judgment, which I guess is standard equipment in your lower grades of cat, and the result was like throwing water on gasoline.

Gasoline on water. Water on a fire. Whatever it is.

Anyways, the brothers got a sudden inspiration to stump a fresh mudhole in the middle of Pete's back, and here they came!

Gasoline on a fire.

"Pete, do me a favor and shut your mouth, will you?"

Fellers, if the chase had gone another hundred yards, we might have been looking at the possibility of throwing baggage overboard to lighten the load, which would have definitely put my new friendship with the cat to a stern test.

But just as the brothers were getting close enough to shorten my tail section, we reached the county road. A truck was coming along and I shot the gap in front of him, made it with inches to spare, and the brothers had to give up the chase.

We had made it!

By that time we were within easy walking distance of ranch headquarters. I slowed to a walk and caught my breath and enjoyed the spectacle of a beautiful Panhandle sunset.

I mean, it was a magic moment. The wind had died to the merest whisper. The western sky had become a fireworks display of red and pink and orange, while off to the north the caprocks were sinking into blue and purple shadows.

I had just pulled off a very impressive rescue mission and had escaped being mauled by the coyotes and had made peace with my very oldest and staunchest enemy.

Just for a moment, it seemed that the whole world stopped what it was doing and joined in on a song to celebrate peace and happiness and friendship and the beautiful sunset. As I recall, it went something like this:

Prairie Vespers

Day is done
Twilight's come
Gone's the sun
And comes the night.
We pray for wisdom
And for health
And for light.

Day is now over
The twilight has fallen
And gone is the sunlight
We're left in the blackness of night
We're praying for courage and wisdom
And for our safe passage from darkness to
    light.

Yes sir, it was an evening to remember. Even Pete caught the feeling of it.

"Well, Hankie, you've put me in a very awkward position. Since you saved me from the coyotes, I may be forced to say thank you."

"Yup, you sure might."

"Which cats don't like to say."

"I've noticed."

"And I might even have to start thinking of you as a friend, which really depresses me."

"I know what you're saying, Pete. I mean, just think of all the years we've invested in a lousy relationship."

"Mmmm, I know. All the nasty tricks and hateful names."

"Right, and all the great fights we've had."

"And now it's finished, Hankie, all gone."

"Exactly, wiped out by one thoughtless act of kindness."

"Well, Hankie, we can always hope that it won't last."

With heavy hearts, we strolled into headquarters. As we were passing the yard gate, I noticed that Pete's head shot up and he said, "Mmmm!"

"What?"

"Oh nothing, Hankie. Thanks for everything and now you run along to your gunnysack bed."

"Well, that's sort of what I . . ." I sniffed the air. Mercy, unless I was badly mistaken, the air had just acquired the fragrance of roast beef. "On second thought, kitty, why don't you run along and find somebody's leg to rub."

"Those scraps are mine, Hankie, because I saw them first."

"Uh no, wrong, incorrect, and wrong. Those are MY scraps."

"He humped his back. I growled. He hissed. I barked. He slapped me across the nose and I made a snap at his tail and . . .

All at once I remembered why I'd wanted to bump him off in the first place and things were back to normal and everyone was happy again. I guess.

Fellers, if you can figger out what happiness is in this old life, you're a better dog than I am. I quit.

**Have you read all of Hank's adventures?
Now available in paperback at $6.95:**

		ISBN
1	Hank the Cowdog	0-87719-130-1
2	The Further Adventures of Hank the Cowdog	0-87719-117-4
3	It's a Dog's Life	0-87719-128-X
4	Murder in the Middle Pasture	0-87719-133-6
5	Faded Love	0-87719-136-0
6	Let Sleeping Dogs Lie	0-87719-138-7
7	The Curse of the Incredible Priceless Corncob	0-87719-141-7
8	The Case of the One-Eyed Killer Stud Horse	0-87719-144-1
9	The Case of the Halloween Ghost	0-87719-147-6
10	Every Dog Has His Day	0-87719-150-6
11	Lost in the Dark Unchanted Forest	0-87719-118-2
12	The Case of the Fiddle-Playing Fox	0-87719-170-0
13	The Wounded Buzzard on Christmas Eve	0-87719-175-1
14	Monkey Business	0-87719-180-8
15	The Case of the Missing Cat	0-87719-185-9
16	Lost in the Blinding Blizzard	0-87719-192-1

*All books are available on audio cassette too! ($15.95
for two cassettes)*

**Also available on cassettes: Hank the Cowdog's
Greatest Hits!**

Volume 1 ISBN 0-916941-20-5 $6.95
Volume 2 ISBN 0-916941-37-X $6.95
Volume 3 ISBN 0-87719-194-8 $6.95